## "IT'S TIME
## OUR AGR

Juliet's tone was matter-of-fact, but she avoided Brady's eyes. "Then come sit down here beside me and we'll discuss things," Brady invited as he pulled a beanbag chair in front of the blazing fire.

"This doesn't seem like a very businesslike atmosphere."

"Honeymoon discussions are rarely businesslike," Brady said, laughing. "They go more like this." He crossed the room in a few brief strides and scooped Juliet up in his arms.

"Put me down," she protested, kicking wildly.

"In just a moment," he promised. But as he leaned over to drop her in the chair, they tumbled down together in a tangled, giggling heap.

"That was supposed to be a classy, seductive maneuver," he said.

"Oh, I don't know," Juliet said, looking into Brady's eyes. "You're first-class all the way...and you're *definitely* seductive."

## ABOUT THE AUTHOR

Virginia-based authors Sally Siddon and Barbara
Bradford got the idea for *The Arrangement* while
scanning the personal ads in the *Washingtonian*
magazine. Sally, a former journalist, and
Barbara, a former teacher, decided to become a
writing team, and the partnership has borne fruit.
*The Arrangement*, their first Superromance, is the
winner of the Romance Writers of America's
"Golden Heart" award.

# Sally Bradford
# THE ARRANGEMENT

# *Harlequin Books*

TORONTO • NEW YORK • LONDON
AMSTERDAM • PARIS • SYDNEY • HAMBURG
STOCKHOLM • ATHENS • TOKYO • MILAN

Published October 1987

First printing August 1987

ISBN 0-373-70281-7

To Pell Palace,
where it all began.

# CHAPTER ONE

BRADY TALCOTT DROPPED the folded magazine on the bar. "Problem solved," he announced, clapping his friend on the back. "I'll be married within a month."

"Married?" Phil Gentry put down his martini and swiveled his bar stool around until he was face to face with Brady. "Exactly who are you going to marry?"

Brady's face broke into a rakish grin. "I haven't met her yet."

"My God! I thought for a minute, there, you were serious." Phil slid down off the bar stool and picked up his glass.

"I *am* serious, dead serious."

"Yeah, and I'm Superman. Come on, let's find a table. What you need is a good stiff drink, and then we've got some business to discuss."

Brady followed Phil toward an out-of-the-way table near the window that gave them a panoramic view of San Francisco, burnished by the late-afternoon sun. "That sounds like my lawyer talking," Brady quipped.

"Your lawyer and your friend," Phil corrected him. "You've got one hell of a problem, buddy, and it's time we quit making jokes about it."

"This isn't a joke," Brady protested, settling himself in a thickly padded captain's chair. He unbuttoned his suit coat and loosened his tie. "I'm trying to tell you, I'm on to something. I really am going to get married. I've finally figured out how to get around my father and his damn trust agreement."

"Your father has been dead for almost two years," Phil observed unnecessarily. He took another sip of his martini, pondering Brady's present state of mind across the rim of his glass. The noise level in the club bar had risen to a low din, about right to give them enough privacy for a serious discussion that was long overdue.

For months Phil had been warning Brady that his time was running out. In another year, Talcott Enterprises was going to be tied up in litigation if Brady didn't meet the terms of his father's trust agreement. Phil could see it coming, and he was powerless to stop it. The hell of it was he couldn't come up with any answers either. Between them they were going to have to figure something out.

"Not only is your father dead," Phil continued, "the terms of that trust agreement of his are coming down to the wire. You can fight it in court—and you'll probably win—but there may not be enough left of the company by that time to make any difference."

"The hell I'll go to court." Brady opened the magazine he'd carried over from the bar and held it near the yellow glow from the hurricane lamp in the center of the table. "If you won't read this yourself, then I'll read it to you. I'm telling you, it's our solution—and don't interrupt till I'm finished."

Brady cleared his throat. He didn't really need the words in front of him. He'd gone over the ad so many times that he'd memorized them. Squinting in the dim light, he read slowly in a carefully controlled monotone:

> SINGLE FEMALE LAWYER, age thirty, in search of professional male, age thirty to forty. Must be good looking, intelligent, open-minded. Object: paternity.

"Paternity! Hot damn, Brady—"

"Quiet! I'm not finished," Brady interrupted. "Where was I?

> Object: paternity. Current references, résumé with photo, and medical history mandatory. Reply to Box 9046, *Bay City Magazine*.

Phil downed the second half of his martini in one gulp. "You are joking," he said tentatively, almost certain but not quite. He'd known Brady for thirty years, since before he could really remember. The thing that bothered him was that this was the kind of damn fool stunt Brady might try because the man was cornered.

Before Brady could answer, the waiter appeared, his footsteps soundless in the carpeted room, his manner one of deference as he waited for a break in the conversation. Brady ordered Cutty Sark for himself and another vodka martini for Phil before he turned his attention back to their conversation. His whole demeanor changed. "I already told you this wasn't a joke." His jaw was set, his eyes hard. "I'm down to the wire. You know it, and I know it. This is a way out, and I am going to take it."

As Brady's voice rose, Phil looked around warily. So far, no one seemed to be paying any attention to them. As even-tempered as Brady normally was, when he got that look on his face it was an unmistakable signal. Anxious to prevent a public explosion, Phil summoned all his restraint. He could see they were going to have to discuss this idea as though it were a reasonable option.

"Let's back up for just a minute." Phil's voice was noncombative. "Try to look at this logically. The ad says paternity. That's not your problem." Brady's face was impassive, and so Phil continued. "What the trust says is that you have to be married before you're thirty-five," he explained patiently. "It says absolutely nothing about fathering a child."

"Hell, I know all that. We've been over it often enough." Brady picked up the jigger the waiter had set in front of him and poured the scotch into a glass of ice. "I'm three steps ahead of you. It's actually pretty basic when you think about it. Some broad placed this ad because she wants a baby. Right?" Phil nodded silently, and Brady took a sip of his drink. "Now, I come along needing a short-term wife, somebody to marry me for a few months. Are you with me so far?" Phil opened his mouth to answer, but Brady raised a hand to silence him. "So what we do is make a trade."

Phil shook his head. "That is a lousy idea if I ever heard one." He looked hard at Brady. There was no sign of humor on his friend's face. Brady really *wasn't* joking. "Look," he tried again, "your father wrote the trust that way because he believed in it. He wanted you to have a wife and kids and all those things he thought really mattered." Phil leaned over toward Brady. "You know that marriage clause probably won't hold up in court. Your father probably knew it, too, but he figured it might shove you in the right direction." With a disgusted look at the magazine, Phil took another drink of his martini. "You'd be better off to go to court than to make a stupid move like this."

"And lose months or maybe years just when the company is on a roll?" Brady shot back. "Talcott Enterprises was on the rocks when my father died. In two years—just two years—I've turned the business around." His eyes flashed with determination. "I've got a good thing going with the new toy line, and I'm not going to put that on hold while I fight a court case."

"Come on, Brady, you're about to make a stupid move because you're mad as hell at your father. You realize, he wasn't such a bad guy—he was just trying to do what he thought was right," Phil observed.

"I know that," Brady grudgingly agreed. And damn! He had to admit he did miss him. There were times he still picked up the office phone to buzz his father when unexpected problems arose. And when he went home to his mother's, especially on holidays, the chair at the head of the table seemed empty, no matter who sat in it. But the terms of the trust were something else. "My father has no right to meddle in my private life—dead or alive." Brady spit out the words.

"True," Phil acknowledged. "But that doesn't change the fact that he's doing it."

"Dammit, that also doesn't change the fact that I'll get married—for real—when I'm good and ready and not by some artificial cutoff date." Anger flashed in Brady's eyes. "I'm not going to have some woman I love always wonder if I married her just because of the trust. You know how I feel about marriage.''

"Yes, I do know how you feel about marriage. And I also know the trust agreement is part of the reason you've pulled back whenever you started to get serious with a woman.''

Brady looked past Phil toward the window where the setting sun had bathed the nearby buildings in gold and had cast deep purple shadows on their neighbors. He and Phil had known each other so long that Phil saw straight through him. Right now Phil was shifting back and forth between the roles of friend and lawyer, and in both capacities he was trying to protect him. Brady wasn't sure he wanted to be protected, not this time. Besides, there wasn't any harm in investigating the idea. If this woman seemed reasonable, he'd be up front with her and tell her about the trust agreement. If she was willing to go along with him they'd both come out ahead. She'd have her baby and he'd have his company, free and clear.

Encouraged by Brady's thoughtful expression, Phil worked on an appeal to his common sense. "I agree you're running out of time, and we're going to have to make some moves. But you're not quite at the desperation stage yet.'' Phil leaned forward, building his case. "We've talked before about arranging some sort of a friendly buy out, and Talcott Enterprises looks good right now. If we could time it just right, we could probably make some sort of deal so your future is safe—''

"Dammit, Phil, no.'' Brady slammed his fist on the table. "You know that won't work. I'm not going to give up.'' His voice dropped lower, the words edged with emotion. "It's not like we sold shoes or paper towels or sheet metal. When you make things for kids—furniture and toys—it gets to be part of you. It's the rest of my life, Phil; it's everything I've worked for. I won't give my company up."

Brady sank back in his chair, withdrawing into a heavy silence, idly swirling the amber liquid in his glass. He knew the ad was a long shot, but it was the best option so far. He'd also known Phil wasn't going to like the idea, but so far his friend hadn't found any fatal flaw in his plan. That was one of the reasons for running it past him. He was going to have to be in on things later anyway. Looking up at Phil, Brady saw the grimace of resignation cross his face.

"All right," Phil sighed. "You've obviously thought this over. Run it by me again."

Brady grinned. He'd figured his friend would eventually come around, at least enough to listen. "It's basically very simple, and the beauty of it is that everybody wins," Brady explained. "I answer the ad. I agree to father the child if she'll agree to a short-term marriage. It's the only way I'd do it anyway—I can't produce a bastard."

Phil shrugged. "I wouldn't think so, but it's often done that way these days."

"Not by me," Brady scowled. "Anyway, we set a cutoff date to end the marriage and then we go our separate ways. Nobody gets hurt. She gets her baby; I get Talcott Enterprises."

"All neat and tidy."

"Right." Brady looked at him smugly and signaled the waiter to bring another round.

Phil picked up the magazine Brady had dropped back on the table and read the ad again, shaking his head. "Come on, buddy. What kind of a broad would run a classified like this? For all you know, she may be playing a nasty practical joke.''

''Maybe...'' Brady hated to admit he hadn't thought of that. ''But I'm banking on the fact that she's a quiet little thing, can't quite make it with men, wants a baby because she's lonely. She'll probably make a hell of a good mother.''

''So what if she comes back later and sues you for support? You can't sign away that responsibility, you know.''

''I never intended to.'' Brady's deep-set eyes darkened and his voice took on a hard edge. ''I'd already planned to set up a trust fund for the baby. I may be an opportunist, but I'm not a heel.''

''I know you're not. As your lawyer I'm trying to keep you out of a mess.'' He looked directly at Brady. ''And as your friend I'm telling you this is a half-assed idea. You're talking about a baby you'll never see.''

Brady took a deep breath. ''I know that. I can handle it.''

Phil's gaze wandered to the window where a panorama of lights punctured the gathering darkness. ''That's what Eileen said when she walked out. She said she didn't give a damn whether she ever saw the boys or me again.''

His hollow voice silenced Brady. Brady knew how Phil felt about his two boys, and how badly his wife had hurt him. He also knew their situation didn't apply to him. He tried again. ''Eileen had problems, or she never would have left. We've been over and over that. What I'm talking about is something entirely different. I've given it a lot of thought—''

''Eileen told me over a year ago that she'd given it a lot of thought, too,'' Phil interrupted. ''She didn't want anything to do with me or the boys ever again. Presto!'' Phil snapped his fingers. ''Instant release from motherhood. Except it didn't work. You know how often she's tried to see Michael and Timmy.''

''I also know what kind of shape she's in,'' Brady added. ''I don't have her problems, and I'm not going to deal with that kind of attachment. I'll never see this baby.''

Phil shook his head. ''All right, let's go at this from another angle. You think it's going to be so damn easy to end this marriage—''

''It's not a marriage,'' Brady cut in. ''It's an arrangement.''

With a sigh, Phil picked up his glass and finished his martini. ''You're really hung up on doing this, aren't you?''

Brady shrugged. ''Not if you can give me an alternative.''

''No alternative—but I'll keep thinking about it.'' Phil signaled for the check. ''Maybe we'll just hope she's already found someone else. Or, maybe...'' Phil looked at the ad again. ''Maybe you won't meet her criteria. Open-minded, yes. But intelligent and good-looking...''

''Cut it out,'' Brady chuckled. He picked up the magazine and stood up, while Phil signed the check. ''And, by the way,'' Brady added, ''thanks for the drinks.''

On the way out of the club, Brady stopped by the front desk to pick up an envelope. Hurriedly he addressed it to the post office box cited in the magazine ad. He pulled a business card from his wallet and dropped it in the envelope. Then he stopped. The ad called for a résumé. If he didn't send one, it might kill his chances. He drummed his fingers on the polished wood counter. He'd never had a résumé, and he wasn't about to write one now.

He deliberated for a few moments before he smiled and sealed the envelope. Sending only a business card could have just the opposite effect. If the lady lawyer had any imagination, she'd be intrigued and follow up the card. The whole damned thing was a gamble anyway. He dropped the envelope in a mailbox on the way to his car.

WHEN THE HASTILY addressed envelope, containing nothing but a business card, arrived in Juliet Cavanaugh's office, she almost tossed it into the wastebasket. Her ad had specified a résumé, and this applicant was the only one who hadn't complied.

She slipped the card under the edge of a brass paperweight on her desk and in the crush of work forgot about it. A week passed before she noticed the card again, and this time her curiosity got the best of her. What kind of man would have the audacity to send nothing but a business card? It might be interesting to interview him and find out, she decided.

When she saw the name J. Brady Talcott on her list of appointments several days later she questioned whether she should have arranged the interview. But that was before Brady arrived.

From the first moment she saw him, Juliet knew she'd made the right decision. Being careful not to reveal her interest, Juliet stood up, appraising him across the expanse of her curved mahogany desk. "You must be J. Brady Talcott," she observed in her controlled professional voice. "Won't you sit down?"

He didn't move, except for one hand that thoughtfully stroked his chin. For several moments he stared at her, his substantial, impeccably tailored frame filling the doorway of her office. He'd known two lady lawyers in his life. One was a tough feminist with a penchant for man-tailored suits. The other was round and dumpy and wore thick glasses. This woman could have stepped off the cover of a fashion magazine. But it wasn't her clothes that captured his total attention. Her light-colored dress faded into the background. All he saw was the shape of high, full breasts, and the curve of slender hips that would be soft to the touch. The rest of her disappeared below the edge of her desk. He wondered what her legs were like. She was one of those women who made him wonder things like that. Aware that she was waiting for him to say something, he found his voice. "You're Juliet Cavanaugh?"

"Yes," came the crisp reply, "I am Ms Cavanaugh."

"Well, I'll be damned," he muttered under his breath.

Juliet fought a smile. His reaction wasn't unusual, but she particularly liked the fact that it came from him. She was quite aware that she didn't fit the stereotype of a woman lawyer, especially one with her credentials. And that suited her just fine. "Won't you come in?" she asked again, extending her hand toward him.

"I will," Brady agreed, striding across the carpeted expanse to the front of her desk. He still couldn't take his eyes off her. Her face was delicate with high cheekbones and a small, straight nose. She had the clear, almost translucent skin of a redhead framed by a thick auburn mane more brown than red. It wasn't until he got closer that he saw her eyes—really saw them, darker green than emeralds but with the same fire.

He took her hand in a brief, firm handshake. "I must admit," he told her, "you're not what I'd expected."

He wasn't what Juliet had expected either, but she didn't see any reason to tell him so. She had already interviewed a dozen men and screened twice that many more applications. She'd found the normal complement of kooks, a few serious contenders, and no one who even vaguely interested her. But something about J. Brady Talcott set him apart from the others. She found herself standing quietly, letting him study her with deep-set brown eyes, nearly the color of bittersweet chocolate. He made her feel more like a woman than like a lawyer.

From a pocket inside his pin-striped suit he extracted a neatly folded clipping, which he opened, scanned quickly to recheck his facts and then dropped in the center of her desk. "Did you run this ad in the *Bay City Magazine*?"

Juliet caught the frown, no more than an infinitesimal crease in the high, broad forehead, and a cold knot began to form in her stomach. Until that moment her plan for having a baby had seemed so logical. Now she saw herself through his eyes and her confidence wavered. Her cool, professional demeanor threatened to desert her. "Yes, I placed the ad," she replied, keeping her voice calm as she sat down. She gestured for him to take the chair that faced her desk.

"Why?" he demanded. He didn't sit down.

"Why?" she repeated, wondering why she felt so defensive. "I thought the ad was self-explanatory."

"It says paternity."

"Right," she confirmed. She'd been pleased with the ad's wording. It was brief and to the point and quite clear. Or at least *she'd* thought it was.

Brady leaned his hands on the edge of her desk and gave her a probing look. "Do you understand what paternity means?"

Juliet stared back at him for a moment, until the question sank in. "Since I was about twelve years old," she told him, laughing softly. She felt herself regaining control. "If you find it a problem, then what are you doing here?"

Brady was beginning to wonder that himself. When he got no response from her in the week after he'd sent his business card, he'd pretty much dismissed the whole thing. By the time she did contact him, he'd lost his initial ardor and was beginning to have second thoughts. Now that he saw her, the whole thing made no sense at all. He couldn't figure out what she was up to, unless she was working for someone else. Maybe she was nothing more than a go-between, somebody to screen the applicants. That would explain everything.

Casually, Brady sat on the chair across from Juliet and leaned forward. "Let's quit playing games. Who are you working for, Ms Cavanaugh?"

"I don't know what you mean."

"Who is your client—the lady who wants to have the baby?" He watched her carefully, figuring she might try to mislead him, but she probably wouldn't tell an outright lie.

Juliet hesitated, and then decided it was best to be direct. "In this instance, Mr. Talcott," she answered evenly, "I am working for myself."

At first Brady just stared at her. Then he laughed, a deep booming laugh that resounded through her office, echoing off the paneled walls and ricocheting through the silence.

Whatever reaction Juliet had expected, it wasn't laughter. She wasn't sure how she felt about this man. He was making her very uncomfortable. "You find that funny?" she demanded.

"Don't you?" he countered, still chuckling.

"Not at all," she replied coldly.

Brady Talcott shook his head. What was this woman after? If she were dull and plain, which was frankly what he had expected, he could have figured out her reasons for placing the ad. But just about any man would be happy to hop in bed with her, no questions asked. She was either naive as hell or there was some gimmick here he hadn't found yet. He tried again. "You mean to tell me that you want a baby and so you advertised for a father? Haven't you ever heard of adoption?"

"Of course. I've investigated it very thoroughly. The kind of baby I want would require waiting for years and then, as a single mother, I'd be too old to adopt at all," Juliet explained patiently. "Besides," she added, "I want to have the baby myself. Really, Mr. Talcott, I've thought this over quite carefully—"

"Then you must have considered artificial insemination," he interrupted bluntly.

Juliet sensed an uncharacteristic burning in her ears. "I want to know without a shred of doubt who the father is."

"So pick your donor," he told her. "How about that place where they guarantee you the father won a Nobel Prize?"

"You obviously haven't read the stories about the doctor who bragged about fathering hundreds of babies because he routinely replaced the donor sperm with his own," Juliet shot back. "I find the whole idea repulsive."

Brady leaned forward in his chair, his eyes penetrating her. "In that case, Ms Cavanaugh, are you familiar with the emotion called love, followed by the institution of marriage?"

Determinedly, Juliet stared back at him. "As a divorce lawyer, Mr. Talcott, I am intimately familiar with both." She had the distinct impression he was trying to intimidate her, and she wasn't going to let him. A growing irritation swelled inside her. "I am also familiar with the havoc that results when marriages fail, which most of them do," she added stiffly. "I figured out twenty years ago that marriage wasn't what I wanted. And everything I've seen since has proven me right."

Brady listened, his face impassive but his mind moving quickly. He had a lot of groundwork to do before he brought up the trust agreement. Funny, in some ways her situation was actually a lot like his. She wanted something she couldn't have the traditional way, so she'd figured out her own approach. Maybe that was part of what intrigued him about her. Before he mentioned the trust agreement he needed to know a lot more about her hang-up with marriage. After all, a marriage arrangement was a critical part of the deal.

"Have you ever been married, Ms Cavanaugh?" he inquired.

"No, Mr. Talcott, I have not."

"Then what's your problem? I thought every woman wanted to get married—at least once." He knew right away he'd hit a sore spot. Her expression barely changed, but her eyes flashed fire.

"I am not 'every woman,' Mr. Talcott," she retorted. "I'm a divorce lawyer. That gives me a window on a lot of miserable marriages."

He knew that explanation was too simple. There was more to it. "I thought you said you'd made that decision twenty years ago. You certainly weren't a divorce lawyer then."

"That's quite true, Mr. Talcott, but that's not the point." Juliet sat up straighter and folded her hands. "We are here to discuss a business arrangement, not my philosophy of marriage. My requirements are very specific, Mr. Talcott. I want to have a baby when I'm thirty. I want to know its father. And I don't want any long-term entanglements with the man. It's as simple as that."

Good, Brady thought. He didn't want any long-term entanglements either. He drummed his fingers on the desk. "I do believe you're serious," he observed.

"Quite serious, Mr. Talcott." The knot inside Juliet's stomach was tightening. For all the same reasons she instinctively knew this man was the right one, she was also wary of him. It hadn't been like that with any of the other applicants. They'd come before her, some with bravado and some with embarrassment, but all of them applying for the position, waiting for her judgment. She'd been in control. With this man, she wasn't. She waited, unable to predict his response.

"In that case, Ms Cavanaugh," he said finally, "if you really are serious about this plan of yours, do you suppose we might proceed from here on a first-name basis?''

His answer caught her off balance. Then the incongruity of the situation struck her. However brief and businesslike their relationship, producing a child required more intimacy than "Ms" and "Mr." Juliet tossed back her head and laughed; it was a soft, melodious sound that swept away the tension between them.

Their eyes met and held for a long moment. Once again she held out her hand. "I'm Juliet," she said softly.

"That's better." He took her hand and held it firmly in both of his. "Call me Brady."

Juliet looked at him as if she were seeing him for the first time. She found herself studying him, breaking the whole into parts—the full lips drawn into an oddly engaging smile, those eyes deeply set beneath bushy brows, the thick dark hair framing an angular face that was almost, but not quite, classically handsome. Nothing was unusual about him and yet everything was. Something about this man was terribly appealing.

She couldn't decide whether that was good or not. She had purposely sought a stranger to help carry out her plan because she wanted to avoid any involvement later. If she'd chosen someone she knew, perhaps one of the men she'd dated, she would have to see him again. There would be no way to make a clean break. He might even try to make some claim on the child and she'd have a real legal battle on her hands, one she might easily lose the way the courts were moving. She couldn't chance that. This was going to be *her* baby.

Realizing with a start that Brady was still holding her hand, Juliet pulled away. She actually knew very little about him and, in any case, it was important to keep her distance. This arrangement was, she reminded herself again, strictly business, whatever they called each other. She needed to get on with the interview. "Now that you've questioned me about my intentions," she began, "tell me about yours. Just exactly why did you answer my ad?"

Brady hesitated. What would she think, he wondered, if he told her the truth right now? Would she laugh and agree to it? Or would she turn him down cold? It was too soon to tell. He decided to wait, and he gave her his other reason. "Absolutely insatiable curiosity," he replied.

"That's all? Just curiosity?"

"What other reason would anyone have? I assume I'm not the only applicant. What reason did the others give you?"

"Most of them assumed there would be a substantial fee—"

"You mean you're going to pay for this?" he interrupted. "A stud fee?" For some reason, an exchange of money had never occurred to him.

Juliet winced. "That's a crass way to put it. Keep in mind, Mr. Talcott, that this is strictly business." When he didn't answer her, Juliet hurried on, anxious to change the subject. "Since I don't have your résumé— suppose you tell me about yourself," she suggested.

Brady shrugged. He couldn't figure this woman out. He was picking up all sorts of sensual signals, subtle invitations to come closer and get better acquainted. The air hung heavy between them. There was no denying the attraction. It had been immediate, and he knew she felt it, too. But the words coming out of her mouth, and even the tone of that carefully modulated voice, were calculated to keep him at a distance. Only in those flashing green eyes had he caught a glimpse of the woman behind the facade, and then what he saw was so fleeting that he couldn't capture it.

Any fool could figure out that his next move was to leave and put as much distance between himself and this woman as he could. But he knew he wasn't going to, and something told him it wasn't just because of Talcott Enterprises. He also wasn't about to submit to her questioning. If she wanted his life history, she could figure it out for herself.

His mouth formed a half grin. "You have my card, which lists my name, and address, and telephone number." He looked steadily into her eyes. "That is precisely the same information I have about you."

"But Mr. Talcott—"

Straightening his suit coat, he stood up. "Brady," he corrected her. "If you want more facts," he added offhandedly, "I'm sure you have the resources to find them."

He covered the distance to the office door in three strides before he stopped and turned to look back at her. Something in the way she was watching him suggested a vulnerability he hadn't expected. He sensed her disappointment, but he didn't change his mind. If she wasn't interested enough to pursue him, she'd never accept his proposition, anyway. He knew that his plan, in its own way, was as radical as hers.

Juliet stood up, and Brady had a sudden, overwhelming urge to go back to her, to suggest they forget what had passed between them and go to dinner like two normal people on a date. But they had already come too far. And they were both carrying too much emotional baggage for that kind of normal relationship to work. He wondered how it would feel to touch the curves beneath her dress, wondered how long it would take to expose the softness of the woman that was hidden inside her. "I don't know the Juliet behind those lovely green eyes," he told her, a huskiness creeping into his voice. "I have no idea whether I would like her or not."

"Is that important?" Juliet inquired.

"Critical." He started to leave and then turned back again. "When you find out whatever it is you seem to need to know about me, and you are ready to have a civilized conversation, feel free to call."

Juliet's voice was icy. "Good day, Mr. Talcott."

"Good day, Ms Cavanaugh," he replied formally, almost tearing himself away from her, not doubting that he would see her again.

Juliet watched him walk away. Once he had disappeared from sight, she paced across her office to the window that overlooked Embarcadero Center and waited until Brady's tall, imposing form emerged from the revolving doors below. Even seeing him from high above, she couldn't have mistaken him for anyone else. There was something about the way his body moved, the way he walked, that set him apart from the other tiny figures bustling along the street. No matter what the consequences, she wanted to know him better.

## CHAPTER TWO

THE NEXT STEP in Juliet's plan was to pay a call to Linda Burke. Somebody had to keep the law practice going while she was busy having a baby, and her former roommate was the logical candidate. But the early-morning visit was only partially business. Juliet greeted Linda with a big hug, realizing how glad she was to see her friend.

"You're looking more and more like a successful lawyer, new clothes and all," Linda observed, standing back and admiring Juliet's designer suit. She tugged at the ribbing of her faded Stanford sweatshirt. "I'm jealous," she said, only half joking. "You make me feel like a *hausfrau*."

"Not for long," Juliet answered, "and that's why I'm here." Walking beside her friend through the low, sprawling house where Linda and Steve had lived for the five years they'd been married, Juliet noted the sharp contrast between her own lifestyle and theirs. Linda's existence was comfortable and homey and obviously geared toward children. Juliet picked up a Raggedy Ann doll that had been dropped half under the hall table, wondering if her life would change the same way once she had a baby. "Where are the kids?" she asked, suddenly aware of the silence.

"Jennie's at nursery school—you just missed her," Linda explained, pushing her short, brown hair back from her face. "And the baby's asleep, outside in the buggy. That gives us a few blessed uninterrupted minutes, and we'd better take advantage of it," she said, leading the way toward the kitchen. "Come on. I'll get the tea."

Juliet watched her friend fill the teapot and put it on the tray with the cups. Linda didn't look like someone who'd had two babies. Maybe she was a little thicker around the middle than she'd been before, but she was still petite. And she had that same sparkle she'd always had. It seemed strange to think of Linda with a family when only a few years ago she'd been as free and independent as Juliet; a young struggling lawyer trying to build a practice. It was time her friend got back to work—they'd both agreed on that. Now, if everything jelled the way she'd planned, Juliet thought, it would be perfect for both of them. Linda could have a part-time practice, and Juliet would have someone to shoulder some of the load when she was pregnant and later, when she wanted to spend time with the baby.

While Linda carried the tray to the large patio looking out across the hills toward the city, Juliet tip-toed to the buggy and peeked in. The baby, sleeping soundly beneath lightweight white netting, still looked very small and vulnerable to Juliet.

"Sh-h-h, don't wake him," Linda warned. "He'll be up soon enough. I want to know what's going on with you. You were really vague on the phone."

Juliet accepted the cup of tea Linda offered and settled back in the wicker rocker. "I think I may have found the father I'm looking for," she announced. "He came in yesterday, and I had this feeling right from the beginning—"

"You're really going through with it?" Linda broke in.

"Of course. I said I would." Juliet was surprised by the question. Linda was the only person she'd told about her plan, the only one she could count on to listen to her instead of being judgmental.

Linda set her teacup on the table. "So tell me about him," she directed, turning her chair toward Juliet. "Everything."

"Well," Juliet hesitated. "Right now there isn't much. His name is J. Brady Talcott and he's president of something called Talcott Enterprises."

"And?"

"That's it, so far."

Linda frowned. "I thought you required a résumé and medical history and all sorts of stuff from these guys."

"This one only sent a business card. I don't know why I even decided to follow up." Juliet took a sip of tea. "But he seems like a good choice."

"You can't get involved in a deal like this with someone you don't know anything about," Linda protested.

"Don't worry," Juliet assured her. "I already called Harry."

Linda nodded approvingly. "Ah, yes, Harry Mechum's one-man detective agency. If anyone can tell you everything there is to know about him, it's Harry."

"That's what I figured," Juliet agreed. "Now, how about you? Are you ready to go back to work?"

"Ready? I'm dying to." Linda leaned forward. "I found an agency last week that provides nannies—they sound absolutely wonderful. Except they cost an arm and a leg. Can we make enough money?''

''We should be able to,'' Juliet answered. ''The practice has really taken off in the last couple of years. There's almost enough work for two of us full-time.''

Linda's eyes sparkled. ''That sounds almost too good to be true.'' She poured another cup of tea for both of them and slowly her expression changed. ''But even with money, it's going to be a juggling act for both of us,'' she warned, looking directly at Juliet. ''Especially for you. A husband can take a lot of the load off sometimes. I know Steve's gone a lot, but when he's home it's really nice to be able to turn it all over to him for a few hours.'' She shifted in her chair. ''You're taking on a lot of responsibility.''

Juliet didn't answer right away. Linda wasn't telling her anything she didn't already know. There were going to be a lot of times when single parenthood would be hard. But other people managed. It was the same kind of caution people had given when she got out of law school. ''Go into a law firm,'' they'd advised. ''It's too hard to make it on your own.'' But she had made it, and she'd make it this time, too.

''You know how I feel about marriage,'' Juliet said slowly. ''It's been good for you and Steve—so far at least—but you're the exception.'' She stood up and walked to the edge of the patio. ''I don't see any reason why I should lose the chance to become a mother just because I don't want to get married.''

Linda's eyes followed her. ''You could adopt a baby, you know. That's an acceptable way to do it.''

''But I don't want to adopt.'' Juliet turned around, her tone unrelenting. ''We've been over that, too. I want to have the baby myself.''

Linda nodded. "I understand that. Having a baby is probably the most profound thing you'll ever do. I'd be the last person to ever try to talk you out of it. But even if you're determined to have it there are other ways—"

"You're about to tell me there are other ways to accomplish that," Juliet interrupted. "We've been over those, too. But this is the only way I can have the baby and be absolutely certain who the father is."

"In other words, you retain total control."

Startled by the comment, Juliet walked back to the chair. "I suppose so. I haven't thought of it exactly that way."

"You like to be in control, Juliet. You always have, and I'm not knocking that either." Linda shrugged. "I just figured we should run through the options one more time."

"Like always?" Juliet grinned at her friend.

"Like always," Linda agreed. "Which brings up the question of you know, what's-his-name...Sam? George?"

"You mean David?"

"Yeah, David. Whatever happened with you and David? You sounded as though you two might actually have been going places. I know it was good...that was written all over you...I thought maybe he'd be the one. At least you know him," she added, pointedly.

Juliet looked out across the hills. Linda was right. It had been good, at least for a while. But she'd never felt complete—as if there should somehow have been something more. They hadn't quite clicked, not the way they ought to have if they were going to risk anything permanent. The relationship had just gone on and on and grown more predictable until finally, one day, Juliet decided she'd had enough.

She looked at Linda. "I think you put your finger on the problem. How long did I go out with him? Two years, maybe? And you couldn't remember his name."

Linda laughed. "I guess we'd call him eminently forgettable."

"Something like that," Juliet murmured.

They sat quietly for a few moments. It was a comfortable feeling, talking with her friend again, Juliet thought. She would be glad to have Linda come into the practice. She'd had reservations at first, wondering whether she would have a difficult time sharing something she'd struggled so hard to build herself. But she and Linda had always been frank and open with each other, going clear back to those years when they were roommates at Stanford. That would make everything easier. And the practice had grown until there was enough work for both of them.

A litany of baby noises, words that weren't words, poured into the morning silence. "Quiet time's over," Linda observed. "Paul's awake—and damn, there's the phone." She stood up and started inside. "Pick him up before he cries, will you?" she called over her shoulder to Juliet.

Juliet folded back the white netting that covered the buggy, and two large blue eyes met hers. The round face broke into a delighted grin. She leaned closer, slightly in awe of the tiny creature. "You lost your rattle," she observed gravely, picking up the small silver rattle she had given the baby when he was born. She held it against his fist and the tiny fingers closed tightly around it. He waved both arms and then stared curiously at his hand when the rattle made noise.

He'd grown in the weeks since she'd seen him, but he still looked so little. Juliet wondered if she'd have trouble leaving her own baby to go back to work when it was still small. But a good nanny would make all the difference, and at first she would work only part-time.

Juliet took off her suit jacket and searched for a cloth to put over her shoulder. She'd learned the hard way that Paul could be very messy. When she turned away from the baby the happy sounds changed to cries. By the time she located a towel, the wailing from the buggy was growing steadily louder. "Come here, Paul," she said soothingly, slipping her hands under the baby's back. "I can tell you don't like being ignored."

Paul continued screaming while Juliet sat down in the wicker rocker and cradled him in her arms. She talked to him softly while she rocked him and in a few moments he was quiet again, his blue eyes fixed on her. He was soft and warm against her body, sweet smelling after his morning bath. Juliet felt a deep sense of longing as she rocked him, and she found herself holding him closer and wondering what it would be like if he were hers.

The baby cooed softly and looked up at Juliet. Yes, she thought, her instincts had been right. She did want a baby, and she wanted one so much that it was worth all she had to go through. She thought about Brady Talcott, framed by the doorway of her office, and hoped Harry Mechum wouldn't find anything damaging about him. The more she thought about Brady, the more "right" he seemed.

Juliet looked up as she heard the patio door slide open. "You two are obviously getting along," Linda observed with a smile. "You'll be a good mother, Juliet. Just make sure you know what you're getting into before you do it."

"I think I do," Juliet answered seriously, "as much as anyone ever does ahead of time."

"By the way," Linda asked, "how are you going to break this to your mother?"

Juliet didn't hesitate. "The same way I'd tell her anything—directly," she answered nonchalantly. "You know how Cass is. She believes in everyone doing her own thing. She won't have any trouble with this. In fact, she'll probably love the idea of being a grandmother."

Linda laughed. "She can't possibly be any happier about her new role than I am about mine. It sounds really good to go into a law practice that's off and running. Mine never quite got to that stage."

"You didn't have time," Juliet replied. Paul wiggled in her arms and she turned him so he was sitting up on her lap.

"Most of the work I had was bar association referrals, and you know how few of those pan out," Linda remembered.

"Bar association referrals," Juliet echoed. She freed her arm from around Paul and checked her watch. "Linda, I'm really glad you said that. I've got a woman coming in this morning—I'd almost forgotten."

"Then you do still take them. If you're already overloaded, why do you?" Linda leaned down to pick up Paul, and the baby reached his arms out toward his mother.

"A couple of reasons, I guess," Juliet said as she stood up and put on her suit jacket. "Sometimes they come to something and..." Her voice trailed off. It sounded sort of hokey to say that was the way she paid her debt to society, but in a way it was true. "Sometimes you can help those people without investing a whole lot of time," she continued. "Remember that big Barker case—the one that really got me going?"

Linda nodded. "How could I forget? It was all over the papers for weeks."

"That started out as a bar association referral," Juliet reminded her.

"I guess it did," Linda agreed. "And besides that," she said grinning, "you've got a big heart, even if you won't admit it. But if we're both going to work at this and make any money—especially when you've got a baby to support—we're not going to be able to spend our time on charity cases."

"Don't worry," Juliet assured her. "My heart's not that big."

Still carrying Paul, Linda walked her to the door. "I'm really anxious to get back to work, Juliet. Thanks for giving me the chance."

"You're the one doing me the favor," Juliet replied. "How do you want to start?"

"Maybe I can come in one or two days a week for a while, till I get into the swing of things." Linda suggested. "I'll call the nanny agency this afternoon and see what I can arrange."

"Fantastic," Juliet agreed, giving Paul a parting pat. She left, feeling that the pieces of the puzzle were all falling into place.

As she drove back toward the office, Juliet mentally sorted through the cases she could turn over to

Linda. Nothing too complicated at first, she decided, and obviously only ones where the retainer was already in the bank. Linda had made her feelings about money pretty clear. And she was right. But in reality, Juliet thought, she only took one or two cases a year without cash up front, and never anything that would take a lot of time. She also decided to call the building management about expanding her office space. Linda would need her own office right away.

A visual image of Brady kept intruding on her thoughts, and she smiled, catching her bottom lip lightly between her teeth. She really would like to know him better. But she couldn't let personal feelings intrude, she reminded herself, and she needed to wait until she talked to Harry to make any final decision. This was, after all, a business arrangement, and it was critical that she keep it that way.

When Juliet walked into her office, the reception room was empty except for her secretary, who was bent over a stack of file folders. "I take it my eleven o'clock didn't show," she said, resting her briefcase on the edge of the reception desk.

Alice peered over her glasses. "Oh, no, Ms Cavanaugh. She's been here more than an hour. She seemed real nervous and so I told her she could go sit in your office. I checked first to make sure your desk was locked up and all."

"Did you have her fill out the background forms?" Juliet held out her hand expectantly. "I'd like to take a look at them before I see her."

"She took them with her, but I don't think she filled them out," Alice said. "She wouldn't even tell me her name."

"That's not a very good start," Juliet muttered.

Behind the closed door a woman sat stiffly on the edge of a light blue wing chair. Her fine blond hair fell like a curtain around her face. Her hands were knotted in her lap. She hadn't moved in nearly an hour. Instead, she simply waited, not really knowing how long she'd been there because she wasn't wearing a watch. The time didn't matter much anyway. She would have waited as long as necessary. This meeting was important. She smoothed her camel-colored wool skirt nervously, pressing out the deep wrinkles with her palms. Her clothes had been beautiful once, and she liked wearing pretty things. This outfit was still presentable. She had worked hard to sponge the stain out of the ecru blouse, and now it was barely noticeable.

Hearing muted conversation in the reception room, she glanced over her shoulder. The lawyer must be in. She fumbled with the clasp on her purse and pulled out a gold compact. Her reflection in the small mirror told her that she looked fine. Well put together. She tried out a smile. Almost gracious. She had to be if she was going to accomplish her goal. She dropped the compact back in her purse and fished around until she found a peppermint under some crumpled tissues. Putting the peppermint in her mouth, she closed the purse and took a deep breath. This wasn't going to be easy. She had known that at the onset. But she could do it. She had to.

The door opened and the lawyer entered. Her hair was a deep auburn and she was younger and much more attractive than the woman had expected her to be. The lawyer didn't look very experienced. The woman clutched a wadded twenty-dollar bill tightly in her hand. That was what the man at the bar association had said she had to pay for a half-hour consultation. She hoped he had referred her to a good lawyer.

Juliet assessed the woman quickly, noting how the hands were knotted nervously together, the angle of the head, the tight lines at the corners of the woman's mouth. They were all common signs. When Juliet extended her hand, the woman stood up. "Good morning," Juliet greeted her, looking directly into the pale blue eyes. "Come on over and sit on the sofa. Would you like a cup of coffee?"

The woman shook her head. Wordlessly, she followed Juliet across the room where she sat stiffly on the far end of the sofa. Juliet watched carefully as she set her purse on the coffee table, moved it to the floor, and finally laid it in her lap. This wasn't the time to pick up the yellow pad she always kept handy by the couch, Juliet decided. She'd dispense with taking notes. It was more important to get the woman talking first. "Why don't we begin with your name?" Juliet suggested.

"No," the woman responded quickly. Too quickly. "I don't want to tell you my name until I'm sure."

"Sure of what?" Juliet prompted.

"Sure you can help me."

"All right," Juliet answered. "Let's begin there. Tell me about your problem."

"I want my babies back," the woman blurted out. For the first time since they'd sat down, she looked at Juliet.

"Your babies? How many children do you have?"

"Two." The woman's voice was flat. She looked away.

"Where are they?"

"With my husband." Again, the toneless voice.

"Are you divorced?"

The woman shook her head.

"Has there been any legal action? Has the court awarded your husband custody?"

Again the woman shook her head, a barely perceptible movement. Her knuckles were white from clutching her purse. Juliet knew they weren't going to get very far unless she could get the woman to open up. The effort was probably going to be fruitless, anyway, but she was so obviously alone and in need of help that Juliet had to try. Juliet asked another question. "How long have you been separated from your husband and children?"

"I'm not separated." She sounded defensive.

At least that was some emotion, Juliet thought. She leaned forward in an attempt to bridge the gulf between them and caught a faint hint of alcohol well-masked with peppermint. "You need to explain more clearly," Juliet told her, beginning to understand at least part of the problem.

For a long moment, the woman searched Juliet's face. "I'm not afraid to tell you, but I want to be sure you can help," she said quietly.

"I can try," Juliet promised, "but I can't do anything unless you tell me what's happened."

The woman took a deep, shuddering breath. "I left last year, one day in the summer. He hadn't been home all week. He never came home anymore."

Now they were getting somewhere. "You haven't been back since?" Juliet questioned.

"I used to go home, but not for a long time now. I miss my children, but when I go back it isn't the same. He won't let me take them anywhere." The woman stared down at her hands. "It's not like really being their mother." When she raised her head, her eyes were filled with tears. "I want to take them home with me. I want them to be mine again."

Juliet pressed her lips together. The puzzle was beginning to take shape and, like so many others, it wasn't very pretty. "Why won't your husband let you take them with you for a few days?"

For a long time the woman didn't answer, and then her voice was barely audible. "He says I can't take care of them."

She was talking now. Before they went further, it was time to lay the cards on the table. "Is it because you drink?"

The woman looked as though Juliet had struck her. Juliet braced herself, not knowing whether to expect anger or denial. She got neither. The woman stared straight ahead.

"I never used to drink. But it got so lonely when he didn't come home. The babies got sick a lot, and I was always so tired, and I never got to go anywhere. I tried to talk to him. But he didn't understand how lonely I was."

The woman's eyes met Juliet's in a plea for understanding. "He sent me to psychiatrists and sometimes they gave me pills, but it didn't help. My husband didn't seem to care about anything but his work. He said I should be grateful because he worked so hard and made so much money. And then he wanted me to have another baby so I would have something to occupy my time. I couldn't stand it anymore." She covered her face with her hands.

"That was why you left?" Juliet probed. "Nothing specific, just because you'd had it?"

"No, not exactly," the woman admitted, placing her hands carefully in her lap, but not looking up. "One day I got really angry at my older boy and I shook him and pushed him against the wall."

"Did you hurt him?" Juliet asked.

"No, but I could have," the woman answered slowly. "The next day, when I thought about it I got really scared." She raised her eyes, her face taut with the pain of the memory. "I was afraid if my husband found out he'd send me away to a hospital. He'd threatened to before. So I just packed and left."

Juliet offered her a tissue from the box on the coffee table, making a mental note to replace the box soon. It was nearly empty again. "Do you want to begin divorce proceedings?" she asked quietly.

A profound sadness settled in the pale blue eyes. "I just want my babies. I want to take them away and start all over again."

"And your husband?"

"I don't know." She blew her nose.

"He hasn't taken any legal action?" Juliet asked.

The woman shook her head. "I don't think so."

"Does your husband send you money?"

"Sometimes," the woman admitted, then added quickly, "but I work as a waitress, too."

Juliet debated briefly about what to do. What this woman needed was some love and understanding from her husband, and if he hadn't cut her off after a year, that was a good sign. It was obvious that she needed a therapist, not a lawyer, and someone to help her fight the alcohol problem when she was strong enough to do it. Juliet knew she might be able to get a court order allowing the woman partial custody, but in good conscience she couldn't do it. At least not right now.

"My first suggestion," Juliet began, "is that you try to talk to your husband again. If the two of you could work out something together, it would be best for you and the children."

"It has been a long time since I've talked to him," the woman admitted. "I don't think it will do any good."

"You need to try," Juliet urged. She stood up, indicating the meeting was over.

The woman came slowly to her feet. "I brought the money. The man said I had to pay you twenty dollars for a half hour."

Juliet accepted the crumpled twenty-dollar bill the woman offered. "If you need further advice, let me know," she said kindly. "We'll discuss payment then."

"All right," the woman agreed, starting toward the door. Even as her hand touched the doorknob, the woman knew that she probably wouldn't come back again. This lawyer sounded like she understood. She sounded like she wanted to help, but she didn't know what to do. No one did. It was all so complicated. Maybe she would find a quiet place and have an early lunch and a few glasses of wine. Then she could get her head together and decide what to do.

When the office door closed, Juliet took a new box of tissues out of the closet and set it on the coffee table. She hoped that somewhere that woman would find the help she needed. She wasn't going to find it in a lawyer's office.

Every time she talked to a woman like that, Juliet understood a little more clearly why she didn't want any part of marriage. This one was a little different than most. Usually it was the man who walked out,

like her own father had. In this case it was the woman.
But it was the same pattern. Two people, happy at the
beginning, slowly grew apart. When the anger and the
disappointment got to a certain level, one of them
usually left. Everyone involved got hurt, especially the
children. Often they got hurt most of all.

Juliet walked over to her desk. She wasn't going to
let that happen. She'd planned her life a different way,
and she'd make her plan work. But first she needed to
know more about Brady, and that required a visit to
Harry Mechum.

# CHAPTER THREE

THE STAIRWAY LEADING UP to Harry's office had a smell of its own. It wasn't dirty exactly, but it bordered on that definition. The pungent smell of permanent waving solution from the beautician's shop down the hall mixed with years of stale cigar smoke and the odor of an old mongrel dog that often slept in the corner of the upper landing. It was a dingy old building, in a neighborhood near the Tenderloin district where Juliet never ventured after dark.

She remembered the first time she'd come, the idealistic young lawyer expecting a spit-and-polish private eye of the Paul Drake variety. Then she'd met Harry, with his doleful eyes and ever-present cigar, stationed behind the mound of clutter he called his desk. Mostly he'd grunted, and she'd left disgusted, never expecting to hear from him again. But when he called, it was to tell her that her client's husband was maintaining a double identity with two wives, two comfortable suburban homes, and two sets of children. The story hit front pages across the country, and Juliet's law practice took off. Ever since then, she'd figured she owed Harry. She knocked twice on Harry's office door, carefully, because it made the glass rattle, and then walked in.

"Morning," Harry grunted as usual, barely looking up. He nonchalantly shifted his soggy cigar from one side of his mouth to the other and pulled a sheaf of dog-eared papers out of one of the piles on the back corner of his desk. "Got that info you wanted. The stuff about the Talcott guy," he said, holding the papers out toward Juliet.

"This is *all* about Brady Talcott?" Juliet asked in surprise as she took the papers from the detective and sat down on one of the wooden chairs crowded into the tiny office. She thumbed through the roughly typed papers, turning them occasionally to decipher Harry's scrawled notes in the margins. Harry certainly was thorough. A newspaper photograph caught her attention, and she picked it up.

"Good lookin', ain't he?" Harry commented. "The broad that's divorcing him is gonna lose a lot. Or maybe get a lot with you workin' for her," he winked.

Juliet smiled at the compliment. She studied the photo of Brady in a sleek, smooth-fitting swimsuit. He was poised on the bow of a sailboat grinning at the large trophy he held in his hand. The caption below the picture read, "J. Brady Talcott III wins Bay Regatta."

"He is good-looking," she said as much to herself as to Harry. Well, she thought, that was one of the requirements she had put in the ad. "Obviously Mr. Talcott sails," Juliet mused.

"Among other things." Harry scraped a wooden match across his shoe sole and lighted the remains of his cigar.

"Such as?" Juliet prompted.

"Flying. The guy used to own his own plane. Tried his hand at racing cars a few years back. Apparently gave that up."

"So, he sails, he flies, he used to race cars," Juliet repeated. "What else?"

Harry reached a none-too-clean hand into the pile of papers Juliet was holding and dug out some notes. He rocked his oak swivel chair backward almost to the point of disaster before beginning. "Let's see here," he drawled with maddening slowness. "John Brady Talcott III. Age thirty-four, turns thirty-five March fifth."

Perfect, Juliet silently approved.

"Born in Boston, public schools there, an engineering degree from M.I.T.—that's the Massachusetts Institute of Technology—" Harry explained.

"I know, I know," Juliet said impatiently. "Go on."

"Father died two years ago, John Brady Jr. Mother surviving, name's Amelia. She's sixty-four. One sister, Sheila, lives in Connecticut," Harry droned on. "She's got a husband and a couple of kids."

Juliet's attention wandered. So, she mentally calculated, Brady was born when his mother was thirty. Good age to have a baby, she smiled to herself.

Methodically, Harry continued. "Never been married..." Harry shot Juliet a puzzled look. "Yeah, I remember now, this is the one I wanted to ask you about. If he's not married, how come somebody's divorcing him?"

"Harry," Juliet responded, "the deal is I don't ask how you get the information and you don't ask what I do with it? Okay?"

"Sure," Harry grunted. "Couldn't find much to spice this up. Doesn't seem to play around much. Did go out a lot with one woman a couple of years ago, but she's married to somebody else. Seems to spend most of his time with his business.''

"Oh, yes," Juliet interjected. She remembered Brady's business card which she had been carrying in her purse all week. "He's chairman of the board of Talcott Enterprises," she noted. "Just exactly what is Talcott Enterprises."

Harry stopped rocking his chair. He stood up and leaned over his desk toward Juliet, blowing the acrid cigar smoke directly into her face. "Now we come to the interesting part," he chortled.

"I'm waiting, and not very patiently," Juliet muttered. She coughed slightly and turned her head away from the cigar fumes. Harry, as usual, didn't pay any attention.

"This guy," Harry tapped Brady's picture, "is worth a mint. We're not talking a couple of hundred thou. We're talking big bucks here. Millions."

Juliet stared incredulously at the picture and then at Harry. No wonder Brady reacted so differently from the others when she offered him money. She'd figured at the time he must be comfortable financially, but she'd never thought about him being wealthy.

"Are you sure?" she countered.

"Yep." Harry nodded his head.

"Where did Brady, er..." Juliet caught herself, but not before Harry shot her a curious look. "Where did Mr. Talcott get all this money if he's only thirty-four?"

"Got the family business when the old man died. Built it into a million-dollar operation."

"And it's all his?"

"Couldn't quite get a handle on that—something odd about the way it's set up but I couldn't nail it."

"Just exactly what is this family business?" Juliet stood up and paced restlessly back and forth across the carpet. She had fleeting thoughts of a line of cruise ships, diamonds, oil....

"Children's furniture," Harry said matter-of-factly.

Juliet stopped pacing and stared at him. "Children's furniture?" she repeated blankly.

"That's what I said," Harry confirmed. He dropped the sheaf of notes into the rubble on his desk and clamped down hard on his cigar. "He designs lots of it himself. Used to be pretty run-of-the-mill, but in the last year or so he's come out with some ritzy new stuff. You probably heard of it—he's got that TV ad. You know the one, that mechanical toy named Hugo that marches around adding pieces to the furniture to make it bigger." Harry stiffened his arms and began to strut around the office, making electroniclike beeping sounds as he rearranged the chairs.

He looked more like a penguin in a greasy tie than a mechanical toy, Juliet thought, and normally she would have convulsed in giggles at the sight. But not this time. She was searching her memory, trying to put it all together. "Now I remember," she cried out. "Last Christmas. Neiman-Marcus, Bloomingdales, Saks. 'The furniture that grows with your child.'"

"You got it." Harry stopped his penguin imitation and reached in his pocket again. "He's apparently test-marketing some other stuff. Started with a spin-off from his furniture—wooden blocks and then snap-together bubbles. He's added motors and remote control hookups for older kids, and a few months ago he came out with some climbing stuff." Harry consulted his notes. "I don't know where he's headed with that. I got a copy of his balance sheet that shows a profit breakdown—''

"Enough." Juliet held up her hand to stop Harry's dissertation. She already had enough information to know Brady Talcott was way beyond what she'd expected. "Now, how about his medical report?" That was the one critical area Harry hadn't covered.

"Talcott's medical report." Harry scratched his balding head. "Why you wanted a medical report is beyond me." He gave Juliet a penetrating look and waited for a response, but she only smiled. Harry shrugged. "Okay, you're the boss. Whatever you want. Anyway, the guy is in great shape."

"You checked his medical background very carefully?"

"That's what you pay me for." Harry scowled. "He had a complete insurance physical a couple of months ago—X rays, blood tests, the whole works. There's probably not a test around that wasn't done on that guy."

"And there is absolutely nothing irregular?" Juliet questioned.

"No, I already told you that," Harry retorted. "Next you're gonna want an affidavit from his doctor."

Juliet didn't answer. She was focused on Brady. His medical exam sounded even more comprehensive than hers had been. It looked as though he filled all the squares. He was smart, and in the right areas. He had math and science abilities to balance her verbal talents. And he was definitely attractive. She pictured him as she had first seen him, standing in her office doorway—dark hair, deep brown eyes, a powerful build that fit nicely into his custom-tailored suit. He was obviously athletic, which she certainly was not. The two of them as parents could be an absolutely dynamic combination.

"Anything else?" Harry's gravelly voice intruded.

She looked up to find him waiting expectantly. "As usual, you've done a fantastic job," she praised him enthusiastically.

"Thanks," Harry answered with practiced modesty. Juliet stood up and reached for the information folder about Brady. Instead of giving it to her, Harry cleared his throat. "You forgot to pay me," he reminded her.

"I'm sorry," Juliet apologized. She quickly reached into her purse for her tapestry checkbook, wrote a check, and gave it to Harry.

"This is a personal check," he noted. "You always pay me with a business check."

"Right," Juliet agreed.

"It's also a hell of a lot more than you usually pay me," he added.

"Right," Juliet answered again.

Harry gave her an astute look. "I don't ask questions. I just do the job," he muttered, handing her the folder.

"Right again," grinned Juliet. "I'll close the door behind me."

She sailed down the stairs, stopping just long enough to give the old mongrel dog a vigorous pat on the head. Once outdoors, Juliet took a deep breath of air, already heavy with afternoon fog, and considered her next move. She had all the information she needed about J. Brady Talcott. She might as well get on with it. Juliet looked around until she spotted a pay phone and then took Brady's business card from her purse. Her pulse quickened as she dialed the number.

Brady answered his own phone.

"Hello, this is Juliet Cavanaugh," she said breezily. There was a long pause, and Juliet's confidence evaporated. It had been a week since the interview. *My God,* she thought, *he's forgotten me.*

"Well, well," Brady finally replied, the business-like tone gone. "I thought I'd be hearing from you pretty soon. You must have made up your mind."

It suddenly seemed important to Juliet not to sound too anxious. "On the contrary, Brady," she hedged, "I haven't made up my mind about anything. Just moved a little more in that direction."

"I understand you've done a background check on me that would make the FBI blush." He didn't try to mask the amusement in his voice. "Did you find my house in order?"

*Damn Harry,* Juliet thought. He could have been more subtle. "Just a few inquiries," she answered, brushing the investigation off as best she could. "I hope you didn't mind."

"As a matter of fact," he answered, "I got calls from people I hadn't heard from in years. My mother said the bank contacted her to find out if I was going to work for the CIA."

Juliet laughed, a soft, throaty sound in the silence. Her own mother would have thought it was funny but, then, Cass wasn't like other mothers. "What did you tell your mother?"

"That someone was doing a credit check—what would you tell her?"

Juliet chose not to answer his question. She was glad she didn't have the problem.

"Well, Brady," she said briskly, "if you're still interested in my offer, I'd like to meet with you in my office as soon as possible to see whether we can agree on a suitable arrangement."

There was another long silence. He must be checking his calendar, she decided. Juliet motioned to a man waiting for the phone, indicating that she wouldn't be much longer. She hoped Brady might be free sometime in the next few days. The contract was ready—all he had to do was sign it, and then... And then, she thought, after Brady signed the contract... Juliet shifted her weight uneasily. That part was still hazy in her mind. She realized she hadn't thought much about the period between finding the man and having the baby. But that would come later.

"Are you in your office?" Brady's abruptness startled her.

"Well, no, I had an errand—"

"Fine," he interrupted. "As long as you're out, you might as well come here. I'll be available in about half an hour."

"But I can't," Juliet protested. "I don't have the contract with me. And it doesn't have to be right away," she added quickly. "I was thinking perhaps later in the week." There was another pause. Juliet thought she heard him chuckle, but she couldn't be sure.

"I'm not sure we're quite at the contract stage yet. Do you have my office address with you?"

"Why, yes—"

"Good," he said, cutting her off. "I'll see you in a little while." Then he hung up.

Juliet stared at the silent phone. It would serve him right if she didn't show up. But inside, she knew she would.

THE BEGINNINGS OF afternoon rush hour had already clogged the streets, which made the cab ride to the Jackson Square renovation district take twice as long as it should have. The delay gave Juliet that much longer to question why she was going to Brady's office in the first place. The cab wound along a route lined with sycamore trees and past old, restored buildings that were a pocket of the past in the middle of the city. When the cab pulled up in front of the address she had given the driver, Juliet found herself on a narrow sidewalk in front of a red brick colonial-style building with two shuttered windows. The brass plaque on the front wall said Playspace, by Talcott Enterprises.

She opened the door and stepped into a quiet showroom where children's furniture was grouped in several softly lit display areas. The nursery caught her attention immediately. She stood by a cradle, idly tracing the outline of a bright red teddy bear on a quilt. She'd need a room like this soon. A sign on a nearby dresser explained that every piece of furniture could be disassembled and expanded, to grow with the child. As she walked past the remaining rooms, she could visualize the change table becoming part of a toy box and then an easel for painting and ultimately part of a corner compartment that housed both a stereo system and a computer center.

The whole concept was ingenious. She wondered whether it was Brady's design. Juliet approached a receptionist sitting at a desk on one side of the room.

As soon as she gave her name, the woman directed her to Brady's office, saying he would join her shortly.

Juliet walked briskly up a flight of stairs and down the hall to the third door on the right. She turned the knob hesitantly and found herself frozen in the doorway of the strangest office she had ever seen. In fact, it didn't look like an office at all. It looked like a playground. There was color everywhere. A vast expanse of bright green carpet—grass green, Juliet thought—blended right into the flower garden stenciled on a wall painted in the palest of sky blue. A brilliant red dome-shaped climber dominated one corner of the room. Across from it was a series of ramps and mazes, which appeared to have been built from a combination of clear plastic tubing and flat multi-colored panels. A collection of small airplanes, gliders, and intricate kites hung from the ceiling. Enchanted, Juliet stepped inside and put her briefcase down near the door.

For several moments, she didn't move. What kind of man could call a place like this an office? Despite all the information Harry had given her, there was obviously a lot she still didn't know about Brady Talcott. At the far end of the room she spotted a desk and telephones and a small conference area with chairs and a sofa—definite signs that someone worked there. But it seemed like a token gesture in the midst of a fantasy.

Slowly, Juliet stepped farther into the room. Walking past an oversized drafting table strewn with drawings and designs, she bumped into a red miniature sports car poking out from behind the table leg. She reached out to touch it and then pulled back, startled when its lights flashed on.

Glancing over her shoulder to make sure no one was watching, she knelt down for a closer look at the car. It reminded her of a toy car she'd seen in a department store window when she was about ten. She'd really wanted that car. But by the time her birthday came, her father was gone and Cass would never have bought her anything like that. She picked up a small remote control that she found leaning against the table leg and curiously pushed a button.

The car doors all opened at once and a horn honked. Delighted, Juliet pushed another button. The car doors closed, the engine revved up, and the car took off, veering to the right and smashing head on into a table leg. "Damn," Juliet murmured. She laid the remote control on the floor and crawled under the table to retrieve the car.

Brady stopped near the doorway, his eyes following her every move. He knew she hadn't heard him come in. There was something very appealing about her in that position, he thought, as he watched her back out from under the table. The way her hips moved, swinging back and forth like that, was definitely sexy. Very sexy. Brady was in no hurry to announce his arrival.

Standing very still, he watched her pick up the remote control and push different buttons, making the car swerve back and forth across the room. There was a spontaneity about her he hadn't seen before. She looked almost fragile to him, not at all like the cool lady lawyer who had interviewed him the week before. His eyes swept across the soft curves beneath her yellow jersey dress and down her legs to her high-heeled pumps. He'd been right. She did have very nice legs. He'd thought she would.

"I see you like the car," he said casually, stepping into the room.

Juliet spun around. "What are you doing here?"

"It's my office," Brady grinned. "I don't usually knock."

"You startled me," Juliet admitted, laying the remote control on the table. "Besides, I don't understand all this. I thought you made children's furniture."

"I do," Brady affirmed. "But after my father died, I expanded the furniture line into a modular system—I assume you saw it on the way in—and now I'm adding toys." He loosened his tie. "Let me show you around."

Juliet shook her head. "Thank you, but I came to discuss business."

"And this is my business," Brady interrupted. He took two steps forward and placed his hands firmly on her shoulders. "Adults are allowed to play, too, you know."

Juliet looked up to find Brady's eyes as warm as his hands. He wasn't laughing at her, she decided, and her body relaxed in the firm pressure of his grip. "This is all foreign to me," she admitted. "I didn't have toys when I was a little girl. My mother doesn't believe in them."

"Doesn't believe in them?" Brady let go of her shoulders. "How can anyone not believe in toys?"

"She doesn't believe in commercial toys," Juliet explained. "Cass thinks children should create their own fun." Juliet could see that he didn't understand at all, but she always had trouble when she tried to explain Cass's theories.

"Cass is your mother?" Brady questioned.

Juliet nodded.

"And you call her by her given name?"

"Well, yes . . ." That obviously seemed odd to him, too, but she had always called her mother Cass.

Brady's rich, mellow laugh reminded Juliet of rare vintage wine. "My mother would faint dead away if I ever called her Amelia." He took Juliet's hand, his touch echoing through her. "Come on," he urged, leading her across the room. "It's time we caught up on your childhood."

"We have to discuss business," she protested, but his hand still covered hers and she walked beside him, realizing that she wanted to accept his invitation.

For the next two hours, Brady introduced Juliet to a world she'd read about and heard about, but never really experienced. They built ramps for the race car, adding bridges and jumps, and Brady produced two more racers along with a tank and a jeep. He found himself as caught up with Juliet as she was with the toys. The tough, self-assured lawyer was suddenly only a cardboard character compared with the intense, vibrant woman underneath. He wanted to know her better.

"Did you really design all of this yourself?" Juliet asked him.

"Just about," Brady answered.

Juliet spread her full skirt around her knees to sit cross-legged on the floor. "You must know little kids pretty well," she told Brady.

"I spent a lot of time with my sister's kids when they were growing up," Brady explained. "I had trouble finding them toys that were fun for more than an afternoon, so I began trying some ideas of my own."

"Do you give them new toys to try out?" Juliet asked him.

"They're too old, now," Brady explained. "But I have a friend living near me with a couple of little boys. They're my official toy testers." Brady watched as Juliet finished building a miniature drawbridge. "You can attach a remote control to that you know." He dropped to his knees beside her, and reached around her to help her secure a connection that would raise the bridge.

With Brady's arms around her, his hands guiding hers, Juliet found it harder and harder to concentrate on what she was doing. He told her step by step how to attach the motor, his warm breath grazing her cheek as he talked. When she finally tried to make the bridge work, it lurched forward, and she convulsed in laughter, leaning back against Brady's chest.

"First drawbridge I ever saw designed to reach out and smack the adversary," he said, laughing with her as his arms tightened around her.

It was a brief embrace and yet it sent Juliet's pulse pounding with the speed of the race cars. She was struck by how easily and naturally she fit into the circle of his arms. He released her, leaving one arm lightly across her shoulders, and moved beside her. She met his eyes, uneasy with what she saw there and even more unsure about her own emotions. But he only smiled and said softly, "You're fun to be with, Juliet." Before she could answer, he squeezed her shoulders lightly and stood up.

Juliet watched his every move. He'd taken off his suit coat and tie and unbuttoned his shirt at the neck. There was something casual and almost familiar about the way he looked, the way he moved. It would be hard not to like him.

"I'll bet you're as hungry as I am," he said, striding across the office and picking up the phone.

"Hungry?" Juliet glanced quickly at her watch. The afternoon was gone. She wasn't quite sure how she'd lost track of time. "I had no idea it was getting so late—" she began, but he motioned for her to be quiet and said a few words into the phone.

Very shortly, Brady was opening the top of a pizza box and Juliet was jabbing straws through the lids of two soft-drink cups. He sat close to her, his knee resting against her thigh. He was pleased when she didn't move away.

"We still have some business to discuss," she reminded him, swallowing a bite of pizza. "Even though I don't have a copy of the contract, I thought we might review the provisions and see whether you have any requirements that aren't included."

He listened, fascinated. She was back to being the consummate lawyer again. He felt her muscles tense as she gathered together her image. Even her speech pattern changed. "You realize this plan of yours doesn't make a whole lot of sense," he said, baiting her.

"It makes perfect sense," she countered. "I thought we straightened that out last week."

He watched her drink her Coke, making hollows in her cheeks as she sucked in through the straw. Her eyelashes were lowered, her thick auburn hair held lightly back from her face with clips. It wasn't just her plan—she didn't make sense, either. "What if a man came along and suggested marriage?" he asked her.

"Wouldn't that be a better arrangement?" It was a trial balloon. He waited for her reaction.

"Marriage?" Her eyes, a darker green than before, were hard with determination when she looked up. He could see this wasn't going to be easy.

"I've already told you how I feel about marriage. It tears people apart and makes them hate each other. I see it every day, every time a new client walks through the door."

Maybe he shouldn't mention the marriage arrangement just yet. "You sound pretty set in your opinion," he observed.

Juliet wadded her napkin into a tight ball and dropped it on the empty pizza carton. "When people get married, they make a commitment that's supposed to be for a lifetime and, as often as not, they turn around and walk out on it. I don't want any part of that kind of hypocrisy."

Brady stared at her, thinking about Phil and Eileen and what an apt description that was of their marriage. He wondered how much pain Juliet had seen to make her so bitter—and how much of it had been personal. At the same time, her objections to marriage wouldn't necessarily get in his way. What he wanted was a short-term arrangement. There would be no commitment involved. "You've apparently given this a lot of thought," he said noncommittally.

"I have," she concurred. She didn't like the direction of the discussion. He kept going back to marriage for some reason she couldn't fathom, and that was totally beside the point. Juliet glanced up at the clock over the fireplace. "It's getting late, and I really need to go." She moved forward on the couch. "Why don't I mail you a copy of the contract? That will give you time to go over it, and you can let me know if you have any problems.''

''That'll be fine,'' Brady agreed. Already he was anxious to see her again.

''Do you mind if I use your phone to call a cab?''

''A cab won't be necessary,'' he told her, pressing one of a series of buttons on a small control board in the center of the table. ''I'll send my driver with you. I'd take you myself, except I have to review a project before tomorrow morning.''

As Juliet approached the office door, Brady moved in front of her. Swiftly he pulled her toward him and bent his head down to kiss her. When her arms stretched up around his neck, he let his mouth linger until her lips softened and parted. He touched her hair, wishing he could loosen the clips so it would cascade freely down her back. Instead, he pressed her tightly against him, reluctant to let her go.

But at that moment Juliet pulled away. Shaken, she leaned over to pick up her briefcase which sat unopened where she had left it, by the office door.

''Thank you for the afternoon, Juliet,'' he said hoarsely.

She looked back but didn't meet his eyes. ''Good night, Brady,'' she responded quickly. She didn't know how else to answer him. Nothing that had happened was the way she'd planned. And when he'd kissed her, her whole being had trembled. She'd never dreamed she would respond to him that way. It left her unsettled and very unsure about what lay ahead.

Brady watched her walk through the lit showroom and disappear in the darkness beyond. ''Juliet Cavanaugh,'' he said softly into the silence, ''you're quite a woman.'' With a satisfied smile, he walked slowly toward his desk. He had a feeling this was going to work. In a few more months he would have met the terms of the trust, and Talcott Enterprises would be solely his. But the thrill of impending victory was brief, dimmed by the lingering image of the woman who had just left him.

## CHAPTER FOUR

MEETINGS KEPT BRADY in the city all week and it was Saturday before he could get home to his beach house near Half Moon Bay. As he loped along the sand, watching the gulls on his way to see Phil and the boys, he shot a longing glance across the calm ocean. He and Phil had been planning to take Phil's Boston Whaler out to fish for longfins. Even though it was early in the season, the weather had been warm and there were reports of catches close in.

But that was before Timmy came down with the chicken pox. Phil had been at home taking care of him all week. Turning up the sandy slope toward Phil's house, Brady checked his jacket pocket one more time. Inside was the contract Juliet had sent him. That was the real reason he was going to see Phil. He'd been waiting impatiently, knowing he had to put together a proposal of his own before he could see her again. He was counting on Phil taking time to assist him right away.

In the other pocket, he had a new black racing car for Timmy and the motor Michael wanted. He always tried to take the kids something. It had been rough for the boys since their mother had left. Brady slowed to a walk. He still couldn't quite figure out what had happened between Phil and Eileen. They had always seemed like the perfect couple—happy, in love, two great kids. But after Eileen started drinking it was all downhill until she left. He supposed seeing that kind of thing was what had made Juliet so bitter about marriage.

"Brady, Brady," came the yell from above him, and Brady braced himself to catch a bundle of seven-year-old enthusiasm that plunged over the deck rail and into his arms. "Timmy's got the chicken pox and he looks really awful," Michael announced with a big grin as Brady set him on the sand. "Did you bring my motor?"

"Sure did." Brady reached into his pocket. He was glad he hadn't forgotten. "I want you to try this with all the hookups and let me know whether it works better than the old one," he directed solemnly.

"You bet!" He grabbed Brady's hand. "You gotta see Timmy. But Dad says we can't laugh when we look at him," Michael added, looking very important. "It'll be hard because he looks really funny all covered with spots."

They found Phil in the kitchen stirring a pan of beef-a-roni. "Brady—just in time for lunch," he offered, pleased at the promise of adult company. He was beginning to understand some of the complaints he used to get from Eileen.

Michael stuck out his tongue as soon as he smelled the food. "Yuk!" he exclaimed, and went off to try the motor.

"Looks like you've had a long week," Brady sympathized.

"That's an understatement." Phil dished some beef-a-roni into a bowl. "As long as Timmy's got the chicken pox, Mrs. Campanelli won't come near him because she's afraid she'll get shingles." It made him realize how much he depended on the motherly Italian woman who had been his salvation since Eileen had left.

"So that's why you haven't been in the office all week." Brady wondered if Juliet had given any thought to the dependency of single parents on their nannies.

"Did you come to look at me?" inquired a muffled voice. A small figure with a tattered blue blanket wrapped around his head tugged at Brady's sleeve.

Brady knelt down and gently unwrapped the blanket. "No way, Timmy. I just came to say hello."

"Then how come you're looking at me?" Timmy demanded.

Brady stifled a grin and took the racer out of his pocket. "Because I want to see if you like your new car." Michael had been right. His brother did look funny.

Suspiciously, Timmy took the car from Brady's outstretched hand and examined it. "Am I testing it for you?"

"I'd like it if you would," Brady answered.

"All right." Timmy's face was serious. "But it better be stronger than the last one, because that one broke." Hiking up his blanket, Timmy started for the stairs.

"Take your lunch with you," Phil called after him, handing him a bowl. "Can I give you some?" he asked Brady.

"Thanks, but I've already eaten lunch. I've got something I'd like you to take care of for me, unless you've got your hands full here...." He didn't want to push Phil, but he was already impatient. Until he had the contract ready to go, he couldn't very well call Juliet.

"No problem," Phil assured him. "Come on into the study." He was glad Brady had business that needed attention. After a whole week with the kids, it would be a relief to do some legal work. "Really sorry about the fishing," Phil apologized, opening the door to his study. "A fella down the way came in with some nice ones yesterday."

"They'll be around for a while," Brady said conversationally. He stepped carefully around a tipsy block construction Timmy had apparently been working on. He always smiled when he walked into Phil's study. When Eileen had been there, it had been Phil's domain, a haven of books and leather and rich stained wood. But in the year since she'd left, a lot had changed. Now a painted rock held down papers on the old roll-top desk, and the boys' drawings were taped to the glass front of the barrister's cabinet. The floor was littered with toys.

"Sorry about the mess. Timmy's been in here a lot this week," Phil explained.

Not answering, Brady walked over to the antique walnut chest under the window and looked at the grouping of pictures: one each of the children and a picture of Eileen, her blonde hair tousled and her lips pursed in determination as she held out the biggest fish she'd ever caught.

"Have you heard from her lately?" Brady asked, staring at the snapshot.

"Not since I got all those calls a couple of months ago when she was in such bad shape," Phil answered. He didn't add that he'd been trying to find her without any luck. He'd tracked her to a restaurant in the

Tenderloin district where she'd worked as a waitress for a while, but they'd told her she left no forwarding address when she quit. It seemed futile after so long. But now that the anger was over with, he couldn't help but think about what might have happened to her.

"Why don't you put the picture away, Phil?" Brady asked. "Having it out only makes things harder."

"I suppose I should," Phil agreed. "But the kids would miss it. They keep hoping she'll come back."

"And you?" Brady asked bluntly.

Phil sat heavily in one of the twin leather chairs. "That's a tough question," he answered noncommittally. For some reason he wanted Eileen's picture there on the walnut chest where it had always been, and he didn't want to have to think about why.

"I guess when you love somebody, it doesn't go away," Brady mused.

"No," Phil answered sadly, "it doesn't. You can hate what they've done. Sometimes you even hate them. But then there are other times—" Phil stared thoughtfully at the picture. Their lives had been such a mess before Eileen left that he didn't see how they could ever work things out. He didn't even know if he wanted her back—certainly not the way she was now. But, at the same time, he couldn't quite give her up.

Brady stared out the window at the deserted beach. "When you love," he said, half to himself, "you give a part of yourself to the person, and you don't get it back." He thought about the two women he'd loved. Both had faded into bittersweet memories, and yet a part of him belonged to each of them and, he supposed, a part of both of them would always stay with him.

Brady leaned over to gather up a handful of crayons from the chair before he sat down. He could understand why, even after all this time, it was still hard for Phil to talk about Eileen. She was gone, but she was still a part of his life.

Turning away from Eileen's picture, Phil deliberately changed the subject. "Now," he said, looking at Brady, "what can I do for you?"

"You can draw me up an agreement," Brady answered, settling back in the chair.

"More hassle over those patents?" Phil asked.

"Nope," Brady told him. "Remember that ad I showed you in the *Bay City Magazine*?" He didn't have to say any more. Phil snapped to attention.

"You mean the broad who wants the baby?" When he hadn't heard any more about it, he'd thought Brady had lost interest. "Dammit, Brady! You're an ass to get involved in some fool scheme—"

"She may be someone you know," Brady continued, watching Phil carefully. "Her name is Juliet Cavanaugh." The significance of the name registered slowly. Brady listened to the old oak wall clock tick away in the silence.

"Juliet Cavanaugh?" Phil repeated. "The divorce lawyer?"

"You've got it," Brady grinned.

Phil shook his head. "No way. There has to be some mistake." Phil didn't know Juliet very well, but he knew what she looked like, and that was enough. No woman with a body like that had to advertise for a man. "She's probably working for some dame who—"

"Wrong," Brady interrupted. "I asked her about that. She's on the level. She wants a baby, but she doesn't want to get married. She figures this is the way to go.''

Phil scratched his head. "Well, I'll be damned." He had to admit that changed the picture, but not much. "She's not going to be a hell of a lot of help to you if she doesn't want to get married," he observed.

"That depends," Brady said, reaching into his pocket, "on how clever you are and how persuasive I am." He handed Juliet's contract to Phil. "She's got all her terms spelled out in there. Take a look."

As Phil flipped through the document, Timmy appeared, still dragging his blanket, and without a word crawled up on his father's lap. Phil instinctively patted him as the little boy wrapped his blanket around his head again and stuck his thumb in his mouth, his eyes drooping. Phil went right on reading the contract, running his finger along the margin as he went. "If I hadn't read it, I wouldn't believe it," he muttered.

"What I want you to do," Brady directed, "is to include all that stuff of hers but add in that we have to be legally married for six months. After that point, either party can terminate the marriage without objections from the other."

Phil leaned back, shaking his head. "And that will get you past your birthday and give you full control of Talcott Enterprises." He could see Brady's rationale. He could also see the pitfalls. "Pretty clever, buddy, except for a couple of loose ends."

"Like what?" Brady challenged. He'd figured on getting an argument.

"Like it will never hold up in court."

Brady grinned. That was the least of his worries. "It won't have to. Juliet won't challenge it—she hates the whole idea of marriage. It's nothing but a statement of intent.''

"Then let's try something a little heavier.'' Phil tucked the blanket around the sleeping child on his lap. "How are you going to just walk away from your baby? Could you go off and leave Timmy if he were yours?''

"I'll never see the baby,'' Brady retorted, more sharply than he'd intended. Phil knew him pretty well, Brady realized. He looked at Timmy—the dark hair, the round face, the surprisingly square chin—all of it so much like his father. What would a child of his look like? Brady wondered. Maybe some day he'd find out. But not this time. This time, he reminded himself, it would never be real, because he would never see the baby. He'd have to make damn sure he didn't.

Phil sat silent for a moment, giving his friend time to think. He knew Brady wasn't as sure of himself as he'd like to appear. He also knew never seeing the baby wasn't the only potential problem. "Now that we know who the woman is,'' he added, looking Brady in the eye, "there's another consideration. What if you fall in love with her? She's made it clear she wants no strings attached.''

That had never occurred to Brady. "Falling in love has nothing to do with this. I'll admit she's damn attractive, but so are a lot of other women. Hell, if I were in love with another attractive woman, I'd marry her and I wouldn't have to do this.''

Phil looked skeptical, but he didn't answer.

"Look,'' Brady said, "she needs me for the baby and I need to marry her to satisfy the terms of the trust. It's a trade-off. That's all. Love doesn't come into it.''

Standing up along with Brady, Phil shook his head. "For your sake, buddy, I sure hope you're right. You could pay a hell of a high price." He wished there were something more he could say to stop Brady from going ahead with the scheme. Phil watched him leave, knowing that what he needed was a real wife, someone who loved him and wanted to have a family the normal way.

After reading over a few paragraphs in the contract, Phil tossed it onto his desk. Damn! Marriage was hard enough without starting out with a load of bricks tied to your back. Maybe that's what had happened to him and Eileen. The bricks had been too heavy—especially for her. They'd been too young, had kids so soon. He stared at Eileen's picture on the chest. Everybody, even Brady, thought the crazy smile on her face was because she was holding the biggest fish she had ever caught. That wasn't the reason at all. She was lit up with happiness because she was pregnant with Michael. It was their anniversary and she had been saving the news as a present. It was the best present she'd ever given him.

Everything had been so good then, Phil thought bitterly. Why the hell couldn't it be like that anymore? That's all he wanted, just Eileen and the kids. Screw the house, the boat, the club, even the law practice. He'd give it all up for life the way it used to be.

"Mommy?" Timmy's eyes fluttered and his thumb dropped from his mouth.

"Mommy's not here right now," Phil gently reminded him. It hurt him to have to say the words. Timmy had asked for her so many times while he'd been sick.

"Is she coming back pretty soon?" Timmy's voice was sleepy and distant.

"I don't know," Phil answered. He looked at Eileen's picture again. They'd sure as hell messed things up. If Brady thought he could do better with that half-assed plan of his, let him try.

MONDAY MORNING Phil sent a contract by messenger to Brady's office with a note clipped to the top. It read: "You sure are a stubborn bastard. Best of luck, Phil."

Brady laughed out loud and reached for the phone. It was time to get together with Juliet. After several rings, her secretary answered only to inform him that Ms Cavanaugh was in court and wouldn't be back for at least an hour. He questioned the secretary closely and, over her objections, he left a cryptic message for Juliet and hung up.

When Juliet returned from the courthouse, she found Linda sitting at Alice's desk eating a carry-out sandwich from the deli. "Stop," Juliet protested. "This is your first day back to work and I'm taking you to lunch, remember?"

"Wrong," Linda said, taking a drink of her Coke. "You have other plans."

"What do you mean?" Juliet set down her briefcase and loosened the belt on her raincoat.

"Alice took the call just before she left," Linda explained, handing Juliet the top sheet from a sheaf of phone messages.

Juliet looked down at the yellow memo. "Union Square. Noon. The bench on the north side by the pine tree. Bring your pen. Brady."

It was the message she'd been waiting for. The news brought a heady exhilaration and, right on its heels, a

surge of panic. He was going to do it. For some reason Juliet couldn't discern, Brady Talcott had gone
beyond curiosity, overcome his reservations, and was
about to sign a contract agreeing to father her baby.
She was going to be a mother! Juliet was aware she
was still staring at the memo, and Linda was grinning
at her.

"Got cold feet all of a sudden?" Linda teased.

"Of course not," Juliet responded. "Except I guess
I didn't think he'd really do it."

"I've got a funny feeling you kind of like him,"
Linda probed. "From what you told me, and from the
stuff Harry gave you, he sounds like quite a guy. Just
one question—why does he want to meet in the park
on a day like this?"

Juliet glanced out the window at the murky fog. "I
have no idea." She picked up the memo and read it
one more time.

"I've also got a feeling you're pretty undone about
this," Linda observed. "Your hands are even shaking."

"Yours would, too, if you were about to become a
mother," Juliet said defensively.

Linda munched on a potato chip. "Speaking of
mothers, what did Cass say when you told her?"

"Cass?" Juliet looked blank.

"Cass—you know, your mother. What did she say
about your having a baby?" Linda shook her head.
"Boy, are you out of it today."

"I am not. I was just deciding whether to walk or
take a cable car," Juliet declared. "Besides, I haven't
mentioned it to Cass yet—the opportunity hasn't come
up."

"I see," Linda answered. "Maybe you ought to walk to Union Square. The fresh air might bring you back to reality."

"I'm going to ignore that," Juliet retorted. But she slipped out of her brown pumps and shoved her feet into a pair of well-worn running shoes. Pulling her raincoat snugly around her green wool dress, Juliet automatically reached for her briefcase before she realized she wouldn't need it. Brady had the contract, which was all that was necessary. Actually, she thought, there wasn't any reason to take a purse, either.

"Anything I can take care of while you're gone?" Linda offered.

"Nothing on the book till four o'clock," Juliet told her.

Linda finished her Coke and dropped the paper cup into the wastebasket. "Oh, I almost forgot—there was a blond woman here to see you," she told Juliet. "I told her I expected you any minute, but she wouldn't wait. She didn't leave her name."

"About our height, thin, short hair?" Juliet questioned.

Linda nodded.

"She's been here before. Don't worry about it. She'll probably come back." Juliet tightened the belt on her raincoat. "By the way," she added, "you might go through those folders I left on my desk. Another week and the doorway should be finished so you'll have your own office."

"Then maybe I'll really feel like a lawyer again," Linda answered, laughing.

"Sorry about the lunch," Juliet called over her shoulder as she headed for the elevator.

"No problem," Linda answered.

Once out of the building, Juliet walked steadily, and within a few minutes she was glad to be outdoors. The exercise was invigorating and the fresh air felt good. She didn't even mind the heavy fog that clung to her skin. As she approached Union Square Park, the wind picked up from behind her and whipped her hair around her face. With a laugh, she turned and walked backward until the long, auburn locks blew back into place and she could tuck them deep inside her collar for protection. When she turned frontward again, she realized she hadn't done that since she was a little girl.

Her pace picked up as she got closer. Meeting outside on a day like this was objectively a dumb thing to do, but the idea was growing on her. There wasn't any need to be indoors for what they had to do—just a quick signature. Maybe they would talk for a while afterward or go to lunch, sort of get better acquainted before they set up their meetings. But they should take care of the business first, she decided, before they did anything else.

As soon as she rounded the corner, Juliet spotted Brady already sitting on the bench directly in front of a neatly trimmed pine tree, just as he had promised. Her purposeful stride slowed while she watched him feeding popcorn to a flock of noisy pigeons. His tie was loose, his jacket hung open, and his hair fell across his forehead as he leaned over to persuade a plump, gray pigeon to take a popcorn kernel from his fingers. *Business,* she reminded herself. *Stick to business*.

"Hi," he called, breaking into a grin when he saw her. He took her in all at once, the curve of her legs above the running shoes, the hair tucked into the collar of her tan coat, the flush in her cheeks that heightened the delicate cheekbones. Every time he saw her, she was more beautiful. He moved over to make room for her. "Come join me before the pigeons start roosting in your spot on the bench."

Making a conscious effort to control the spring in her step, Juliet approached him slowly. "You really have a following," she teased, shooing the pigeons aside so she could sit down.

"Just my magnetic personality—and my popcorn," he replied. "Have some?" he asked, offering the red-and-white box to Juliet.

"No thanks." Juliet shook her head. Despite her resolve to focus only on the contract, she couldn't help but notice he had a wonderful grin that deepened the cleft in his chin and crinkled the corners around his eyes. Suddenly, she was quaking inside. What was she doing? In a few minutes the contract would be signed and then, well, then what? She hadn't ever really considered the exact logistics before. She had just assumed that somehow everything would happen the way it should and in nine months—give or take a few weeks—she would produce a baby. Just exactly when, or where, or how the encounters would take place... That part was all a little vague. She was going to have to give some thought to the logistics.

Brady leaned over to feed a pigeon and his leg pressed more firmly against hers. Would they go to her apartment or his? she wondered. Would he take her to dinner? That wasn't in the contract, of course. Maybe he would expect her to take him to dinner. The pigeon waddled away and Brady sat back, his shoulder touching hers. She had to get a grip on herself. Everything would work itself out. First the contract.

"Did you bring it?" she asked, trying to sound casual.

"Bring what?" Brady emptied the last of the popcorn directly from the box into his mouth and tossed the empty box toward a trash can, scoring a direct hit.

Juliet took a deep breath. "The contract." Her stomach tightened and she began to feel uneasy. "The agreement for us to...um, ah..." Inexplicably she was at a loss for words.

"Oh, *that* contract." Brady sat up straight and pulled the papers from a pocket inside his jacket.

Relieved, Juliet took the document from him. "I assume you've signed this?"

That was the opening Brady had been waiting for. "Not yet. There's one more thing we have to add first."

Juliet frowned. "I expected you to contact me if you wanted changes. I suppose we can initial them if they aren't major."

"This one may require some discussion," Brady began. "You're entering into this agreement because you want a baby, right?"

Juliet nodded.

"Then it's only reasonable that you should make some concession to get what you want," Brady continued.

"What are you getting at?" Juliet asked skeptically. "If you're asking for more money—"

"We can forget the money entirely," Brady interrupted her. "I don't consider that a concession."

Juliet was growing more and more uneasy. He had lured her to the park with a message saying he was ready to sign the contract, and now he was hedging. She thought back to the exact words her secretary had written down. Actually all she'd said was "bring your pen."

"Exactly what is it you expect me to do?" Juliet demanded.

Brady looked directly into Juliet's eyes. "I want you to marry me."

For a few moments, the word "marry" stunned Juliet into silence. Then she sprang to her feet, positioning herself directly in front of Brady.

"We never discussed marriage as an option, and we're not going to now," she sputtered. "The contract stands as written. I'm hiring you to father my child. Take it or leave it."

Watching her calmly, Brady leaned forward, resting his hands on his knees. "Those are your terms. Now I've added mine," he asserted in a low voice. "If I'm going to father your child, I'm going to marry you first. If you'll sit down and listen for a minute, I'll explain why."

"You can explain anything you want to and it's not going to make a bit of difference." Juliet sat on the bench as far away from Brady as possible.

Brady went right on talking. "When my father died, he left Talcott Enterprises in trust, with me as the beneficiary," he told her. "My father was a real family man, and he wanted me to be the same way. As he got older, he got more and more domineering."

"I don't see what that has to do with this marriage arrangement you've concocted," Juliet declared.

"That's because I haven't told you yet." Brady brushed a stray popcorn kernel off his pants. "When my father wrote the trust agreement he put in a provision requiring that I be married by the age of thirty-five or the company would be sold and the proceeds go to some rather questionable charities.''

"But you could fight that—" Juliet interrupted.

"And probably win," Brady added. "But in the meantime I could get tied up in litigation that would drag on for years.''

"It's still an insane idea," Juliet argued. "If you think I'm going to marry you just because—"

"Actually, there's another thing to consider," Brady cut in. "Maybe you should think ahead. When the child grows up, wouldn't it be nice to be able to say you were married when he or she was born?'' It was part of his preplanned argument, but the words came out with a conviction that surprised him.

Juliet hesitated. She'd never thought of it that way. "Times have changed," she asserted. "Marriage doesn't matter any more." She'd always believed that. She had to believe it. Otherwise, this wouldn't work.

Brady's voice was firm. "I don't care how much the world has changed. It's easier for a child who has a father—a legitimate father.''

"And I suppose you would want it to have your name?''

Brady flinched. The idea appealed to him. But if he wasn't going to see the child, that was out of the question. "I don't care what name you give the baby," he answered. He hadn't meant to sound so harsh. He reached into his pocket and took out a neatly folded paper. "I had my lawyer prepare a contract that spells out our revised agreement.''

Juliet knotted her fists, her green eyes blazing. "I'm not marrying you or anybody else," she announced evenly. The words barely out of her mouth, she wheeled around and took off down the sidewalk.

"There's a six-month escape clause written into the contract," Brady called after her. Juliet kept on walking, her back stiff and unyielding.

He realized she hadn't heard him. *Now she's mad as hell,* Brady thought. He settled back on the bench and pulled a crossword puzzle out of his coat pocket. Unless he missed his guess, Juliet would be back. But it might take a while.

By the time she turned the corner out of sight of Brady, Juliet was ready to explode. "Damn," she swore aloud. *I should have known he was after something. It was all too easy.* Too angry to even begin to sort the snarl of thoughts, she slowed her footsteps and tried to figure out what she was going to do next.

*This is stupid,* she lectured herself, realizing she had lost all perspective. What she had to do was take the overall objective, analyze the obstacles, and choose the best option. Same as any other problem. She looked for a place to sit down, but there wasn't a bench in sight. Perching herself on a fire hydrant, which was very uncomfortable, she managed to come up with a pencil stub from her coat pocket and began making notations on the back of an old grocery receipt.

Objective: Have a baby, as quickly and simply as possible.
Problem: Need a father
Solution: Advertise for one
Problem: Nearly 300 replies, ten possibles, but only one really desirable and he demands marriage
Solution:

Juliet scrawled "Damn!" across the sheet. The obvious solution was to accept his terms or find another father. She didn't want to do either one. Juliet shifted her weight, wishing she had found a bench to sit on, and then finally stood up. She wasn't getting anywhere. She began to walk, idly, aimlessly, hands stuffed deep in her coat pockets. It had all seemed so simple until Brady came up with that stupid marriage demand, she thought, kicking at a clump of grass that grew up through a crack in the sidewalk. She scrunched her shoulders and buried her chin in her coat. The air was damp and heavy and the sky leaden, threatening rain.

Juliet shivered. She didn't want to start all over and find another father. Brady was prefect. She thought about him sitting on that bench feeding the pigeons, and about the light in his eyes when he looked up and saw her coming. There was no way she could talk him out of marriage and still get him to cooperate. That was his bottom line, just like having the baby was hers. Well, she thought, if she couldn't refuse his demand, maybe she could modify it. Suddenly Juliet stopped walking and turned on her heel. If she couldn't do this on her terms, she'd do it on his terms—but her way.

In long determined strides, she retraced her steps. Somehow she knew Brady would still be sitting right where she left him. But this time she was going to be in control.

"Hi," she called out to Brady, slowing to a normal pace.

"You're back," he observed, stating the obvious. It hadn't taken her as long as he'd thought it might, and everything about her told him she'd come to some decision.

"That's right," Juliet confirmed. "I'm back." She sat down on the bench next to him, but still as far away as possible.

"Are you ready to read my contract?" Brady asked, putting the crossword puzzle in his pocket and again offering her the papers.

"Not quite," Juliet responded. "I've considered your offer, and I've decided to negotiate."

"It doesn't seem to me there's much to negotiate where marriage is concerned," Brady noted. "You either do or you don't."

"Not quite," she corrected him. "If you expect me to make a concession and agree to marriage, then you can make an equal concession and agree to release me from the marriage at any time."

"Fine," he shrugged.

She stared at him. It was too easy.

"If what you're trying to say is that you want an escape clause, it's already in here," he noted mildly. "It applies equally to both parties."

"Why didn't you tell me all that in the first place?" Juliet demanded.

"I tried to tell you." Brady broke into a grin. "But you stalked off." He laid his contract gently in Juliet's lap. "Maybe you should read this before we discuss it further?"

Juliet slowly picked up the papers and began to read. She wondered if the churning inside her was because he seemed to have the best of her—again. She suspected that wasn't the only reason. If he insisted on marriage, an escape clause was obviously the only sensible approach. But she'd liked it better when it was her idea.

After studying the contract carefully, Juliet had to admit it was simple, to the point and scrupulously fair. It spelled out that after six months either one of them could dissolve the marriage. But the whole thing didn't make sense. She knew she should take a few days to think it over. Instead she turned toward Brady. "Do you have a pen?"

"Sure thing." Quickly he reached in his pocket. He'd won. She was going along with it. He was about to get what he'd gone after, and for an instant he wasn't sure he wanted it. Phil's warning echoed in his ears: *You could pay a hell of a high price.* He handed Juliet the pen.

Within moments the document was signed in duplicate and Juliet was folding one copy to put in her pocket. "Well, that should do it," Juliet said awkwardly. She stood up and extended her hand.

Brady rose quickly to his feet. "Right," he agreed. He shook her hand. What an inane way to seal a marriage proposal, he thought to himself.

"Then I guess that's it." Juliet patted the pocket that held the contract. "I'm tied up in court next week, but my calendar is reasonable after that. Phone me when you've set the wedding date." She started to walk away.

Suddenly he couldn't let her go, not like that. "Juliet!" Brady's hand was on her shoulder, turning her around. "We forgot something else." He gave her no time to think, his lips closing over hers as he pulled her to him. They were alone in the mist, the intimacy of their mouths at odds with the awkwardness of the agreement that separated them. Her lips were incredibly sweet, and Brady sensed the fleeting promise of something that might have been.

He held her very tight before he slowly released her. Juliet didn't want him to let her go. She was frightened by what lay ahead, overwhelmed by the scope of the commitment they'd just made. For those few brief moments they shared the immensity of what they had done, but when she walked away, she'd be on her own.

"I'll phone you, Juliet." She heard the uncertainty in his voice. Then he turned on his heel and disappeared into the mist.

OVER THE NEXT FEW DAYS, Juliet persuaded herself that their compromise was actually quite reasonable. She would have her baby—not exactly the way she'd planned—but the marriage would be only a brief inconvenience. And maybe Brady did have a point about legitimacy. She could decide later how to discuss its father with the child. At least this gave her another option. When Linda called to see how things had gone with Brady, Juliet told her they'd signed the contract, but she didn't mention the marriage provision. She decided she'd explain that part the next time she saw her.

It wasn't until Juliet found herself standing at the door of her mother's art studio in Sausalito that her confidence wavered. She couldn't quite put her finger on the problem. Cass was a free spirit if there ever was one, accepting of nearly everything. Juliet had intended from the very beginning to discuss the plan for a baby with her, but she kept waiting for the right moment. Now she didn't have any choice. If she was going to be married, her mother had to know. She opened the door slowly, with a gnawing feeling that dealing with Cass on this one was going to be a little tricky.

"Juliet?" Her mother's red head popped up from behind her easel. "Come give me a hug—but don't spill the turpentine. Why didn't you phone and tell me you were coming?"

"So you could stop your work and break out the silver tea service?" Juliet teased. Relishing the familiar smell of paint, she leaned carefully around the easel and gave her mother an affectionate squeeze.

"Silver tea service, my foot," laughed Cass. "I've never owned a silver tea service in my life. Besides, if I don't get these illustrations to the publisher pretty soon, he'll have the sheriff after me." She wiped her brush with a rag and stood it upside down in an old mayonnaise jar. "However," her face lit up, "I do have a brand new juicer. How about some fresh carrot juice?" Without waiting for an answer, Cass breezed into the kitchen, her paint-splotched smock billowing like a parachute around her wiry frame.

Juliet grimaced but followed along behind, ducking low to avoid the bundles of fragrant herbs drying over the kitchen door. Once she got the conversation rolling, she would ease into the subject of the baby and go from there, Juliet decided as she perched on a tall stool next to the butcher-block counter. Her mother would laugh and congratulate her. After all, Cass had been a single parent for most of Juliet's life. And once she got excited about the baby, she'd be able to take the marriage idea in stride. She'd understand why it had been necessary to compromise on the marriage as soon as she found out it was only temporary.

"Why did you drive all the way to Sausalito on a weekday afternoon?" Carrot in hand, Cass gazed intently at her daughter. "It must be bad news," she determined, raising her voice over the hum of the juicer. "My horoscope said this morning that—"

"No, it's not bad news," Juliet interrupted. She took a glass of carrot juice from her mother. As many times as she had rehearsed the speech, she couldn't seem to get into the opening statement.

"What is it then?" Cass prompted impatiently. She took a sip of her juice.

That's my cue, thought Juliet. She took a deep breath. "How would you like to be a grandmother?" she began. She knew immediately it was the wrong approach.

Her mother's eyes flew wide open and her mouth dropped. "My God," she whispered hoarsely. "You're pregnant. I knew it was bad news."

"Oh, no," Juliet reassured her. "No, no, not yet."

Cass heaved a deep sigh of relief.

"But I'm going to be," Juliet forged ahead. "Very soon, I hope."

Cass blinked several times and downed the rest of her carrot juice like it was a well-fortified martini. "Juliet," she said firmly, "you know I pride myself on being liberal—some people might say too liberal—but this tests my limits. Now, you start at the beginning and give me a full and complete explanation. Don't try to spare me. I am in excellent physical condition, and I want all the details."

Juliet felt a smile begin to cross her lips but quickly suppressed it. Maybe a marriage was going to be easier to explain than a baby, after all.

"All right," Juliet agreed. Setting her glass of carrot juice on the butcher block, she looked directly into her mother's worried eyes. "I'm going to get married." She paused to let the concept sink in. After all, she had been proclaiming for most of her life that she would absolutely never get married.

When she saw the slightest hint of a smile on her mother's face, she continued. "And then, I'm going to get pregnant as soon as I possibly can. I got a little ahead of myself with that part," she explained.

Her mother broke into a glowing smile. "Oh, I see," she babbled with great relief. "You're going to get married first and then have a baby. That's perfect. The wedding and then the baby. That's really the best approach." Cass was regaining her usual aplomb. "It's wonderful, Juliet," she exclaimed. "Absolutely wonderful. I can't imagine what was wrong with my horoscope."

Juliet's laugh was hollow, but her mother was too excited to notice. Underneath it all, Cass apparently wasn't the free thinker she'd have people believe she was—at least where her own daughter was concerned. Discussing the agreement she had with Brady would be a terrible mistake, Juliet realized. In fact, the less said the better. It would be easier to just deal with the divorce when it happened.

"Aren't you even going to ask me who I'm marrying?" Juliet inquired.

"As long as you love him, dear, it doesn't matter," Cass responded blissfully.

Juliet almost spilled her juice. This wasn't at all the kind of reaction she had expected from Cass. She had no idea what to say next, but Cass didn't seem to expect anything more.

"Now," her mother continued, "we have to make plans. There's a church, a place for the reception, flowers, invitations, a photographer, and..." She reached out to Juliet and held her close. "And a wedding gown," she finished in a dreamy voice.

Juliet realized she would have to put a halt to that kind of thinking immediately. "Cass," she said gently. "I'm not sure how to break this to you, but I...er, we don't want a big wedding. We're both really busy," she hurried on. "We need to keep it simple—there's not enough time for a big wedding."

"Not time for a big wedding? Juliet, you're my only daughter! What do you mean not enough time?"

Juliet had never considered having a problem like this with her mother, and she wasn't prepared. "Brady—that's his name—Brady and I want to be married as soon as possible. I have several important cases coming up and he's...well, he's busy, too, and can't take time from work. We thought we'd just have a small ceremony in front of a judge."

"Juliet!" Her mother looked her square in the eye. "Are you sure there isn't something you aren't telling me? This all sounds rather unusual. Very rushed. Are you sure you're not pregnant?"

"Of course not, Cass," Juliet answered uncomfortably. She'd always been open with her mother, and she didn't like this deception. "I just don't want to make a production out of a wedding."

Cass nodded knowingly. "I must remember I'm talking to the woman who vowed she would never get married under any circumstances."

"That's right," Juliet answered.

"I'm really glad you've changed your mind," Cass said softly. "I've always worried that your father walking out and leaving us had a permanent effect on you. And maybe it did—maybe it made you wise enough to wait until you were sure."

Juliet swallowed hard. "You're probably right," she managed to agree, momentarily overwhelmed with guilt. Then she added quickly, "You've been as terrific as any other two parents could have been. I was perfectly happy having a single parent."

"Raising a daughter is the most meaningful thing I've done in my life," Cass told her, and Juliet looked away, seeing the misting in Cass's eyes.

"Even more than winning the publishers' art award last year?" Juliet tried to redirect the conversation and escape the emotion.

But her mother remained serious. "It far surpasses that," she answered, her voice unsteady. "Bringing a child into the world is an enormous responsibility, Juliet. And trying to raise a child alone and give it all the guidance and love by yourself..." Cass's voice broke and she hugged Juliet again. "I'm so glad you'll have a man to share it with." She was speaking almost in a whisper. "I want so much for you to be happy."

Juliet froze. All these years she'd never known how Cass felt, never imagined that her mother felt doubt or uncertainty. When she'd decided to have a baby, she'd been so sure of her mother's support. But Cass would never be able to accept what she was doing. That didn't matter, she told herself. It was going to work.

"Now young lady..." Cass's tone changed, breaking the tension between them. "Your nutritional habits will need significant improvement if my grandchild is to arrive in robust condition." She frowned dramatically and picked up Juliet's untouched glass. "Here," she directed, "drink your carrot juice."

"Mother," Juliet groaned, emptying the glass. She hated carrot juice.

"My name is Cass and has been all my life," her mother reminded her. "Now, let's discuss having this fiancé... Brady, you said his name was? Let's discuss having this Brady to dinner. Is Thursday a good night for both of you, and does he eat sushi?"

Juliet sighed. This was another one of those details she hadn't given much thought to, but she supposed—even if they were going to be married for only a few months—that Brady would have to meet Cass at some point. Thursday dinner was as good a time as any.

# CHAPTER FIVE

JULIET WAS SHAKEN when she left her mother's. She thought she knew Cass. But it appeared that Cass's libertarian ideas applied to everyone else but her daughter. Regardless, Juliet reassured herself, Cass would be delighted when her grandchild was born. And it was the long term that mattered. The immediate future wasn't all that important.

Except for one thing. Cass was planning to have them for dinner Thursday night. That meant she needed to talk to Brady as soon as possible. She didn't even know whether he'd accept the invitation. Dinner with in-laws wasn't part of their agreement.

She followed the line of traffic around the ramp and nosed her Nissan into the center lane on the Golden Gate Bridge. If Brady hadn't insisted on marriage, none of this would have happened. She could have explained him away as an indiscretion. As it was, he would simply have to make some sacrifices, too.

Impulsively, she decided to drive by his office on her way home and invite him in person. It wasn't really all that much out of her way to go to Jackson Square. She changed lanes again, noticing that when she thought about seeing Brady, she started to feel a little better.

By the time she got to Talcott Enterprises it was late afternoon, and Juliet was afraid Brady might already have left for the day. She was sure of it when she walked in and found the reception desk empty. Deciding to check Brady's office anyway, she walked hesitantly through the showroom and up the stairs.

When Brady met her at his office door, looking enormously happy to see her, a warm glow filled Juliet. She was instantly glad she'd come. He wrapped one arm around her shoulders, leaning down to give her a brief kiss on the lips. "Boy, am I glad to see you," he told her. "You couldn't have come at a better time."

Juliet wanted to believe he'd missed her, and that he simply couldn't wait to be with her, but something didn't ring true. She looked at him more closely. His shirt sleeves were rolled up, his tie was askew, and he was carrying a bottle of calamine lotion in his hand.

"I've got a big favor to ask—"

"That's funny," Juliet interrupted. "That was going to be my opening line."

"I beat you to it." Impatiently, Brady checked his watch. "What do you know about chicken pox?"

Juliet frowned at the bottle of calamine. "A little bit," she answered suspiciously.

"Great! Then you can stay with Michael while I catch the last half of an important meeting." Brady was already rolling down his sleeves.

"Wait a minute!" Juliet didn't like the sound of this. "Who's Michael?"

Brady rapidly buttoned his cuffs. "A seven-year-old buddy of mine who's staying with me because his father's in court today. Here, hold this." He thrust the calamine into her hand and straightened his tie. "You'll need it. Michael caught the chicken pox from his brother. But he's not contagious anymore—he's all scabbed over."

"Brady!" Juliet brandished the calamine. "I didn't come to baby-sit with—"

"Sh-h-h." Brady glanced over his shoulder. "I need you." He was already walking back into the office. "Come meet him." Reluctantly, Juliet followed Brady. She felt herself being railroaded.

A loft bed had been attached to standards on the wall near the dome climber, and as they approached, Juliet saw a small figure almost lost in a tangle of sheets and blankets.

"Michael, I want you to meet Juliet," Brady said cheerfully. "She's going to stay with you while I go to a meeting."

Michael looked at her with obvious hostility. "I don't want her to stay with me. I want you." He kicked the sheet off entirely.

"I won't be long," Brady promised, putting on his suit coat. "And your dad will be here soon." He leaned close to the boy. "Juliet's okay," he confided. "She's my friend."

Michael didn't answer.

"Be back as soon as I can," Brady called over his shoulder, and Michael and Juliet were left alone.

Michael turned toward the wall. Juliet considered telling him she wasn't any happier about the situation than he was. No wonder Brady had been glad to see her. He'd have been glad to see anyone who could take over this job. Michael squirmed uncomfortably. "Have you had the chicken pox long?" she asked, for lack of anything else to say.

"Forever," he answered glumly.

"It probably seems that way," Juliet observed. She looked at the boy more closely. He lay on his back on the bed, staring at the ceiling, his hands rubbing his pajama shirt roughly against his stomach. His face, his neck, his feet—every exposed inch of skin was covered with spots. Judging from the pink streaks of lotion in his short blond hair, he probably had scabs on his scalp, too. He was obviously miserable.

Juliet began to feel more sympathetic. "Do you itch a lot?"

"Everywhere." For the first time since they'd been alone, he looked at her, the startling blue eyes still skeptical. "Brady put calamine on me," he added pointedly.

Juliet hesitated. "Would you like me to do that?" She didn't really want to touch him, but he looked so unhappy she offered anyway.

"I suppose," he muttered.

Determined to at least give it a try, Juliet took off her linen suit jacket and rolled up the sleeves of her green silk blouse, thinking that she'd have dressed differently if she'd known about this. She uncapped the bottle. "Where do you want me to start?"

"My feet. They itch really bad." Juliet dabbed some calamine on her finger and began rubbing it gently on the bottom of Michael's left foot, trying not to recoil as her fingers moved across the rough scabs. "Yeah, right there," he encouraged her.

She liked making him feel better. "Mr. Talcott said your name is Michael. What's your last name?" Juliet dabbed on more calamine, thinking about Brady. He owed her one for this. There wouldn't be any way he could turn down dinner with Cass.

"My name is Michael Allen Gentry. And I don't call him Mr. Talcott. I call him Brady. I work for him," the boy added proudly.

Then Juliet remembered. "You must be one of the toy testers Brady told me about."

"Yeah, me and Timmy. He's my brother, but he's too little to be much good. He's the one who gave me the chicken pox." The boy wiggled uncomfortably. "Can't you hurry up? You're still on the same foot."

"This method isn't very efficient," Juliet admitted. At this rate it was going to take her all afternoon to coat his spots. There had to be a better approach. "Maybe if I can find you something to do...." Looking around the office, she saw some brushes and paints in one of Brady's open shelves. "I've got it!" she exclaimed.

"Just hurry up," Michael pleaded.

Juliet dumped the paper clips out of a ceramic box on Brady's desk, wiped it clean with tissue and filled it with calamine lotion. Then she grabbed the biggest paint brush she could find and went to work on Michael's other foot.

"Hey, what are you doing?" he demanded, half sitting up.

"I'm painting you." Juliet ignored the lotion that dribbled on the sheet. "Pull up your pants legs."

Michael appraised her with new admiration. "Even Brady didn't think of that."

Since when was he the ideal? she asked herself. It made Juliet feel good that she was the one who'd come up with a better method. In a funny way, it restored some of the confidence Cass had shaken. She would be able to take care of her own child, just as she was able to take care of Michael. Juliet quickly painted him with calamine, feeling his muscles relax as she worked. He dipped his own fingers in the bowl and rubbed them on his scalp. She finished the job with a flourish of the brush on his chest. "There, does that feel better?"

His eyes were no longer angry. "A whole lot," he said gratefully.

No longer apprehensive about touching him, Juliet patted him on the shoulder. She liked Michael. "Maybe I could read to you," she offered, "if I can find a book."

He watched her search through the shelves. "My mom used to read to me."

"She doesn't anymore?"

"Nope."

Juliet absently continued the conversation. "Why did she stop?"

"She's gone."

No emotion. Just a statement of fact. Juliet began to pay attention. "Is she coming back?"

"Daddy says maybe someday."

Juliet's heart went out to him. She remembered the loneliness after her own father left. It was worst of all when she was sick. "I found a book," she told him, pulling a chair up near the bed. "Has anyone read you *The Lion, the Witch, and the Wardrobe*?"

"Never heard of it. Does it have detectives?"

"No, but it has a witch who turns living creatures into stone. It was written by C. S. Lewis," she added. "He was my favorite author when I was a little girl."

Michael didn't comment, and so Juliet began to read. She had just finished the second chapter when she hard an unfamiliar voice behind her. "Michael?"

"Daddy!" Michael sat up and held out his arms. Stepping around Juliet, the man leaned over to hug his son. She could sense the bond between them. Even as they talked, the boy was still clinging to him. Even if

Michael didn't have a mother around, he obviously had one parent who cared.

When the man turned back toward Juliet, their eyes widened in mutual recognition. "Phil Gentry!" she exclaimed in surprise. He had the same brilliant blue eyes as his son.

"Juliet, what are you doing here?"

"She's a friend of Brady's," Michael answered for her. "She painted me all over with calamine lotion and she's reading me a neat book."

"Juliet, I really appreciate this...." He hadn't seen her for months, and than only in passing at the courthouse and at occasional bar meetings. She was more beautiful than he remembered, and he knew by looking at her that his gut reaction had been right. Brady was playing with fire.

"Brady had to go to a meeting, so I stayed with Michael," Juliet explained. "We had a good afternoon," she added, almost surprised to realize that they really had. "I'm sure Brady won't mind if you take the book we were reading—"

"And the paintbrush," Michael interjected.

"And the paintbrush," Phil agreed. "Where'd you learn about that?" he asked Juliet curiously.

She shrugged. "Necessity sparks lots of new approaches."

*Right,* thought Phil, *and doubly right where you're concerned.*

Once they were gone, Juliet wiped the calamine lotion out of the ceramic dish and replaced the paper clips. She wandered around the office, impatient for Brady to come back. She found herself thinking about Michael and about the kind of man who would offer to keep a sick child in his office all day. She liked the things she was learning about Brady. She was walking over to the bed which was still in a tangle, when she heard his voice.

"Juliet, great, you're still here." Brady burst into the room. "Where's Michael?"

"His father picked him up," she explained, turning toward Brady with a smile.

Brady pulled off his suit coat and tie, watching her straighten the sheets on the bed. "I'll bet Phil looked harried. This is the second time around with the chicken pox." Brady dropped his coat on the chair. "Had you ever met Phil before?"

"Only professionally." Juliet fluffed the pillow and her auburn hair tumbled down around her face. "I understand he's a good lawyer."

"He is," Brady agreed. "And with both kids sick, he's had a hell of a time keeping up. The baby-sitter won't come near them."

"Their mother's not there?" Juliet remembered what Michael had said. She wondered what the real story was.

"Nope." Brady didn't want to elaborate. He couldn't take his eyes off Juliet. When she stood up, her blouse settled over her breasts, outlining them subtly. Brady's mouth was dry. "How did you and Michael do, this afternoon?"

Juliet stretched her leg down from the ladder that leaned against the loft bed. Her calf was slender and shapely, the kind that invited a man to stroke it.

"Just fine. We talked for a while and I read him a book—" She felt Brady behind her, his hands cupping her elbows.

"I really appreciate this, Juliet." He turned her around to face him, his eyes apologetic. "I pushed you into doing it—"

"I'm not angry, if that's what you're thinking," she assured him.

That wasn't what he was thinking at all. He was thinking about her breasts and how they thrust, high and firm. He ran his hands lightly along her upper arms. Her blouse was silky to his touch and her skin warm beneath it. "Well, anyway, thanks for taking care of Michael for me." He was acutely aware of the rising and falling of her breasts when she breathed.

"I didn't mind staying with him, Brady, at least not after I got to know him." His touch warmed her everywhere, a rippling warmth like a slow electric current running through her. His hands tightened on her arms. His eyes were soft as velvet. She opened her lips and found his, cool and sweet, waiting for her. Juliet wanted the moment to last forever, so she could press still closer to him, his arms binding her body against his.

Instead, she opened her eyes slowly and forced herself to come back to the present. This wasn't the answer, not here, not now, not under these circumstances. "What are we doing, Brady?" she whispered, pulling away.

He felt the tightening in his groin and wanted her against him again. He slipped his hand under her hair to find the sensitive skin on the back of her neck. "We're getting to know each other. We're about to get married, remember?"

Juliet's whole body stiffened. "That's turning into a real problem, Brady. It would have been a lot simpler my way."

"Meaning?"

Juliet took a deep breath. "Meaning my mother wants us to come for dinner."

From her reaction, Brady had been expecting a crisis. This hardly qualified. "So why not?" he shrugged. "Can she cook?" He was about to reach for her again when she paced across the office.

"Of course she can cook, but she's a little...um...original sometimes. She asked if you eat sushi."

"Raw fish?" Brady groaned. "I owe you one for this afternoon, Juliet. I want you to know you're collecting. When do we do this?"

"Thursday night. I can ask her to change the menu."

"No," Brady declined, "let's stick with sushi. At least I know what that is." He made a note on his calendar. "I take it she knows we're getting married?"

Juliet grimaced. "She's very excited...full of plans."

*Plans.* He drew back sharply. "Wait a minute. What kind of plans? You're not going to dress up like a real bride are you?"

The prospect horrified Juliet. "Of course not—why would I do something like that?"

Brady felt better. "I just wanted to be sure," he said. They looked at each other in silence, wondering what they'd gotten themselves into.

CASS CALLED JULIET three times in the next three days about the dinner plans, which was three times more often than she had ever called about any social event. Juliet felt herself getting more and more involved when everything was supposed to be so simple.

She worked late Thursday, and by the time she locked the office door it was already seven o'clock. That was when she was supposed to be downstairs meeting Brady. Juliet had just stepped out of the elevator and was hurrying across the building lobby when she heard someone calling her name. "Wait, please wait, Miss Cavanaugh."

She turned toward the sound of the voice and saw a blond woman hurrying toward her. Juliet recognized her immediately. She was the one who wouldn't give her name, the one with the children. Checking her watch, Juliet decided whatever the woman wanted would have to hold until later. Brady was probably waiting for her, Cass was expecting them, and she was already late.

"I'm sorry," she said as the woman approached. "My office is closed for the day, and I'm late for an appointment."

"But I really have to talk to you," the woman persisted.

For an instant, Juliet wavered. This woman desperately needed help. But there wasn't enough time just now. "If you'll call the office in the morning..." Juliet said, walking faster. She left the woman standing alone in the building lobby, and tried hard to block out the look of disappointment in those pale eyes.

The blond woman watched the lawyer go through the revolving door. The lawyer made her angry. She had said it was all right to come back anytime, but every time she came the lawyer was busy. She probably wouldn't even have time to make a phone call. Just one phone call that could get her babies back.

For a moment the woman considered making the phone call herself. There were pay phones just outside the building. She would just call her husband herself and tell him she wanted the boys. That was what she'd wanted the lawyer to do, because he would listen to a lawyer. But now she'd have to do it herself.

She headed purposefully through the revolving doors and toward the row of phones. When there was no answer at home, she tried his office, but his secretary said he had left for the day. Now she didn't know what to do. It was just like before. He was never there when she needed him. She'd even thought about telling him she might like to come home for a while. But it didn't matter anyway. The last time she told him she might come home he'd wanted to put her in the hospital first. She didn't want that. She just wanted her babies back.

Turning away from the phones, the woman walked briskly, leaving Embarcadero Center behind. She slowed as she passed the liquor store and then picked up her pace again when she turned the corner. That proved she didn't need to be in any hospital. It had been over a week since she'd had a drink, except for a few glasses of wine, and they didn't really count. If she really had a drinking problem she wouldn't be able to stop drinking. She'd be like one of those bums staggering down the street taking swigs from an open bottle. And she wasn't like that at all.

The woman paused for a moment and stared at her reflection in the window of a portrait studio. Automatically she smoothed the fine blond hair back from her face and stood up a little straighter. Inside the studio, propped up on an easel, she could see a picture of two children about the same ages as hers. Their mother was probably fixing them dinner now. That was how it was supposed to be.

Discouraged, she walked down the street. Her husband was using the children to hurt her, keeping them from her when she had a right to them. She wouldn't let him get away with it. She'd keep calling him and when she got him, she'd make him listen. And, if he still wouldn't, she'd go back to the lawyer and wait no matter how long it took. And, one way or another, she'd get her babies back.

JULIET STOOD ON the corner for several minutes before Brady pulled up. No matter how hard she tried, she couldn't get the woman off her mind.

"You look like you've seen a ghost," Brady told her as she slid into the car.

"No, just a client with some enormous problems," Juliet replied. "She seems so lonely, and so defeated, and there's not much I can do to help her."

Brady found a break in the steady stream of traffic and pulled the car away from the curb. "It must be hard not to get involved in their problems," he said thoughtfully.

"It is sometimes," Juliet agreed. She wanted to tell him more about the woman, because the incident was bothering her. But at the same time, she wanted not to think about it. She turned toward Brady with an apologetic smile. "Enough work for one day," she said. "I'm sorry I'm late."

"It doesn't matter. I got tied up in traffic anyway," Brady answered. "Your mother obviously doesn't commute, or she wouldn't live in Sausalito."

"Cass? Commute?" Juliet laughed, realizing how little Brady knew about her mother. "Of course not. She's an artist "

"What kind of artist?" His BMW purred softly as they took their place in a line of cars stretching back from an interminable stoplight.

"She illustrates children's books."

Brady began to look interested. "And she's good enough to make a living at it?"

The comment struck Juliet as peculiar. She'd always pretty much taken her mother's talents for granted. "Did you ever hear of *The Beetlebob and Ellie*?"

"Sure," Brady revved his engine and made it through the light on yellow. "I read one of those books to Timmy not long ago—he's Michael's four-year-old brother. You mean she illustrates that series?"

"Along with a couple of others." They crested a hill and Juliet looked down to see cars flowing smoothly across the Golden Gate Bridge to about midpoint in the bay where they vanished into nothing as the fog rolled toward the city. Her mother's timing had been perfect. The crunch of traffic was thinning out.

"Has your mother always lived in Sausalito?" The BMW zipped across the bridge and made a turn.

"Since I was little. She has one of those old houses that used to be dirt cheap before all the tourists came. For a while she considered living on a houseboat," Juliet laughed. "She's really kind of... kind of different."

"I knew that when you told me we were having sushi." Following Juliet's directions, Brady turned down Cass's street. "I can promise you that my mother will serve a more traditional meal when you eat at her house."

"Your mother?" Juliet echoed. This was getting more complicated.

"Don't sound so surprised," Brady answered.

"And I suppose she serves roast beef, mashed potatoes, that sort of thing?" Juliet inquired.

"Yeah, Mother's big on roast beef—standing ribs for company," Brady confirmed.

Juliet couldn't remember her mother ever cooking roast beef, and when Cass was in one of her vegetarian phases, she was disdainful of all red meat. Juliet had the distinct feeling Brady wasn't ready for Cass. "Where does your mother live?" she asked.

"Boston," Brady answered. "She went back there to live with her sister after my father died." He slowed the car as they neared their destination. "I'll have to take you there to meet her. She doesn't travel much anymore."

Juliet barely heard him. She was resolving that she would not, under any circumstances, fly to Boston to meet Brady's mother. A paper marriage was one thing. Getting involved with all the relatives was something else. She wished she'd told Cass the truth right from the beginning.

"So this is where your mother lives," Brady observed, turning off the engine. Juliet glanced at Brady, who appeared to be studying the house with great interest. She followed his gaze across the tangle of wildflowers where the front yard should be, and on to the weather-beaten frame structure almost hidden by tall trees.

"Maybe we shouldn't have come, Brady," she said suddenly.

"Why not?" He hesitated, his car door half open.

"Cass isn't at all like the people you're used to."

"I think she'll be fascinating—"

"But Brady, she thinks we're really getting married," Juliet blurted out.

"So that's it." He shut his door and turned toward her, taking her hands in his. "Have you changed your mind?"

"Not about the baby, but all the rest of this—"

"Look, Juliet, it's a lot easier to explain a baby with a marriage than a baby without one. I thought you said your mother was excited."

"She is." Juliet answered glumly.

"Then let her have the fantasy." He held her hands tight. "In the long run it'll be easier for her, too."

Brady wished he felt as confident as he sounded. He squeezed Juliet's hands reassuringly and hurried around to help her out of the car. It was no wonder she was apprehensive. He'd never considered mothers as a part of all this either. Boston was far enough away that they could probably avoid a trip there since they only had a six-month agreement. But Sausalito was just across the bridge.

As they approached the door, which was painted bright turquoise, Brady slipped his arm around Juliet's shoulders. She was tight as a knot. Might as well make the best of it as long as they were there, he decided, reaching for the brass peacock knocker.

"You're here," Cass exclaimed, flinging the door open.

"Cass, this is—"

"I know, I know," her mother interrupted. "This is Brady." She threw her arms around him and gave him an enormous hug.

Barely keeping his balance, Brady managed to lean over and give her a kiss on each cheek. "You're even more delightful than I'd anticipated," he told her. Juliet had obviously been trying to prepare him, but he hadn't been ready for a middle-aged woman dressed in a purple Japanese kimono, especially one who embraced him like a long-lost love even before they'd been properly introduced. She was obviously Juliet's mother—the resemblance was striking—but the similarity stopped there. "If I were to guess," Brady said with a twinkle in his eye, "I'd wager that we're having Japanese food for dinner." He wondered if the gardenia tucked into Cass's flaming red hair would simply continue to wobble precariously or if it ultimately would drop into the nearby fish tank.

Cass patted his arm. "Indeed we are dining Japanese tonight," she said approvingly, "and I like to create the proper atmosphere right from the start, so if you two will just leave your shoes here at the door..."

"Sorry," Juliet whispered to Brady as she bent down to slip off her black pumps.

"It's okay," he whispered back. "I can tell this evening is going to fall in the category of 'one of those enriching experiences....'" Brady untied his shoes and set them alongside Juliet's pumps on the terrazzo floor of the foyer.

"Come along now," said Cass, taking Brady's arm and leading him into the living room.

"Hey, this is great." Brady grinned and dug his toes into the thick white carpet. She was obviously the eccentric artist, and he had to admit, despite the effusive welcome, there was something about Cass he liked.

"I can tell that you and I are going to get along very well," Cass told him, "and I am a very good judge of character." She led the way among piles of bright, multicolored pillows that had been strewn across the carpet and folded herself into a perfect lotus position as she sank down on a pink satin cushion. Juliet and Brady followed her example and settled themselves around a black lacquer table. Brady choose a green cushion that was firmer and thicker than the rest.

Juliet had long ago accepted the fact that her mother didn't have chairs in the living room, and had no illusions about Cass changing her style at this late date. She wondered what Brady was thinking and stole a sidelong glance at him. His attention was focused totally on Cass, and he looked as though he was enjoying himself.

"Now," Cass began, "I want to hear all about these wedding plans. First of all, when is the big event going to take place?"

Juliet looked at Brady. If he'd set the date yet, he hadn't told her about it.

"A week from Saturday," he answered smoothly, as if it had been an accomplished fact for some time.

"A week from Saturday?" Cass repeated. "You mean the Saturday just after this one?" The gardenia in her hair bobbed dangerously.

"I did warn you that we were going to do this soon," Juliet interjected quickly. It obviously wasn't the time to tell her mother that the actual date was news to her, too.

"You did tell me," Cass agreed, "but by 'soon' I didn't realize you meant immediately. You were obviously hatching these plans for a while before you got around to telling me." She gave Juliet a pointed look.

"Oh, no . . . well, yes," Juliet corrected herself. She judiciously avoided Brady's eyes. "You see, both Brady and I are very busy," she hurried to explain.

"Not too busy for a honeymoon, I hope. You are going to take a honeymoon, aren't you?" Cass demanded.

*Honeymoon?* The idea had never crossed Juliet's mind.

*Honeymoon!* thought Brady. *Damn!* That did follow the wedding.

They opened their mouths simultaneously. "No," answered Juliet. Her higher pitched voice was almost drowned out by Brady's deep, resonant "Yes."

"Well, which is it?" Cass looked back and forth from one to the other. "No or yes?"

Juliet paused, not wanting to get in any deeper than she already was. She could tell her mother was already suspicious of their relationship.

"It's yes," Brady replied firmly. "We are definitely going on a honeymoon."

"We are?" Juliet looked at him, puzzled.

"It would appear you're not quite of one mind on this," Cass noted. Juliet shrugged helplessly, and so Cass focused on Brady. "Where are you going?"

"To Carmel," Brady answered. He hoped the inn had a room available for the week. "I had been keeping it a bit of a surprise," he added coolly.

"Oh, I hope I didn't spoil anything," Cass exclaimed. "But, to Carmel—" Her deep green eyes, so like her daughter's, sparkled with excitement. "How romantic! The ocean, the quaint little shops, the rolling hills . . . we need to drink a toast." Quickly she stood up and disappeared into the kitchen.

"Brady," hissed Juliet. "First you didn't tell me when the wedding was, and now you're talking about a honeymoon. I never agreed to a honeymoon. There isn't a word about Carmel in our contract."

"Don't blame me," he hissed back. "It was your mother's idea."

"She's not the one who said we were going to Carmel." Juliet's voice began to rise.

"Sh-h-h." Brady warned her. "She is, however, the one who assumed—and, I might add, correctly so—that there is a normal progression from wedding to honeymoon."

"That doesn't mean I've agreed to it," Juliet whispered defensively.

"Maybe not," Brady grinned at her, "but you're the one who wants the baby. That could be a hell of a good start."

Juliet felt the color rising in her cheeks. Fortunately, Cass returned to the living room at just that moment, carrying a tray with three porcelain wine cups and a plate of delicate sushi.

"Warmed sake," she announced as she handed each one of them a cup. "To a long and joyous future," she toasted happily, looking first at Brady and then letting her gaze linger on Juliet. "My goodness, dear," she said after a sip of rice wine, "your color is better than I've seen it in ages. Obviously this pending marriage agrees with you."

Juliet thought for a moment she might choke on her drink.

"To us," Brady added his own toast, obviously aware of her discomfort and, she realized, no doubt enjoying it. He leaned over and kissed Juliet on the cheek, stirring sensations that raced through her faster than a large gulp of the smooth, warm rice wine.

*Stop that,* Juliet thought. *Stop that instantly.*

"You two are perfect for each other," Cass pronounced. "I can tell just by watching you together. And, in case there is any doubt, I'll do a chart comparison."

"Cass!" Juliet protested. For some reason she didn't want to know whether hers and Brady's astrological signs were compatible. It was all nonsense anyway.

"No kidding." Brady looked up with interest from the sushi he had been dipping in soy sauce. "Does that really work? I'm March fifth—Pisces." He downed the sushi as if he'd been eating it all his life.

"Of course it works," Cass proclaimed, "even for a strong-minded woman like Juliet. But it might take me a few days to reach my astrologer. She isn't always available." Cass stood up gracefully. "Now, if you'll excuse me one more time, I'll get the sukiyaki."

"Let me help you." Juliet sprang up behind her mother, anxious to avoid any more private conversations with Brady.

"I wouldn't think of it—sit down, Juliet," her mother ordered. "You have a fiancé to entertain. I won't be a minute."

Reluctantly, Juliet sank back on her yellow silk cushion, giving Brady a sidelong glance to see how he liked being referred to as a fiancé. But his thoughts were elsewhere.

"It's fun to watch you take orders for a change," he commented with a wicked grin. "Your mother is fantastic."

"That's not exactly the word I'd choose," Juliet noted dryly.

"Then you underestimate her," Brady asserted. "Just one thing I can't figure out."

"Only one?" Juliet jibed.

"Tell me," Brady continued, "how did an eccentric artist like Cass Cavanaugh end up with a daughter like you?"

Juliet rolled her eyes helplessly. She'd often wondered how she'd ended up with a mother like Cass.

Brady and Cass launched into a lively discussion of children and creativity, while Juliet mostly listened, wishing they didn't get along quite so well. It was just going to make bookshelves more difficult when the marriage came to an end. On the way home, Brady talked enthusiastically about the illustrations Cass was doing for her latest book. The doubts that had shadowed Juliet all evening grew even more disquieting. There would be no trip to Boston to meet his mother, she resolved again, and as little contact with Cass as possible until the six months were over. The marriage was nothing but a formality, and it would stay that way.

As they neared her apartment, Brady also lapsed into silence. He sensed that the evening had disturbed her, and the fact that he'd thoroughly enjoyed himself probably didn't help. He made no move to touch her when they pulled up in front of her apartment building and she quickly got out of the car. He'd wait and let her phone him—which, he realized, would have to be soon. Their wedding day was just a little more than a week away.

Brady chuckled softly as he drove away. It was going to be a hell of a funny marriage—two people who didn't want to be married to each other going through the motions. Too bad in a way. He wished he'd met Juliet under different circumstances. He really did like her. But getting married like this would no doubt destroy anything that might have developed between them. Turning the corner, he gunned the engine. Phil had been right. This whole damned thing wasn't going to be all that easy.

It wasn't until the next day that Juliet realized she had been so preoccupied with Brady meeting Cass that she didn't have the basic information she needed to plan her schedule. She had spent an entire evening with Brady and they hadn't even talked about the time of the wedding, or anything about the honeymoon he'd sprung on her.

"Just which details did you want to discuss?" Brady inquired over the phone.

"Oh," replied Juliet breezily, "a few minor things like the time and place of the wedding."

"Three-thirty next Saturday afternoon. Judge Baldwin's office on Geary Street," Brady said promptly.

Juliet made a quick note in her appointment book and then started to laugh.

"What's so funny?" Brady asked.

"Oh, nothing," Juliet said, scanning the page, "except it looks a little odd when you pencil in your wedding the same way you'd write down a trip to the dentist."

"I don't know. You said yourself this was purely a business arrangement," Brady pointed out.

"Yes, I know I did...." Juliet's voice trailed off. Somehow it was different now. "Well, then," she continued briskly, "I also need to know what the honeymoon plans are. I may have to rearrange my schedule.''

"Just block out the week following the wedding," Brady directed.

"An entire week?" Juliet gasped, looking at the neat notations sprinkled all across the calendar page. "You've got to be kidding. I've got a load of appointments and two cases I'm getting ready for trial. I can't possibly take a week."

Brady held firm. "A proper honeymoon requires at least a week."

"How about we settle for a long weekend?" Juliet proposed.

"Nope," Brady asserted. "A week at least."

"What will we do all that time?" Juliet regretted the words the instant they were out of her mouth.

There was a long silence on the other end of the phone line. "Apparently we do have some details to discuss." Brady's tone of voice offered no clue as to what he might be thinking. Juliet decided that might be just as well.

"We can talk about it over dinner tomorrow," he suggested. "I'll pick you up at eight."

Juliet frowned. Sitting at her desk, she could maintain a strong bargaining position. But over dinner... "Couldn't we just take care of it now—over the phone?"

"I've got an appointment in exactly...actually I'm late now. See you tomorrow."

Juliet hung up slowly. She'd just have to be firm, she decided. A whole week simply wasn't necessary. She could see if Linda could take over for a few days, but any longer would be asking a lot of her this soon.

Linda should be in by now, Juliet realized. She'd stayed at home for the last week, getting her house in order, as she'd explained, and waiting for the workmen to finish with her office. Yesterday, movers had delivered knocked-down bookcases, a dozen cartons of books, and a desk, and today Linda planned to get organized. Although they'd talked on the phone two or three times, Juliet still hadn't mentioned her upcoming marriage. It seemed better to discuss it in person.

The door to the new office was open, and Juliet found her new partner in jeans and a sweatshirt, pounding a recalcitrant bookshelf into position with the heel of her shoe. "Sure glad I saved these bookcases when I closed down my practice," Linda said, giving the shelf a final smack.

Juliet surveyed a long line of cardboard cartons. "You've got enough books here to open a law library."

"It just looks like a lot when they're boxed." Linda wiped her hands on the back of her jeans.

"You should be pretty well settled by next week," Juliet observed. "How's your schedule look for the week after that?"

"Free as a bird," Linda answered. "That new nanny is a gem. Jennie loves her and she's wonderful with Paul. What have you got in mind?"

"Well..." Juliet hesitated, trying to decide how to lead in gradually. "I told you things went really well when I met with Brady—"

"And that's all you said," Linda interrupted. "What's up?"

"I'm going to get married a week from Saturday," Juliet announced. There didn't seem to be any way but the direct approach.

"Married!" Linda exclaimed. "You hardly know him."

"It's not like it sounds," Juliet added quickly. "His father left a trust agreement that says he has to be married by the time he's thirty-five. That's the real reason he answered my ad. He offered to father the baby if I'd marry him for six months."

"You've got to be kidding." Linda stared at her. "I knew he sounded too good to be true."

Juliet paced across the office. "I didn't want any part of it at first," she admitted, "but actually it's not that bad. It's not really a marriage—it's just an arrangement for six months. And, as he pointed out, it might be easier this way when the baby grows up."

"I can't believe this is you talking." Linda sank onto the only available chair, which was still covered with brown paper. "Wait a minute—when did you say you're doing this?"

"A week from Saturday," Juliet repeated.

"Oh, Juliet," Linda moaned. "I can't come. That's my Dad's sixty-fifth birthday and my mother is giving him a surprise party. She'll kill me if I don't show up."

"That's okay," Juliet shrugged. "I really didn't expect you to come. This isn't for real. It's just going to be a quick thing in the judge's chambers to make it legal."

"When am I going to meet him?" Linda asked.

"I don't know." Juliet frowned. "It's no big thing, and it's going to be really brief, just till I get pregnant. That's part of the deal. I don't want to get involved.''

"It sounds to me like you're already involved, Juliet," Linda observed quietly. "Are you sure you want to do this?"

"Why not?" Juliet questioned, but she didn't feel as casual about it as she was trying to sound.

"I'm not sure why not," Linda answered. "It just seems like you're in pretty deep. How's Cass handling it?"

"She's ecstatic because her only daughter is getting married."

"You didn't tell her the circumstances?"

"No," Juliet said, "and that turned out to be a problem, because she insisted on having Brady to dinner and then asked where we were going on our honeymoon. He said to Carmel, so I guess we are." Juliet sat on the edge of the desk across from Linda. "I thought maybe you could come in for a few days that week...."

"Of course," Linda agreed, "if you'll give me some idea of what's coming up. Stay away as long as you want—if you're going to be married to him, you might as well get to know him."

"A couple of days will do it," Juliet assured her. "I'll put together the background you'll need and we can sit down next week and go over all of it." Juliet started toward the door, and then she paused. "Just one other thing, in case I forget," she said, turning around. "Do you remember that rather subdued blond woman? I think you saw her that first day you came in."

Linda looked thoughtful for a moment, then her face brightened. "Oh, yes—tall, thin...could be really pretty?"

"She came back just as I was leaving last night and I didn't have time to talk to her," Juliet said. "There's no file on her because she won't give her name, but in a nutshell, she wants custody of her kids and she's got an alcohol problem. There's something about her, Linda. She's so lonely—"

Linda nodded. "I get the picture. Don't ever let it get around town what a soft heart you have or we'll both starve to death."

Laughing, Juliet went back to her office. It had been time to take in a partner, and Linda had been the perfect choice. She let out a long, satisfied breath. Everything was going pretty much as she'd planned it. Except the wedding, and, in the overall scheme of things, that was only a bump in the road.

# CHAPTER SIX

JULIET LET HER BODY slide down the slick porcelain bathtub, wondering how many years it had been since she'd taken a bubble bath. Tonight she was going to dinner with Brady, and next Saturday they were getting married.

Checking her hair, which she had piled high on her head and secured with a ribbon, she sank lower until the water touched her chin and the bubbles tickled her nose. *I'm getting married in a week,* she thought incredulously. Of course the ceremony was just a formality. She blew a long trench in the sea of bubbles. But then...then they would drive to Carmel and then...

Despite the steamy water, little chills ran through Juliet. She'd never really thought about getting in bed with the man who was going to father her baby. At least she hadn't thought about it in concrete terms. And it was different now that it was one specific man. *Brady.* She considered what making love with him would be like. She couldn't quite imagine being totally naked with him, but maybe that wouldn't be necessary. She probably wouldn't need to undress. He could slide her nightgown up....

The sound of the doorbell ringing punctured her reverie. She ignored it, wondering what Brady wore to bed. Some men slept in the nude. Sinking just a little deeper in the soft, perfumed bubbles, Juliet thought that over. Under these circumstances, she decided, Brady would probably wear pajamas.

The doorbell rang again, insistently. "Go away," she called out. "Nobody's home."

There was absolutely no one she wanted to see in the middle of her bubble bath. She tried to revive the image of Brady in bed, but whoever was outside her door leaned steadily on the bell. She heard a muffled male voice shouting from outside. Annoyed, Juliet stood up. It was always possible there was a fire or some kind of emergency. Mounds of bubbles ran down her slippery skin. "All right, all right, I'm coming," she shouted, wrapping a huge, thick blue terry towel around her body.

After making sure the security chain was firmly in place, Juliet opened the door a crack. "Yes?" she said impatiently, water dripping around her feet.

"Boy, are you slow," replied Brady's cheerful voice. "How about letting me in?"

"Brady!" gasped Juliet, pulling the towel tighter. She wondered irrationally if he somehow knew what she'd been thinking. "What are you doing here?" she demanded. "You're not supposed to come until tonight, and I'm in the bathtub."

"No, you're not," Brady countered. "You are standing at the front door of your apartment, wearing a towel, probably freezing, and arguing with me. Open the door."

"Can you wait till I get a robe?"

"Open the door," Brady directed impatiently. "I promise I won't attack."

"Oh, all right," she agreed. Taking a firm grip on her towel, Juliet removed the chain, poised for a speedy retreat to the bathroom.

But after Brady closed the door behind him, he stopped directly in front of her. "You, my dear, are a vision of loveliness," he said admiringly, flicking at the bubbles that still clung to her shoulder. "I want you to know that it is only because I am a man of my word—"

"Stop that, Brady Talcott," she demanded. "What are you doing here anyway? You said you'd pick me up at eight. That's hours from now."

"I got impatient." His fingers still toyed with her shoulder, removing the final traces of the bubbles and leaving a tingling sensation in their place. "Besides, it's a perfect day to fly a kite and I've got a new one I want to test. Put your clothes on, and we'll go to the beach. I'll show you my house."

Juliet hesitated. There were probably a thousand reasons why his suggestion was a bad idea, but she couldn't think of one. "Make yourself at home," she said with a smile. "I'll go get dressed."

Brady watched her disappear in the direction of the bathroom, wishing the towel she had clutched around her would flap open a little more when she walked. Then he wandered into the dining room, curious about how Juliet lived. He surveyed the graceful lines of the Queen Anne table and chairs, all in gleaming mahogany. Her taste was impeccable, he decided, but very conservative. The living room was more inviting. He studied the room, a blend of peach and aqua and yellow, coordinated by an expanse of light peach carpeting. They weren't his colors, but he liked the room anyway. It had a friendly feeling about it.

Checking his watch, Brady looked for the kitchen. You got a feeling about people by walking through their houses, he realized. Everybody put things together a little differently. He checked the refrigerator for beer and settled for orange juice. Juliet apparently didn't cook very much, he decided, looking around the immaculate kitchen which was decorated in pale yellow. Maybe because of the subtle striped wallpaper—or maybe it was the shutters—the room didn't look cold. But it didn't look used, either.

Brady wasn't sure what to make of Juliet. She was a series of contradictions. Cold lady lawyer wants a baby, negotiates a contract. But there had been nothing cold about her that day in his office. And she didn't look very formidable in that towel, either. He smiled to himself as he mentally undressed her. Tantalizing was a better word. Yet she didn't seem to be a closet homemaker who had made a nest and wanted a child to complete the fantasy. He was putting the orange juice back in the refrigerator when he heard Juliet's voice.

"If you'd like something to drink, help yourself," she called to him.

Orange juice in hand, he went in search of the sound. He caught her on her way to the bedroom, still in the towel. "You haven't made any progress at all," he complained. "Hurry up."

"I've still got roughly six hours before you're due to pick me up," she retorted, shutting the door behind her. "And I am hurrying," she called out through the closed door.

When she appeared in the living room in a white warm-up suit with a jacket slung over her shoulder, Brady let out a low whistle. Her skin glowed, framed by that thick flowing hair that was pulled loosely back except for a few damp tendrils that had escaped. She smelled fresh and new, like spring flowers. But what drew him most, what always drew him, were those eyes, those magnificent green eyes.

"I take it that whistle is a compliment. Thank you," she told him.

"Well deserved," he murmured, still staring at her. Whatever else Juliet was, she was also beautiful. He was almost sorry he'd decided to take her to the beach. He'd have liked to stay there with her. But he also wanted to fly the kite. "We need to get going," he said, taking her arm.

BRADY WAS RIGHT, Juliet decided, as soon as they stepped out into the sunshine. The day was perfect for flying a kite or for almost anything else, as long as it was outdoors. The blanket of fog that had hung heavily until mid-morning was gone entirely, leaving the city sparkling beneath a brilliant blue sky. With the jutting skyline disappearing behind them, the BMW purred south on Route 1.

The highway rose above the coastline and curled through the hilly farmland emerging atop rocky cliffs where surf crashed below. Brady had left the sun roof open, and Juliet drank in the sea-scented air. "I'm glad we're going to the beach," she said happily. Brady only smiled.

As they approached Half Moon Bay, the cliffs gave way to a gentle slope that overlooked an endless white sand beach. Brady turned the car onto a side road that wound its way through the dunes. Sprawling contemporary homes were scattered along the shoreline high above the water. They pulled alongside a house built

of weathered cedar with tall rectangular windows facing the road.

She knew immediately why he liked it, and yet it
seemed a strange place for a bachelor furniture maker
to live alone. The more she got to know Brady, the
more he seemed to be a series of contradictions.

"See, what did I tell you?" Brady demanded as they
got out of the car, the wind whipping his hair. "Have
you ever seen a better day for kite flying?"

"Never," Juliet agreed. She watched him gather the
tightly rolled kite out of the back seat, and followed
him down the sandy slope to a flat expanse of beach
stretching like a ribbon along the sapphire-blue ocean.
She sensed his excitement, and it was contagious. Juliet watched Brady lay the kite train on the sand, three
kites in a row—one yellow, one red, and one an electric blue, attached together with an intricate web of
kite string.

He was as engrossed in what he was doing as she
might have been in preparations for a major trial,
checking the wind, adjusting the kite string, freeing
the tails. He seemed to do everything with his whole
being. A wind gust whipped Juliet's hair, and she
shivered, sliding her arms into the jacket she had been
carrying over her shoulders.

She steadied the kites for Brady until he tightened
the lines, and the kites rose swiftly, their noses pointed
into the sun, their tails flowing behind in perfect par-
allel. They hung dead still overhead, before Brady
brought them careening down almost into the sand. At
the last moment they swerved sharp right and raced
sideways toward the breaker line before climbing again
to swirl their tails in graceful loops.

Juliet remembered the last time she'd flown a kite. It had been with her father, one of the last things they'd done together before he left. The kite they'd flown had been a simple diamond; the only challenge had been getting it launched in the first place. From then on it had been at the mercy of the wind. But Juliet could still remember the thrill of watching it fly free, sure that at any moment it might touch the clouds.

As she walked up the beach toward Brady, she never took her eyes off the kites racing in gleaming streaks of color across the sun. They were typical of Brady, in their grace and precision. "They're magnificent," she called out as she approached him. He was clearly proud of them. His cheeks were flushed, his eyes glistening with victory.

"You want to fly them?"

Juliet nodded, reaching for the handles, but then she pulled back. She didn't want to fly a kite. She wanted to keep her memory of the day with her father intact, just as it was. "I'd rather watch you," she told him, her voice subdued.

Brady frowned, sensing the change in her. "What's the matter, Juliet?" Taking a piece of twine from his pocket, he secured the handles to a piece of wood buried deep in the sand, letting the kites soar unattended.

"I just don't feel like flying a kite."

Brady put his hands on her shoulders, his fingers pressing into her fleecy jacket. "You're too serious about life, Juliet. You've never learned to play."

Juliet looked past him, her eyes following the jerky movements of the sanderlings racing away from the leading edge of the surf. The tone of his voice softened the accusation, but the truth of his statement was stinging. "My father used to say things like that," Juliet remembered. "He was an expert at playing."

Brady felt Juliet trembling beneath his hands. "Cass said the other night your father walked out when you were little. Is that why you've never mentioned him?"

"There's not much to say." Juliet shoved her hands into her jacket pockets. She didn't like to talk about her father.

"Is he the real reason you're so opposed to marriage?" Brady asked thoughtfully. "You're afraid the same thing will happen all over again?"

"Don't you dare analyze me," Juliet snapped, pulling away from him. "I'm not afraid. I have my life all planned and I'm not afraid."

Brady reached out and grabbed her arm, drawing her back to him. She braced both hands against his chest but he held on, locking his fingers around her upper arm. "Walk with me for a while," he whispered softly. "The kites will be all right here." She didn't answer, but slowly he felt her resistance lessen. They turned and began to walk together, their footprints stretching far down the deserted beach before either of them said a word.

Gusts whipped the froth from the breakers, spewing a fine spray across the sand. Juliet's mind churned, searching for the reasons behind her sudden burst of anger, trying to understand the memories. "Whatever you're thinking, I don't hate my father," she said finally, raising her voice so the force of the wind wouldn't blow away her words. "I know what the experts say: a daughter abandoned by her father at an early age learns to distrust men. My problem with my father is that he couldn't set priorities. All he wanted to do was play."

"And that's why playing makes you feel guilty?"

"It does not," Juliet retorted. She knew the words were empty, and probably Brady knew it, too. Work had always come easily to her—hard, driving work that had led her to more and more impressive successes. But play seemed so frivolous, so unproductive. There were always so many more important things to do.

Almost as though he'd heard her thoughts, Brady continued, "Playing is how you get in touch with yourself." He reached for Juliet's hand. "I have a hell of a lot of fun with my life. I also work—I work damn hard. But that's not what life is all about."

"Just exactly what is life all about?" Juliet heard herself asking him.

Brady didn't answer right away. It was one of the questions he'd wrestled with since as far back as he could remember. He hadn't come to terms with the meaning of life until after his father died and probably he wouldn't, completely, until the trust agreement was also dead and buried. "Life is about people." His words came slowly. "It's about people and the links that hold them together. It's about families and the kids who grow up to carry it all on."

His answer surprised Juliet. "Then why aren't you married?" she asked bluntly.

Brady didn't hesitate. "The right woman hasn't come along. It's as simple and as complicated as that." Letting go of Juliet's hand, he leaned down to pick up a broken seashell and skip it across the waves. "I want a wife to be the reason for my existence and I want our children to be an outgrowth of our love."

Juliet sifted his words uneasily. In his own way, Brady obviously felt as strongly about marriage as she did. His feelings were a stark contrast to their paper agreement. She walked along beside him, feeling very much alone, watching the breakers froth and curl before they dashed up on the sand. The seagulls screamed into the wind, flying free, diving for their supper and then soaring again to float on the air currents high above the blue-black water. She would be free like the gulls, and she would teach her child to love that freedom. The child. A sense of anticipation stirred inside her. Cass had said raising a child was the most meaningful thing she'd ever done. It would be the same for her. She couldn't get tangled in her feelings about Brady. He was temporary. The child would be forever.

The kites were fluttering in the distance, and Juliet looked ahead to see a tiny figure in a bright red sweatshirt running toward them down the beach.

Brady saw him, too. "Here comes Michael," he said grinning, automatically bracing himself.

Without breaking his stride, the boy leaped into Brady's arms, nearly sending them both tumbling into the sand. Regaining his balance, Brady spun him around twice before setting him down feet first.

"You gain two more pounds, and your human dynamo days are over," Brady warned him sternly. "I can't believe you're only seven years old."

Michael grinned. "I thought you said you were going to take up weight lifting."

Brady groaned. "No amount of weight lifting would prepare me for you, the size you're getting to be." He tousled the boy's sandy hair.

Only then did Michael seem to notice Juliet, who was trying hard not to stare at him. She had forgotten how dreadful children looked on the downhill side of chicken pox when the crusty scabs turned black. But Michael's liquid blue eyes had a sparkle in them now. As awful as he still looked, it was obvious that he felt much better.

"We finished the book," Michael announced, dispensing with any greeting. "Daddy said we could start *Prince Caspian* next week—that's the next one. There's a whole bunch of them."

Juliet smiled. "Did you like the part in the book about Lucy having tea with the faun?"

"Yeah, but I liked the part about Edward running away better," Michael answered. He turned back to Brady. "We came down to the beach right away when we saw your kite. I told them I'd find you, but Timmy thinks you fell in the ocean and got eaten by a shark."

"Then maybe we'd better go straighten him out," Brady suggested.

Michael didn't budge. "Do I get to fly the kite?" he demanded.

Brady smiled. At seven years old, it was obviously necessary to settle the important issues first. "You can fly it as long as you want," he agreed seriously.

"Before Timmy?"

"I suppose," Brady sighed, realizing he'd fallen into a carefully set trap.

"All right!" Michael grabbed both their hands. "Hurry up, will you?" He broke into a half run between them.

With Michael binding them together, Juliet and Brady avoided each other's eyes, staring straight ahead as he pulled them along. Like a flying wedge, the strange triangle moved swiftly down the beach.

Phil saw them coming long before they saw him. *What a perfect family portrait,* he thought, *and how deceiving looks can be.* As he watched them, bittersweet memories flooded back. Eileen's hair was blond, fine and straight like the boy's. And Michael had been smaller then, his short legs pumping furiously. When he couldn't keep up any longer, they each wrapped one arm around him and lifted him up, running in step with the boy between them, laughing together with the wind in their hair. It seemed an eternity ago instead of only a couple of years.

Phil brought his heel down hard on a shell, crushing it into the sand. Those first years after they'd moved to the beach had been so good. Maybe if he hadn't been gone so often, it would have stayed good. He'd warned her that it was going to be a tough commute, and that he wouldn't be home as much. She'd said that would be all right. They'd work it out. But even he hadn't realized how grueling the schedule was going to be and how often he'd end up spending the night in the city.

He'd stayed over more and more often as the distance grew between them, Phil realized. And when he did come home near the end, she was usually asleep, and the empty bottle was in the trash. After a while, he gave up trying to wake her. Maybe he shouldn't have pushed her to have another baby. He'd thought it would help. But it had only made everything worse. The psychiatrists hadn't helped much either. Maybe if he'd encouraged her to go into a rehabilitation program . . .

Hell, none of it mattered anymore, anyway. You played the hand life dealt you. At least he had the boys. He watched Timmy digging a giant hole near the surf, making his own ocean he called it. God, he loved them. Despite everything else that had gone wrong, his kids made life worthwhile. Even if they did get the chicken pox, he thought, grinning.

"Daddy!" Michael shouted, dropping both Brady and Juliet's hands and racing ahead. "I do get to fly the kite. Brady said so."

Phil shook his head as Michael raced for the kite. Brady had been a godsend with the boys. By making them his official toy testers, he'd given them a purpose in life after their mother had first left, something to take their minds off how much they missed her. It had been especially good for Michael. He was older, and he remembered so much more.

As Brady and Juliet came nearer, Phil waved a greeting. They were walking side by side now but a safe distance apart. "Brady, Juliet . . . good to see you again." Phil extended his hand, and Juliet clasped it briefly. He wondered if she realized he was aware of the arrangement between her and Brady.

"Nice to see you, Phil," Juliet said. "I'm glad Michael feels better."

"Me, too," Phil agreed. "That paintbrush idea of yours was definitely inspired."

"Paintbrush?" Brady interrupted, looking from one to the other.

"Didn't Juliet tell you?" Phil had figured Juliet probably told Brady all about her time with Michael. Maybe they didn't talk about things like that. He wondered what two people with a relationship like theirs did talk about. "She painted the calamine lotion on Michael and then gave him the brush to take home," Phil explained. "I could tell right away when he started to get better. He began painting calamine pictures on his stomach."

They all laughed, but at the same time, Brady found himself looking at Juliet with surprise. For some reason, that kind of novel approach to a child's illness wasn't something he would have expected her to think of.

Feeling a pressure on his leg, he looked down to find Timmy tugging at his pants. "You look a whole lot better," Brady told him, "almost as if you didn't have the chicken pox at all."

"I didn't get ugly like Michael," Timmy said proudly. "So I think I should get to fly the kite first— and because I'm only four."

"Not first this time, because I already promised Michael," Brady explained, wishing he'd brought along an extra kite. "You let him do it for a little while and then it will be your turn."

"I'll go tell him that," Timmy announced, racing across the sand toward his brother.

Within moments, he was back. "Michael says I can't fly it till he's through and that will probably be all afternoon," he wailed.

Juliet watched Phil kneel down on the sand and talk to his son quietly. Phil seemed to know exactly the right things to say, because after a while the tears stopped, and Timmy sniffed. Would she know the right answers in situations like this? Juliet wondered.

Phil patted Timmy, not seeming to notice the dirt streaks that appeared when the little boy wiped his face across his sleeve. "We need to go have a talk with Michael," he explained as he stood up. "We'll bring your kite back later, Brady."

"Keep it for a few days," Brady called after them. "Let them give it a good workout."

"Thanks," Phil called over his shoulder.

Juliet smiled as Phil reached down to take Timmy's hand, shortening his stride to walk in step with his son. "He likes being a father," Juliet said softly, "and he's got two really nice little boys."

"It's a lonely road for one person," Brady replied.

"But even alone he's obviously done a good job of it," Juliet pointed out.

Brady tossed a shell at the breakers. There was no arguing that Phil had done well with Michael and Timmy. But no one outside could possibly understand how hard it had been. Brady had caught only glimpses of his friend's agony, a few words over a drink, a look in his eyes when they talked about Eileen, which they rarely did anymore. "He didn't have much choice," Brady said quietly. He took her hand, not wanting to talk about Phil's situation. "It's starting to get cold. Let's head back to the house."

With the setting sun at their backs, they started to climb the slope that led back to the beach house. Without looking up at Brady, Juliet asked cautiously, "Do you think my plan will work?"

"What plan?" he asked.

"My plan for single motherhood."

"If you're asking me if it's all right to back out of this deal, the answer is yes. I won't sue you for breach of contract."

"That isn't what I meant," Juliet answered. Their pace slowed. "I just wondered what you thought about it."

"You're having second thoughts?" he pressed.

"Not exactly." But something was bothering her.
"It's just...well, watching Phil with Timmy...I guess
it made me think. Babies grow up and, well..." Juliet paused, not sure what she was trying to say and
sorry she'd ever begun to explore it. "I guess I was just
thinking that another life is a whole lot of responsibility for one person to take on." She reached down to
pick up a fragment of shell, polished soft pink in the
pounding surf, and rubbed her finger rhythmically
across it.

Brady stopped walking and studied Juliet carefully. She looked very vulnerable at that moment, he
thought, and very beautiful, with the sun burning red
behind her, shimmering off her tousled auburn hair.
He resisted the urge to take her in his arms, knowing
he needed to answer her.

"Well, Juliet, you are biting off a big chunk," he
began. She listened, not moving at all. He understood that it was important to choose his words carefully. "I think a baby is a lot bigger step than most
people realize at the beginning," he continued
thoughtfully, "although I suppose if anyone can do it
well, you can."

Juliet looked relieved. "Thank you," she answered.

He couldn't leave it there. "But it would be easier
to do it with two parents."

Juliet turned toward him, her eyes clouded, suspicious. "Are you trying to say something else, Brady—
about our arrangement?"

"Not at all," he assured her. "I was simply pointing out that parents normally come in pairs."

Juliet started walking again, bringing her feet down hard on the sand. There it was, the same old argument. The Noah's ark syndrome. The great American dream that wasn't true anymore. "They may start out in pairs—but they don't stay that way." Juliet didn't try to hide the bitterness in her voice. "And you can't tell me that broken homes and broken trust make children better off. They're a whole lot better off with love they can count on—love they can keep."

Brady matched her stride. "Love doesn't come with guarantees, Juliet." He watched her, wondering how many people, if any, had seen the sensitive, frightened woman beneath her polished exterior. She was looking for a way to beat the system, to ultimately make life better for herself and for this baby she wanted so much. If it was a mistake, it was an honest one.

They were still at the edge of the chasm, Brady realized, with nothing tangible between them except a piece of paper that could be torn up. Nothing was irrevocable—yet. They walked faster. The approaching evening had tamed the wind gusts, but brought with it a pervasive chill. "Are you sure you want to go through with this, Juliet?"

Her response was immediate. "Of course I'm sure," she answered with a cool assurance she didn't feel. She sensed his uncertainty. If she wanted out, this was the opportunity. But she'd already made her decision, after months of thinking it through. She wasn't going to change her mind now. "Are you backing out?" she challenged.

Brady hesitated.

"Well?" Juliet prompted. She turned toward him, her eyes flashing.

"No," he said finally. "I'm not backing out. The contract stands."

"Good," she answered smoothly.

He took her extended hand but held it instead of completing the handshake. "We'll take it one day at a time," he said evenly. "First we'll be married. Then you'll probably get pregnant—"

"No probably about it. Definitely," Juliet interrupted. "I've got it all figured out, the timing and everything. There's no reason why it shouldn't work."

Brady couldn't suppress a laugh. "Sometimes the best plans in the world have to be a little flexible—"

"I know that, but—"

"But you figure if you've got it all mapped out ahead of time, you've got a better chance," Brady chuckled.

His response didn't faze her. The wall of doubt between them was thinning, for some reason Juliet couldn't quite put her finger on. Nothing had changed. But she saw an acceptance in his eyes that hadn't been there before. "You're getting to know me," Juliet smiled back. "Maybe you'll pick up some of my good habits."

"Don't count on it," Brady answered softly. He let go of her hand and wrapped his arms around her. All afternoon he'd wanted to do that.

Juliet buried her face in his chest, giving in to the unexpected pleasure of feeling sheltered and protected. A steady wind off the ocean swirled around them, but in the circle of Brady's arms, Juliet was secure.

The embrace tightened, and she knew he was going to kiss her. Brady barely touched her at first, holding back until she moved her head toward him. Then his mouth pressed down hard on hers.

At first she savored his salty taste and then she felt the warmth all through her. It might have been heat from the late-afternoon sun burning into her back, except it moved when his hands moved, stroking her rhythmically. Gently, his tongue parted her lips and traced a tantalizing path across them. She opened her lips wider, letting him explore the softness within.

When she felt Brady's hand against the curve of her breast, inside her jacket against the soft, fleecy fabric of the warm-up suit, it seemed right and natural. But then he moved away. She wondered how much he could read in her face.

"The air is getting colder, Juliet," he said.

"I guess I hadn't noticed." She lowered her eyes.

"There's a fireplace in the house. We can warm up there and have something to eat."

"I'd like that," Juliet agreed. She wanted to be with him for a little while longer. Turning toward the sprawling beach house, its weatherbeaten siding blending in among the sandy hills dotted with mossy ice plant, they walked silently, hand in hand in the deepening twilight.

Juliet followed Brady into a large room that stretched all across the back of the house. The sun, sinking toward the horizon, poured through a wall of glass. Brilliant streaks of red shimmered off the crashing surf that pounded the beach below. Juliet caught her breath.

"Like it here?" Brady asked, and Juliet was aware of him standing beside a white fireplace that seemed to recede into the stark wall behind it.

"How could anyone be less than enchanted?" Her eyes followed the sun rays across the room, watching them dance in splendor on a myriad of tiny silver sea-gulls suspended from the ceiling. "If I had a place like this, I don't know whether I'd ever go anywhere else."

"I guess that's the real reason I moved out here," Brady admitted, as he stacked wood in the fireplace. "It's damn inconvenient, but it's worth the drive." He dusted his hands together before wiping them on his jeans. "Maybe we should come here instead of going to Carmel for our honeymoon," he mused.

His suggestion brought Juliet back, away from the hypnotic surf, to the memory of why she was with him. They were supposed to be talking about going to Carmel. Maybe it would be better to honeymoon at his house, instead.

She looked at the room itself more carefully. It was simply decorated but all the more striking because of it. The only chairs, if you could call them chairs, were huge blue beanbags. Several small glass tables with driftwood bases were placed among them on the nat-ural-fiber area rug. Brady's house was casual. And close. And not as much like a honeymoon as a trip to Carmel. "This would be a nice place to spend a cou-ple of days," Juliet agreed.

"A week," Brady corrected, striking a match to the paper strips he had stuffed under the logs.

Juliet winced. She wasn't ready for a week. Ac-tually, she wasn't ready for a honeymoon at all. What she'd expected was a paternity agreement and then a few arranged meetings, carefully timed. "We ob-viously have some things that need discussing," Ju-liet observed.

Brady put up the firescreen. "First, we eat," he determined. "That'll give the fire time to get going."

Juliet couldn't argue. She'd been hungry for an hour. Brady's kitchen turned out to be well stocked—actually better than hers. They took thick, meaty lentil soup from the freezer, then prepared a large salad and hot buttered bread. They both ate hungrily after the day outdoors, not slowing down till the end of the meal when they wiped out their soup bowls with the last pieces of bread.

Brady took a swallow of coffee, studying Juliet over the rim of his mug. He still couldn't figure her out. She seemed so damned together most of the time, as though she didn't need anyone or anything. But out on the beach, when he'd touched her, she'd wanted more. He'd seen it in her eyes, and he never misread that in a woman. He'd wanted her this afternoon, when she'd greeted him in that towel. Brady set down his coffee cup. "I like you in blue," he told her.

"But, Brady—" Juliet's eyes dropped to the warm-up suit. "I'm wearing white."

"You weren't this afternoon."

At first Juliet was confused. Then she felt the heat in her cheeks. She'd known he was studying her. Now she knew what he'd been thinking. It didn't make her angry—that would have been easier to deal with than the unmistakable sensation stirring deep inside her. "I guess I *was* wearing blue," she acknowledged.

Anxious to change the subject, Juliet stood up abruptly and took her dishes to the sink. "I feel much better after eating," she told him as she rinsed off her plate. "But we still haven't settled anything about next week—"

"Then come sit down and we'll discuss it," Brady invited as he pulled a dark blue beanbag chair in front of the blazing fire.

Juliet stopped at the edge of the room. "This doesn't seem like a very businesslike atmosphere."

"Honeymoon discussions are rarely businesslike," Brady said laughing. "They go more like this." He crossed the room in a few strides and scooped Juliet up in his arms.

"Put me down," she protested, kicking the air.

"In just a moment," he promised. But as he leaned over to drop her in the beanbag chair, she grabbed him tightly around the neck and they tumbled down together in a laughing, tangled heap. "That was supposed to be a classy maneuver," he noted.

Juliet tried to shift her weight off him, but he pulled her back. "You're not heavy," he told her. "Unless you don't like it here—"

"Well . . ." She lowered her thick lashes till they brushed her cheek. "It is warm," she murmured.

Brady stroked her hair, smoothing it into place. He liked her this way, so open and free. He trailed his fingers along the side of Juliet's face, and then, with one finger, lifted her chin and leaned down to cover her lips with his. Her mouth was soft and yielding. "You seem happy, Juliet," he whispered, sliding his arm under her and cradling her head against his shoulder.

"I am happy," she confirmed, smiling up at him. He was leaning over her, the deep red of the sunset bathing his face, softening his rugged jawline and illuminating the darkness of his eyes. She felt very close to him. "The last thing in the whole world I'd have done on my own today was to come to the beach," she admitted. "But I liked it. I liked the kite, and I liked the way the wind felt in my hair, and I like ... I like being here with you."

Juliet stopped talking because she didn't know what else to say. She didn't understand her own happiness and she didn't want to analyze it. She didn't want to lose it. Not forever, but just for the moment, she wanted to be here, with him, just the way she was.

For a long time they lay together, quiet and content, watching the darkness gather and the orange and yellow flames dance in the fireplace. After a while, Brady began to stroke the smooth, fair skin of Juliet's cheek, slowly and gently with the back of his hand. Juliet turned slightly in his arms and snuggled closer to him. She ran the tips of her fingers up and down the length of his arm, enjoying the feel of his coarse, springy hair.

His body felt so different from hers, so firm and hard. His scent was as masculine as he was, a musky smell Juliet realized she had come to associate with Brady. His breath was warm, barely grazing her ear. Juliet closed her eyes. She could hear the ocean waves rolling up on the beach and then sliding back to the water's edge. Up and back, up and back. Over and over in a rhythm as old as time itself. Juliet felt her body begin to undulate in rhythm with the waves. She reached around Brady and pressed close to him, tilting her head up, waiting, knowing how delicious his lips would taste.

"My God, you're lovely, Juliet," he whispered into her ear.

Juliet floated in his arms, trailing kisses down the side of his neck. He tasted salty from the sea breeze and the afternoon by the ocean, a delicious taste. She twined her fingers in his hair and pulled him down, until his mouth covered the hollow in her throat. Still the ocean waves rolled up and back on the shore and Juliet continued to match their rhythm.

Brady buried his face in her breasts for only an instant. Then he raised up to look at her, a debate raging inside him. He had to decide quickly or there would be no decision. His body was straining, ready. He thought he might explode when she rocked against him.

But when he reached down to touch her, she changed, her muscles drawing taut, the gentle rocking gone. *Oh, God,* he thought, *not now.* She didn't push him away, or offer any real resistance, but he knew. She might have let him take her. Under other circumstances, he'd have tried. But she wasn't ready, and he knew it. She might not even realize it herself, but she would afterward, and they had too far to go together. For one more moment he pressed hard against her, his body screaming for relief.

When he drew back, Juliet caught her lower lip between her teeth, biting down, waiting. The passion that had engulfed her, almost strangling her, had ebbed. She was disappointed but not surprised. It was what usually happened.

But he didn't move back against her. "No," she found herself protesting. "Don't stop." In a strange sort of way she still wanted him. She opened her eyes wide and saw Brady above her, silhouetted in the firelight, looking down at her.

"The rest will have to wait until the honeymoon," he said softly.

What had happened? No man stopped at that point. "Why?" she asked, her voice barely audible.

"Because it isn't time now." He kissed her lightly on the lips. "I want it to be good for both of us."

Again Juliet heard the breakers crashing against the sand and the low whistle of the rising wind outside. She reached up to touch Brady's cheek, and felt the tension in the hard set of his jaw. When he turned his head slightly, she saw the fire in the dark brown of his eyes.

"About the honeymoon, Brady," she began slowly.

"Yes?" His voice was choked.

"I think I can clear my calendar for a week." Right then, she wasn't sure a week would be long enough.

## CHAPTER SEVEN

STILL IN HER SLIP, Juliet tucked a sweater in the corner of the suitcase that lay open on her bed. Shoes, lingerie, robe, slippers—slippers! She couldn't go on a honeymoon without slippers. Juliet hurried to the closet. Maybe it would have been better not to have left the packing until the last minute, she thought, feeling almost panicky. She always packed at the last minute but for some reason, this time, she couldn't seem to get it all together. And she couldn't be late for her own wedding.

The sharp jangle of the phone startled her so much that she dropped one of the wedge-heeled satin slippers on the floor.

"Yes, Mother, I'm ready...no, I haven't left yet...well, yes, I'm almost packed...no, I'm not quite dressed...yes, I know you're already there." Balancing the phone on her shoulder, Juliet started pulling clips out of her hair. "Look, if I don't get off the phone I'll never be ready." She stretched the phone cord to its very limits and grabbed her brush off the dresser. "No, of course I'm not nervous," she added defensively, hearing the laughter on the other end of the line.

Tossing the slippers toward the already bulging suitcase, Juliet dashed back to the closet. Still struggling with the buttons and loops on her organza blouse, she stepped quickly into her suede pumps and then took them off again to pull on her white wool skirt. The zipper stuck and she tugged at it, already on the way back to her dresser to get her pearls. Catching sight of herself in the dresser mirror, she stopped and slowly counted to ten.

"Get hold of yourself," she commanded aloud. This wasn't really her wedding day, she reminded herself for the tenth time, only a brief arrangement, a necessary formality.

The doorbell rang, and Juliet raced to answer it, glancing nervously at her watch.

"Delivery for you," said the uniformed messenger, handing Juliet a shamrock plant wrapped in floral paper. As she closed the door, Juliet fumbled with the card, wondering who had sent it. She knew the moment she saw the handwriting.

"For luck," Linda had written. "Relax and enjoy. I'm thinking about you." Juliet smiled, wondering if Linda could have guessed she'd be coming apart. *She's right,* Juliet decided, touching a tiny white flower. *If I could just relax—pantyhose!* she thought suddenly, when the hem of her skirt brushed her bare leg. She hurried back to the bedroom and kicked off her shoes one more time. At this rate, she thought ruefully, Brady will end up marrying my mother because she's the only one there.

ON HANDS AND KNEES, Brady shoved his hand as far as it would reach under his dresser and patted the thick gray carpet. It had to be in there somewhere—a cuff link didn't just disappear. "Damn," he sputtered, crawling to the other end of the dresser to try again. The doorbell rang, and he ignored it. He could almost feel the fuzz from the carpet coating his charcoal-gray suit pants. The bell rang again, steadily, until Brady finally withdrew from under the dresser and shouted angrily, "Can it, will you? I'm coming."

"Say, buddy," Phil noted calmly when Brady's unfastened French cuff flapped in his face at the front door, "you seem to have forgotten something."

"Stupid cuff link dropped in the carpet," Brady muttered. "Look for it, will you, while I close the suitcase?"

Phil folded his arms across his chest and grinned. "I'm your lawyer, remember, not your valet."

"Well, today you're my best man," Brady corrected him, leading the way to the bedroom. "It's somewhere over there by the dresser—start digging."

Phil couldn't remember ever seeing Brady this way. "You sound almost like a real groom." He crouched down and studied the carpet. "I thought this wedding ceremony was just filling a square in your father's trust agreement."

"That's exactly what it is," Brady said explosively. He brushed vigorously at the carpet fuzz on his pants.

"Then why are you so nervous?" Phil casually picked up the lost cuff link from behind the leg of the dresser. He reached for Brady's shirt cuff. "You haven't answered my question," he persisted.

Brady wished Phil would leave him alone. He couldn't answer. He had no idea why he felt the way he did. He'd been like that since he got out of bed. "Anyone would be nervous if he had to rely on you for help," Brady muttered. He shoved his arms into his suit coat, which Phil held for him.

"Now, do you have everything?" Phil asked, more and more amused. He remembered the day of his own wedding when the situation had been reversed. Except his marriage had been for real. He dismissed the memories and grabbed the suitcase off the bed.

Brady dug in his pockets, still muttering to himself. "Let's see . . . got the license in here, the hotel reservations here, the ring in this pocket—"

"Ring?" Phil interrupted. "You got her a ring?"

"It's a wedding, isn't it?" Brady retorted.

Phil frowned. "It's supposed to be a business arrangement. You didn't have to get her a ring."

"Well, I did." He hoped it wasn't a mistake. It had seemed the right thing to do when he bought it yesterday.

"I suppose you got her a bouquet, too?" Phil's voice was heavy with sarcasm, but Brady didn't notice.

"A bouquet? Damn! Never occurred to me." Brady grabbed Phil by the arm. "Come on, we've got to hurry."

"What's the rush?" Phil inquired mildly, nearly running to keep up with Brady. "We don't have to be in Judge Baldwin's chambers for more than an hour."

"Yeah," said Brady, "but first we've got to find a florist willing to put together a wedding bouquet on short notice."

ALL THE WAY up Geary Street Juliet mentally reviewed the contents of her suitcase, absolutely certain something vital was missing. Money! She'd meant to stop at the bank and pick up some traveler's cheques. They hadn't discussed how they were going to pay for this honeymoon, but she assumed since it was Brady's idea he'd pick up his half. Too late now—at least she had her credit card.

After she paid the cab driver, Juliet stood for a moment at the curb, her crimson leather suitcase in one hand, her makeup case in the other, and her purse tucked tightly under her arm. The street was nearly deserted. She didn't know what she'd expected, but it seemed that maybe Brady—or somebody—might be around.

When she walked into the reception room outside the judge's chambers and found Cass waiting for her, Juliet felt an enormous surge of relief.

"You are absolutely lovely, dear," Cass bubbled. "I'm so glad you wore that white suit. Here, put down your things and smile while I take your picture."

Feeling like a little girl on display at her birthday party, Juliet obediently gave the camera a radiant smile.

"No, no," Cass told her, shaking her head. "You aren't buttoned." Juliet looked down to find the entire center section of the organza blouse gaping open. "You obviously need a mother's touch," Cass clucked, quickly going to work on the buttons. "I had no idea you'd be so nervous, but I should have expected it. It isn't every day a girl gets married."

*No,* thought Juliet, *and it isn't happening today, either, not really happening.* The whole thing was absolutely ridiculous. She hadn't had this many butterflies the day she took the bar exam.

After giving her daughter a final once-over, Cass resumed the picture-taking session and Juliet posed patiently. "Good," Cass beamed. "Now turn your head to the right just a tad."

Juliet followed Cass's instructions and, in doing so, caught a glimpse of a clock on the wall of the reception room. Brady was ten minutes late. What if he didn't come? In some ways, it might be better if he didn't.

"That should do it," Cass declared, setting the camera on a nearby table. "Now, one more thing." She produced a flat white box which she handed to Juliet.

Both surprised and deeply touched, Juliet untied the ribbon. She hadn't thought about presents because this wasn't a real wedding. But Cass didn't know that. Cass was giving away her only daughter with the same hope and joy and tugs at the heartstrings that any mother would feel. Juliet lifted the lid and slowly unfolded the tissue paper inside.

"Oh, Cass," she gasped. "Grandmother's mantilla." She blinked back tears. How could she wear the exquisite lace veil, with all the meaning it held, to her wedding which wasn't really her wedding at all?

"I knew you'd be pleased," her mother said, glowing. "Hurry and put it on so I can take some more pictures. Brady will be here any minute."

"Oh, Cass," Juliet began, "I can't—"

"Nonsense," Cass dismissed her protest. "Just because this isn't a church wedding doesn't make it any less real." She took the delicate mantilla from its bed of tissue and draped it gracefully over Juliet's silky auburn hair. "Perfect," she declared, picking up the camera. "Now, smile."

Juliet produced a wavery smile, but inside she was quaking. She'd never bargained for all this.

"Once more—lift your chin a little," Cass directed.

Juliet sighed. Whatever she should have done, it appeared she was going to have to deal with what she had done. Like it or not, she was going to look like a bride—veil and all.

As the camera flashed again, Judge Baldwin appeared from his chambers. "I see the blushing bride has arrived," he commented jovially, still fastening the front of his voluminous black robes. "How about the groom?"

Right on cue, Brady strolled through the reception room door looking for all the world as though he got married every day. But when he caught sight of Juliet, he stopped, his lips parted, and he didn't say a word. What was she doing? She'd promised she wouldn't dress up like a bride. But, God, she looked beautiful. He stood transfixed, unaware of the others gathered silently around them.

"Hello, Brady," Juliet said softly. "I'm glad you're here...I was beginning to worry about you."

"I...I'm sorry I'm late," he stammered. "I...Juliet you're beautiful."

"Thank you," she answered.

"I have something I wanted to give you...." Brady looked helplessly at Phil, who produced a nosegay of pastel flowers edged in lace, with white satin streamers flowing almost to the floor. "Here," Brady said, holding the flowers toward Juliet.

Juliet stared at the bouquet. "Brady, you didn't have to...I mean...Oh, Brady, I love them." Suddenly, everyone in the room was talking at once. When the chatter settled, they all had been introduced to each other and Brady was standing beside Juliet, his arm tightly around her waist.

"Now," began Judge Baldwin, with an expression that said he clearly enjoyed weddings, "let's get down to business. We'll complete the preliminaries first.

Choosing to be married in a civil ceremony does not diminish the sanctity of the institution of marriage," he added sternly.

Juliet avoided looking at Brady, and she sensed that he wasn't looking at her, either. Her hand was shaking as she signed her name and then handed the pen to Brady whose usual ruddy complexion was several shades of gray. *He looks like he's as scared as I am,* she thought, waiting silently while Phil and Cass signed as witnesses. Why are we doing this? Juliet asked herself, and at that moment she almost backed out. Then she looked at the flowers clutched in her hand and lightly, almost reverently, touched the lace mantilla that flowed gracefully to her shoulders. She'd come too far. She wouldn't change her mind now.

Judge Baldwin talked for several minutes about the commitment of marriage and the responsibility a husband and wife have to one another. Juliet clutched her bouquet tighter and tighter, trying to shut out his words, wanting to scream for him to get on with it. Everything was so real. She had thought when the papers were signed, it would be over. But this—this was like really getting married.

Juliet heard herself almost inaudibly repeating the vows the judge recited, and she heard Brady's voice break when he said the same words. But when Brady took her left hand to slip a gold band on her finger, her response was loud and clear. "Brady! You never said anything about a ring." She pulled her hand back. A ring was so . . . so tangible.

"I suppose if you don't want one—" Brady answered.

Juliet realized everyone was staring at her. "It's not that," she added quickly. "It's just, well, I guess I was

surprised.'' Feeling very foolish, she extended her
hand and Brady slid the ring on her finger.

She was still staring at the shining gold band when
she heard Judge Baldwin say, ''Now, Brady, you may
kiss the bride.''

For the first time since the ceremony began, their
eyes met and held. Brady lowered his mouth to hers.

THEY WERE in the car on their way down the coast
before Juliet stopped shaking. She glanced sideways
at the man next to her. The radio was set to a pop rock
station, and he was tapping his fingers on the steering
wheel in time to the music. His eyes were fixed on the
road, a curving, twisting highway that hugged the
coast. He had been quiet for a long time, but then so
had she. It didn't make any difference that they'd gone
through the ceremony. You couldn't be married to
someone by just signing some papers and repeating
empty words. Not really married. Still, she'd done the
thing she'd sworn she'd never do, with a man she'd
known only a few weeks. Even if it wasn't a real marriage, it was a sobering experience. The sun glinted off
the gold band on her finger.

Brady saw her staring at it. She looked frightened
and unhappy. Buying the ring had apparently been a
mistake, probably one of many. ''I'm sorry about the
ring, Juliet,'' he apologized. ''I walked by a jewelry
store yesterday and saw it in the window. I bought it
on a whim. You don't have to wear it.''

Juliet didn't answer right away. In fact, she didn't
want it. But she didn't want to take it off, either. ''I
guess maybe I'll wear it for a while, while we're in
Carmel, anyway. It'll remind us we're on a honeymoon.'' Juliet winced. She hated that word.

Brady tuned the radio to a classical station. "Do you think we'll need reminding?"

"Well, we barely know each other and here we are—"

"You're sorry, aren't you, Juliet?"

She looked out the window at the rocky cliffs rising from the ocean far below. "I don't know." She twisted the ring on her finger. "I didn't expect so much ... so much wedding. I thought we were just going to sign some papers and that would be it."

"So did I."

"You mean you didn't arrange all that?"

"Hell, no." Brady slapped his hand down on the steering wheel for emphasis. "All I did was phone the judge and set up the time. Phil told me he liked to do weddings."

"Obviously." Juliet frowned. "But, Brady, what about the flowers ... ?"

Brady squirmed uncomfortably. "I got them on the way. Phil brought the idea up, and I thought maybe it was something I should do. And then when I got there and saw you—" His face softened as he remembered. "You were beautiful. But you told me you weren't going to dress up like a bride."

"I didn't!" Juliet exclaimed, suddenly defensive. "At least I didn't mean to. My mother brought Grandmother's mantilla and there wasn't anything I could do."

"I didn't mind, you understand," Brady added. "You looked—" He stopped. How could he tell her that when he walked in and saw her, she was like a fantasy, like a beautiful dream? "You looked nice," he finished lamely.

"Thank you," Juliet murmured. The wedding had apparently had an impact on him, too. "Were you nervous?"

"Nervous?" He remembered the missing cuff link and how irritated he'd been with Phil. "No, not really. How about you?"

Juliet thought about the haphazard packing job, the pantyhose she'd forgotten. "Well...having my mother there was sort of unsettling."

"At least it's over," Brady sighed. He didn't add that the good part was still ahead of them. Ever since the night at the beach, he'd wanted her. She'd crept into his fantasies, soft and sensuous, her body moving rhythmically against his, an invitation to soothe the raging heat that drove him. Whenever he thought about Juliet, he felt the familiar aching in his groin.

They lapsed into silence again. Juliet stared out the window at the ocean whipping by. It wasn't over. Getting married was a carefully programmed activity, with a very specific set of built-in expectations. The next one down the line was the wedding night. They were speeding toward it, drawing closer with every passing mile. She couldn't back out now. That was the whole reason she was doing this. The faster she could get pregnant, the faster all this would be over, and the sooner she could quit pretending, she reasoned. But logic didn't help at all. Her stomach tightened and she felt almost as though she might be sick. "How much further?" she asked. The voice didn't sound like hers at all.

Brady glanced at her. She was huddled as close to the door as her seat belt would allow. "We're just coming in to Monterey," he answered. "Is something wrong, Juliet?"

She swallowed, her throat dry. "No, nothing's wrong. I just wondered." But he hadn't quite answered her question. "Is the place we're staying at far from here?"

"The inn? Maybe twenty minutes." He looked at her again. "Are you sure you're all right, Juliet?"

"My stomach feels sort of odd," she admitted.

So that was it. "Nerves and a long car ride," he diagnosed. "I was going to suggest dinner, but maybe you'd like to stop and get some fresh air. We can walk down on the wharf."

Juliet gave him a grateful smile. "I'd like that, Brady." She relaxed slightly. A walk would give her a little more time.

The sky was cloudless blue when they stepped out of the car. Juliet tilted her head upward, drinking in the fresh salt air. The wind off Monterey Bay whipped around her legs and tossed her hair playfully across her shoulders. "Maybe we can eat some squid while we're here," she suggested.

"That's the fastest transformation I've ever seen." Brady brushed a long auburn strand of hair from her face, noticing how Juliet's emerald eyes sparkled in the sunlight. "You sure your stomach's all right?"

"Fine," she assured him. "Except I'm hungry."

"That's easy to fix if you can handle dinner out of a cardboard box on your wedding day." He laughed easily. "Of course I don't see any reason we can't make our own rules. We have up to now."

Juliet wasn't sure why, but she suddenly felt better than she had all day. They ate fried squid and drank coffee from Styrofoam cups balanced between them on a wooden bench. Juliet could hear the seals barking and the haunting sound of the fog horn that signaled the coming of evening and, with it, the approaching fog. When the last bite of squid was gone, Brady chucked the box in a trash can and took her hand.

"Are you ready?" he asked.

"Oh, no." The answer had been too quick. "What I mean is, I'd like to go out on the pier and look at the seals."

"You couldn't possibly have a case of bride's jitters, could you?" Brady asked.

She saw the amusement in his eyes. "Of course not," she snapped. "I'm not even sure what you mean."

"Good." He put his arm around her waist, slipping his hand under her suit jacket to brush her breast suggestively. "Because anticipation's half the fun."

Juliet's cheeks flamed and she didn't answer him.

His arm still around her, they walked out on the wharf, moving slowly so that Juliet's heels didn't catch between the rough hewn boards. A mixture of smells, laced with caramel corn and frying fish assailed them. As they drew near the end of the wharf, Juliet wrinkled her nose. "Ah, fresh ocean air."

"That smell, my dear, is coming from those very picturesque seals off to your right," Brady informed her.

She leaned her elbows on the railing and scanned the horizon. In the distance she could barely make out a group of seals on a pile of dark rocks. She supposed if their barking carried that far, their smell could, too. Her eyes drifted upward to follow a seagull, and then she felt Brady behind her, his body pressing against hers. She tensed, her thoughts moving ahead. The anticipation, he'd said. She shivered.

Seeing something floating in the water, Juliet leaned over the rail for a better look, relieved when the movement separated her from Brady. "I think it's a sea otter," she said.

Brady bent over the rail beside her. "Sure enough, and she's got a baby."

Juliet stared at the brown furry creature bobbing on its back. It was a mother cradling a tiny baby with black beady eyes that stared fearlessly at them. She felt Brady's arm around her as he leaned close to watch. He didn't seem so threatening now, sharing the same fascination she felt.

"She seems totally contented, doesn't she?" Juliet observed. "Like she had nothing better to do than just lie there and let the waves rock them."

"Maybe she doesn't." Brady held Juliet tighter. "She's got a full belly, and probably a place to go for the night. What more could she want?"

Juliet nodded silently. It all seemed so simple.

Brady straightened, putting his hands on her shoulders. "We've got a place to go for the night, too. Are you ready?"

Juliet turned toward him, and his eyes, dark as midnight, locked with hers. His meaning was clear. Silently, Juliet looked away, staring out at the rolling ocean. The sun was setting, a glowing red ball fading beyond the horizon, and the sky had turned to a smoky-purple dusk. He was waiting for an answer, and there was only one she could give him. "Yes, Brady," she said softly. "I guess it's time to go."

THE ROOM WAS DECORATED in a modified country theme, a delicate balance of casual and elegant. Juliet didn't notice. Her eyes were riveted on the bed. A huge bed with ornate posts rising at its corners to support an arched lace canopy. The bed dwarfed everything else in the room, and the longer Juliet stared at it, the bigger it got.

"I hope everything is all right," the bellboy said politely. His job finished, he stood near Brady, waiting.

"Just fine," Brady assured him, reaching for his wallet.

Juliet didn't say anything at all. She glanced around the room, but found her attention drawn almost immediately back to the bed.

"Well, here we are," Brady said conversationally after he handed the bellboy a tip and the young man left.

"Yes, here we are." *And what in God's name are we doing here?* she thought.

Brady laid the room key the bellboy had given him on a small table near the door. He looked around. The room was everything the desk clerk had promised on the phone. "Do you like it?" he asked Juliet.

"Like it?" She hadn't moved. "It's really big."

"Big?" Brady looked at her curiously. That was an odd comment for someone as cosmopolitan as she appeared to be. "Well," he said skeptically, "I suppose as hotel rooms go..."

"Oh! You mean the room." She hadn't been paying attention. Looking around carefully for the first time, she managed a weak smile. "It's a lovely room," she answered sincerely.

Brady walked toward her, still puzzled by her response. "What did you think I meant?"

"Well, I don't know...." Juliet searched for a graceful way out. "This is a really nice inn. Have you been here before?"

Maybe her thoughts had been elsewhere, Brady decided. "I took a trip down here when I first came to San Francisco," he replied, "and I made up my mind right then if I ever went on a honeymoon, this was the place."

"I see," Juliet murmured. This was an insipid conversation. Why was she so flustered? Obviously, it had something to do with going to bed with Brady. But why? She was no prude. That night in the beach house she'd wanted him, really wanted him. She thought back, trying to recapture those feelings. It didn't work.

Brady put one hand on her shoulder and then lightly stroked her arm. She could feel his eyes on her, but she didn't look up. Maybe if she had just a little more time.... Her eyes darted around the room, she searched for something, anything, to divert him.

"Oh, Brady!" she exclaimed enthusiastically. "This room has a fireplace."

Brady frowned, moving his hand away from her arm. "Of course it has a fireplace. Did you just notice it?"

Juliet approached the corner fireplace, a prominent feature in the room with its raised hearth and rough-hewn mantel. Developing a sudden interest in the decor, she touched the patterned blue-and-white tiles that bordered the sides of the hearth. "How pretty," she said. "Maybe we can have a fire."

"A fire?" Brady gave the wood box a cursory glance. "I guess it *is* a working fireplace," he conceded, "but why don't we wait till tomorrow to build a fire?" Raising his arms over his head, he stretched expansively. "It's getting late, and it's been a long day." He approached Juliet again, standing behind her, his hands on her upper arms. "You must be tired, too."

"Oh, no," Juliet answered quickly, turning to face him. "I'm not tired at all." She noticed a bouquet of mixed flowers in the center of a table between two large, blue chairs. "I like the flowers," she commented to fill in the silence. "Did you order them specially?"

Brady turned to see what she was talking about. "No, they must come with the honeymoon suite."

"Honeymoon suite?" she repeated. "We're in the honeymoon suite?"

"It seemed appropriate," Brady remarked. "After all, we are on our honeymoon." He scrutinized her carefully. This had gone far enough. "Juliet..." he began, his fingers tightening on her arm. He waited till she looked up at him. "Juliet, are you..." he began again. Something stopped him, as though he sensed she was begging him not to push her and not to ask the intimate questions that were on his mind. "Juliet," he asked gently, "would you like a glass of champagne?"

"Yes." Her eyes were grateful. "I'd like that very much."

While Brady picked up the bottle of champagne that had been chilling in an ice bucket near the fireplace, Juliet sat down in one of the blue chairs, slipping out of her shoes and tucking her feet underneath her so she occupied the whole chair seat. She was going to have to come to terms with her problem, whatever it was—and quickly. Maybe it was getting married, she speculated, but quickly realized that while the ceremony had been profoundly disturbing, it was over and she didn't feel any more married than she had before.

Here at the inn, with the day behind her, she should be breathing a huge sigh of relief. Instead her hands were icy cold and her stomach was in a knot again. Juliet watched Brady unwrap the foil from the top of the champagne bottle. Again, she thought about that night in his beach house, that night when she had felt so very differently.

Brady popped the cork and it shot to the ceiling, bouncing off a beam and landing across the room. "To us," he said, handing her a glass of the bubbling champagne and taking a sip of his own.

Juliet took a large gulp. "Brady," she asked suddenly, "which side of the bed do you sleep on?"

"Well—" he grinned, sitting on the edge of the other blue chair and leaning toward her "—it just depends. Most nights, I sleep right in the middle."

"Oh." Juliet replied in a small voice.

Brady worked hard to control a smile. "Do you have a favorite side?"

"I always sleep on the right side," she proclaimed. "But maybe that's just because my night stand is on that side, and I like to be near the phone...." Her voice trailed off.

"That's all right," he assured her. "You can have the right side. It shouldn't be much of an issue after a night or two anyway."

Juliet shifted in her chair and took another large drink of champagne.

Brady drained his glass and set it on the table with a deliberate clank. "Juliet, we've had a full day. It's time we got ready for bed."

Juliet's eyes widened. In one quick motion, she emptied her glass. "Do you think I could have some more champagne?" She held the glass out to Brady who promptly refilled it. He did not, she noticed, pour any more for himself.

"Would you like to go into the bathroom first or shall I?" he inquired.

"Well, if you're really tired—"

A fleeting frown shadowed Brady's eyes and he looked hard at Juliet. "I'm not 'really tired,' and neither are you," he asserted flatly. "That has nothing to do with it. Now, would you like the bathroom first?"

"No, no," Juliet demurred. "You go ahead. I'm still finishing my champagne."

"I didn't know you liked champagne so much," Brady remarked as he opened his suitcase.

"Oh, yes." She took another sip, drawing it straight down so it didn't touch the sides of her tongue. "It's so bubbly," she added. She watched Brady loosen the straps that held his clothes in neatly folded stacks. He removed a robe and a shaving kit, then walked back across the room and set them on a table beside her. She didn't see any pajamas. Maybe he did sleep in the nude, after all.

Brady began casually unbuttoning his shirt. "Today has been a lot to handle, Juliet—more than either one of us expected." She watched his fingers move with agility as he progressed to the next shirt button. It was hard to remember the day. She had a flash of her loneliness when she'd stepped out of the cab onto that deserted street; of that look in Brady's eyes when he first saw her just before the wedding; of Cass near tears when she lovingly arranged the mantilla.

The last button unfastened, Brady pulled out his shirttail. "We haven't had very long to get to know each other, Juliet."

She watched him pull his arms out of the shirt-sleeves and wad the shirt into a ball.

"Even if this is only a short-term arrangement, I guess it's natural we might have some qualms about it," he continued, pulling his V-neck T-shirt off over his head.

His chest was broad, Juliet noted, and covered with thick, tightly curled hair. She'd never seen him without his shirt before. She watched in fascination as he slipped the undershirt inside the wadded shirt and tossed both in the direction of his suitcase. He leaned over her, naked to the waist, not touching her. Juliet lowered her eyes, waiting. He lightly brushed her hair with his fingertips and asked softly, "Juliet, would you like some more champagne before I go into the bathroom?"

Juliet look at the half-empty glass on the table and then up at Brady. "No, thank you, I don't want any more." Whatever her problem, more champagne wouldn't solve it.

He picked up his robe and shaving kit and kissed her lightly on the cheek. "I won't be long," he called back to her before he closed the bathroom door.

Juliet sat perfectly still, watching the bubbles rise and burst in her champagne glass. The night in the beach house, Brady had stopped. He had sensed the change in her. No other man had ever done that. Most men were satisfied with a willing participant. Brady obviously wanted more. Again her eyes were drawn to the bed, its French-blue coverlet trimmed in lace that matched the edging on the dust ruffle. Deep inside,

Juliet knew what Brady wanted. It was a part of her she had never been able to give any man. The problem was, Brady knew the difference. That made the wedding night like a command performance, one Juliet knew already she could never complete.

She stood up, stretching her stiff, tight muscles. She could hear water running in the bathroom. Slowly, she began to pace diagonally across the room and then back again. Her legs were shaking. Passing the bed, she stopped and pushed on the mattress with her hand. When it didn't give under the pressure, she tentatively sat down on the edge and bounced up and down a few times. Then she poked at the pillow.

Juliet swallowed hard, trying to contain the turmoil inside. Maybe she should have talked to Brady, told him...told him what? That she liked sex even though she couldn't let herself go completely? That he shouldn't expect so much of her?

She picked up the edge of the coverlet, tracing the patterns in the lace with the tip of her fingers. Her attitude shouldn't make any difference anyway, she told herself. She could still get pregnant, and that was the point of all this. Or was it? Abruptly, Juliet stood up and walked across the room to open her suitcase. That was the heart of the problem, she realized suddenly. However all this had started out, it wasn't strictly business anymore. Brady had made his way into her life and her thoughts. Even after everything she had said about no entanglements...

Juliet rummaged in the suitcase until she located her white batiste nightgown at the very bottom and pulled it out with a swift tug. Frowning, she held it up in front of her. It was perfectly plain except for a sprinkling of tiny yellow flowers at the neck and eyelet lace at the armholes. Hardly the right thing for a wedding night. Juliet wished she'd planned ahead.

She was still holding the nightgown when the bathroom door opened and Brady emerged wearing a deep blue velour robe. His hair, damp from the shower, was curly. He smelled of soap and shaving lotion and yet, as he came closer, Juliet realized that he still smelled like Brady.

"Sorry to take so long," he apologized, "but that shower felt good."

"I . . . I didn't mind," Juliet answered quickly, bending over the suitcase in search of her other slipper.

Brady laid his trousers across his open suitcase and put his shoes on the floor under the ledge before he turned toward Juliet. "Your turn," he prompted.

"You mean in the bathroom?" Juliet asked. She stood in front of him, her nightgown over her arm, her slippers hugged against her body, and her small case filled with toiletries clutched firmly in her free hand.

Brady tried to control his impatience. "From the looks of things, that would appear to be where you're headed," he noted wryly. "I'll be waiting."

"Right," said Juliet. She hurried toward the bathroom.

For several moments after she disappeared, Brady stared at the locked bathroom door, shaking his head. "I'll be damned," he muttered to himself. The signs were unmistakable. For some reason that was beyond him, Juliet Cavanaugh was scared to death. Only she wasn't Juliet Cavanaugh any more, he reminded himself. She was Juliet Talcott. "Damn!" he swore out loud. What the hell had he done?

Stuffing his hands in the pockets of his robe, Brady paced back and forth in short, quick steps. Except she wasn't Juliet Talcott either. That was only on paper. No wonder she was confused. He went to the side of the bed and turned back the coverlet, leaning across to smooth the other side. Her side. She said she always slept on the right.

He began pacing again. He should have taken her that night at the beach house. Then making love now wouldn't be such an issue. He thought about her body, soft and beautiful in the firelight, and the texture of her skin, like spun silk, and her hair that glistened in the red of the sunset. His body stirred, and he pulled the belt on his robe tighter. Methodically, he turned off all the lights in the room except for a small hurricane lamp by the bed, and then he sat down by the fireplace to wait. Damn, she was slow.

# CHAPTER EIGHT

THE BATHROOM DOOR opened, pouring light into the darkened room. Brady sat forward expectantly. Juliet was a study in hesitation, emerging barefoot, her auburn hair flowing to her shoulders, the nightgown dropping in soft folds to the floor. She stopped when she saw Brady and reached back to turn off the bathroom light.

Instantly Brady was on his feet, moving toward her. She watched his approach as if in a dream. "You're beautiful, Juliet." His voice caressed her. Still studying her face, he slipped a hand under her gleaming hair.

Feeling very shy, Juliet avoided his eyes. "I'm sorry I didn't get an appropriate nightgown," she told him. "I guess I didn't think about..."

Brady held her at arm's length, a puzzled expression on his face. "What could possibly be more appropriate?" he asked her. When she didn't answer, Brady continued, "But if you don't like it, we'll take care of that right now." In one swift motion, he caught the hem of her gown in both hands and pulled it off, dropping it on the floor beside her.

"Brady!" she gasped.

He never took his eyes from hers. "You are now more lovely than you could possibly be in any nightgown ever created," he assured her. His hand brushed her cheek. "If they were giving awards for wedding night attire, you'd be the unanimous choice for best dressed."

Juliet's mouth quivered, but she forced a smile. "I do feel very naked."

"You didn't turn and run."

Her smile widened, slowly becoming genuine. "I never even thought about it," she admitted.

Brady's eyes crinkled at the corners. "That means we're halfway there." He scooped her up in his arms and carried her across the room.

"That's twice, Brady," she warned mischievously. "I'm going to begin to expect this kind of service."

"Your turn next time," he promised glibly. "Equality, you know." He put her down gently on the crisp white sheet and stood above her. "I know, wrong side," he muttered playfully. "You always sleep on the right. But I'll share just this once."

He untied the belt and let his robe fall backward off his shoulders. Juliet caught her bottom lip between her teeth, watching his every move. His body was trim and strong in the soft lamplight. Dark hair curled in a soft, springy mat on his chest, thinning toward the flat muscles of his abdomen. She could see those muscles, flexed and taut, drawing in at his waist.

Juliet averted her eyes. "Do you think we could turn out the light?" she asked in a small voice. Except for the flush high on her cheekbones, her skin was almost as white as the sheet.

Sitting beside her on the bed, Brady frowned. The moon had set early, and without the dim lamp they would be in total darkness. Brady wanted to taste and touch Juliet, but he wanted more than that. He wanted to relish her with all his senses. He wanted to watch her face, as he had in the firelight, when his touch and his kisses consumed her. "Why do you want the light off?" he asked her.

"Well, I just thought it might be more...more..."

"It would make you more comfortable?"

"Maybe...well, yes...no..."

Brady moved closer to her, his lean hip pressing against her gentle curves. "I don't want the light off, Juliet." He stroked her cheek with two fingers, which felt cool against her burning skin. "I want to see your face. I want to savor all of you." He lowered his mouth to hers and flicked his tongue across her lips, softening and moistening them until they melted into his.

He touched her, gently at first, his hands moving and exploring. As fire rose rapidly within him, he grew insistent and then demanding. He could feel her breath coming in little gasps, and he stretched out his body until he was lying against her.

Something wasn't right. Brady opened his eyes and looked at Juliet. Her eyelids were squeezed shut, and her hands were clenched into tight fists at either side of her head. He sensed she was literally holding her breath, waiting.

"Juliet," he said hoarsely. "What's wrong?"

Slowly she opened her eyes and in the jade-green depths he saw that he'd been right. Her little gasps had not been breaths of passion. She was scared.

"Talk to me, Juliet," he demanded, forcibly restraining his desire.

She turned her face away. "I don't know what to say, Brady. You expect so much of me and I—I don't think I can do it."

"Look at me, Juliet," he demanded. Slowly she turned her head. She looked so fragile, so vulnerable, her green eyes huge in that fair, fine-boned face. "Ju-liet," he asked gently, "are you a virgin?"

"No," she said in a barely audible voice.

His forehead wrinkled. He tried to sort it out. "Then what is it? What is it you think I expect of you?"

Juliet wanted to crawl away and hide. She had to try to tell him, but she didn't know how. These were in-timate, hidden feelings she had never verbalized. "It's just that when you...we...get to a certain point, I don't...I don't feel the same anymore. It isn't that I don't like it...I just don't feel quite as...quite the same." It was so hard to talk about. His eyes were dark as midnight, inscrutable. She had no idea whether he could even begin to understand, but she couldn't seem to go on.

Brady sat silently for a moment, thinking over what she had said. "What you're telling me is that you have a shut-off button, and when I hit it, it's over for you."

Relief washed through Juliet. In an odd way, he did understand. "But I want you to go ahead," she added quickly. "I just—it doesn't work to wait for me."

"But you weren't going to say anything about this, were you?" he demanded accusingly. "You were just going to let me go ahead—"

"That's what I want you to do," she interrupted. Maybe he didn't understand after all.

Tenderly he stroked her hair back from her face. "Oh Juliet, Juliet," he murmured softly. "You're so damn determined to be superwoman and handle everything on your own that you have no idea what it can be for two people together...." His voice trailed off. "Trust me, Juliet," he directed. "For this one time, this one night, let yourself trust somebody else."

Juliet wasn't sure what he meant. "I'll try, Brady," she agreed tentatively. "I'm not doing this very well."

"Dammit, Juliet! We're not having a contest," he exploded, raising his body almost to a sitting position. "This is one area where your standard measures of accomplishment don't apply. There's no right or wrong. Think you can handle that for a little while?"

He was so intense he frightened her. "Are you angry, Brady?" She almost wished he wouldn't answer.

"No, not angry." He shook his head. "Just trying to figure out how to get to you. My grandfather had this saying. He said there weren't any cold women— just bad lovers. You need to start by believing that. Grandfather was a very wise man."

"I . . . I'm not cold, Brady," she answered defensively.

"No, Juliet, you're not cold. But I don't think you have any idea how really passionate you are. I think it's time you found out."

"I guess I can try," she agreed again, this time reaching her arms around his neck to pull him back to her. But he didn't move. "Not that way, Juliet. This way." He took her hand, patiently unclenching her fist, and very gently stroked her palm.

She wasn't sure what he was doing, but he kept on until slowly her hand began to relax and Juliet found her entire being focused on the sensation. "M-m-m... That feels good, Brady." She didn't try to hide the surprise in her voice. There wasn't much point in trying to hide anything from him now.

"All right," he told her. "It's your turn. I want you to stroke my hand just the same way."

His suggestion seemed easy enough. Juliet cradled his hand against her stomach and gently touched him. After a while, she was amazed to feel a stirring deep inside her. She was almost disappointed when he took his hand away and touched the inside of her arm.

He moved his hands with deliberate slowness, until the shell of fear melted away and he found the softness of the woman waiting for him. She was sensual and lovely, and it took all his determination to harness the passion building in him. He could have touched her, but to share, she had to also give to him. He took a deep breath, anticipating the delicious agony.

Juliet was beginning to drift into a pleasant oblivion when Brady stopped and lay back on his side, waiting. She raised up one elbow, her fingers outlining the roughness of his jaw and then moving quickly to explore the thick hair on his chest. Brady seemed willing to let her go on touching him, but she was growing more and more restless. She moved her hand downward, to the taut skin at his waist, and felt him draw a sharp breath. His response was like a lightening bolt that shot through her in an incredible burst of heat.

"Touch me, too, Brady," she urged him. She pulled his hand down to her breast. "Oh . . . oh, Brady, that makes me feel like—"

"Like more and more," he breathed.

"Oh, yes."

"Not quite yet," he whispered, feathering kisses downward until Juliet gasped with pleasure.

He wrapped one leg around her, and she lay back on the pillow, moving against him. Her hands began to explore Brady hungrily, twining in the tightly curled hair on his chest and then running downward along his firm, taut hips. Juliet's entire body seemed to be on fire. The more she touched him, her hands, her mouth, her tongue flicking across his skin, the more the driving, burning sensations welled up in her.

"Don't you feel it?" she whispered in desperation. "Don't you know what's happening inside me?"

"Tell me," he commanded in a hoarse whisper. "Tell me how you feel."

At first she didn't answer, unable to focus on anything except his hand on her waist.

"Talk to me, Juliet," he demanded. "Tell me what you're thinking."

"I'm not thinking." She fought to form the words, reaching downward, touching him as he was now touching her. He moaned softly.

"Oh, Brady, more...I..." His fingers were moving rhythmically upward along her thigh. Juliet arched her back, her body writhing against his.

"Brady," she cried out. She felt it happening, her response unbearable, consuming. Driven by a passion that exceeded all her fantasies, she dug her fingernails into his shoulders. "Don't stop, please don't stop," she pleaded.

"God, no, Juliet," he rasped. "I want you." His mouth found hers, open and ready, as she clutched him, grasping his hips to pull him down. He plunged deep inside her, and she cried out again, a piercing cry amidst the shuddering gasps pulsing through her.

Finally, her body trembling, she dropped back against the pillow, overwhelmed by him and by herself. She felt his hand gently enclosing her breast. His breathing slowed until it was deep and steady, and when she opened her eyes, he was watching her, his face peaceful, his eyelids heavy.

"It was good," Brady said.

"Very good," she murmured, her voice dazed and soft.

He studied her, sharing the peace that had settled around them. "You trusted me, Juliet. You let yourself be you, instead of fighting."

"But I didn't make it happen, Brady. When I touched you, I had these feelings—"

He smiled, knowing she couldn't describe her feelings because there were no words. He also knew that what they'd done had forged a bond between them that was irreversible. A man and a woman couldn't share together what they had shared and come out of it unchanged. However much they might someday want to, they could never go back. He stroked the damp tendrils of hair away from her face. She smelled of musky springtime, a delicious smell that tempted his senses. He leaned over to kiss her breast, moving with the heaviness of approaching sleep.

"Can I stay nestled here against you Brady?" she asked him, knowing it would produce a grin.

He nuzzled her lazily. "You mean on the wrong side of the bed?" He liked the sound of her melodic laughter.

"I guess I hadn't noticed." She snuggled closer to him, her eyelids fluttering and falling closed. "I think I'd like to sleep right here tonight."

BRADY AWOKE WITH Juliet in his arms. He felt his body stirring even before he opened his eyes. Her breathing was light and regular. He knew she was still asleep, although the sun already streamed through the windows. He shifted slightly against her soft, warm flesh. Her hair was draped across his arm, glistening in the early light, framing a face innocent in sleep. She'd bared her soul to him. He'd asked for trust, and she'd given it all. The heat was building in him. He kissed her lightly, knowing it would awaken her.

When Juliet felt his lips brush her mouth she sighed softly, opening to him, inviting him. She never was sure when she crossed the threshold of consciousness, or whether she ever did. Afterward, when she lay against him, she could only remember the passion that had consumed her and the fulfillment that followed. It took great effort to finally open her eyes.

Brady lay beside her, looking as languid as she felt. "Good morning," he greeted her. "Almost good afternoon."

"Is it that late?" She was surprised, but not the least bit concerned.

"Do you suppose we should get up?" he asked, propping his head on his elbow so that he could see her face.

Juliet didn't feel very ambitious. "Why should we get up? Is there somewhere we have to go?"

Brady laughed softly. "That's right. You were the one who was worried about what we were going to do for a whole week."

Juliet lowered her eyelids seductively. "I guess I wasn't fully aware of all the available activities."

"There are others," Brady suggested. "But I can't promise any of them will be quite as much fun." He ran his fingers slowly through her hair. "For example, we could get up and go eat. Or even take a walk."

Juliet gave him a look of wide-eyed innocence. "You mean before we go back to bed?"

Brady chuckled, and gave her a hard whack on the backside. "You don't do anything halfway, do you Juliet?"

"Ouch!" she yelped, grabbing for him as he sprang out of bed.

It was early afternoon by the time they both dressed. Brady ordered sandwiches and soft drinks from room service while Juliet took a shower. She ate with him, wrapped in a large terry towel. "I'm beginning to think that's one of your regular outfits," he teased her, eyeing the beige towel. "But I think I prefer you in blue."

After they'd dressed and left the room, they wandered aimlessly around Carmel, poking through the shops, exploring the tiny art galleries that dotted the narrow, sloping streets. They lingered in a toy shop, rearranging an entire display of wooden soldiers much to the amusement of the owner, who had been having a very slow day. By sundown they were both incredibly hungry. Juliet was ready to stop for a sandwich, but Brady intervened.

"We ate out of cardboard boxes for our wedding dinner and off a tray for lunch. Tonight," he announced, "we will dine."

After a glass of wine and some cheese and crackers from room service to stave off their hunger, they showered and dressed. When Juliet emerged from the bathroom with its combined dressing room, Brady let out a low whistle. He started at her feet, letting his eyes move from her high-heeled sandals up the shapely curve of her legs. He lingered on the midnight-blue dress that draped her hips and torso above the soft folds of the skirt. Finally, he let his eyes rise to her face—fair skin framed by thick, flowing auburn hair and those eyes—those magnificent green eyes.

"You are absolutely smashing, my dear." He kept his tone light and playful.

She gave a low curtsy. "Thank you, kind sir."

"Shall we go?" he asked, offering his arm, knowing that if they lingered, they wouldn't go at all.

The evening air was sweet with the smell of flowers that lined the long stairway up to the restaurant. Inside, candlelight flickered across the faces of the diners in the softly lit room, and the subdued conversation faded into the sound of the grand piano, which filled an entire corner of the intimate restaurant. The maître d' seated them at a table near an expanse of windows where they could see the moon rising across the bay.

From the wine, through perfect Beef Wellington, to fresh fruit, the moon turned from soft yellow to silver, its reflection shimmering on the foaming surf. The moonbeams turned the sun-cured grasses white beneath the rugged silhouette of a single Monterey Pine. Juliet stared at the stark outline, letting it form shapes and patterns in her imagination. The man at the piano played a familiar love song that touched a chord deep within her. She felt Brady's fingers curl protectively around hers as he asked her to dance.

Juliet stood up slowly, his hand warm and sensual on her back. Once on the dance floor, Juliet moved in his rhythm, letting him lead her with his eyes and his body until nothing else mattered but the music, and the night, and the two of them. Her fluid movements matched his as he whirled her, light as a feather, in perfect time to the music. The piano player chose a slow love song, and their tempo kept pace with his.

Brady silently pressed his cheek against her hair, and Juliet closed her eyes, drifting with him on a cloud of music. In those moments, untouched by the world outside, her life was perfect.

She became aware slowly that the music had stopped, but Brady was still holding her. For a long moment, neither of them moved. In the soft amber glow of the lights above the dance floor, Juliet caught a glimpse of her own feelings reflected in Brady's dark eyes. She sensed that something had changed between them. But she refused to think beyond that.

She felt Brady's hands on her shoulders, guiding her toward their table. Quickly Brady paid the check, and they hurried back to the inn.

It was past noon nearly every day when they emerged from their room. One morning they did wake up with the dawn, and by ten o'clock that same day they were on their way south, driving down toward the Big Sur to look for migrating whales. They both knew it was too early in the season, but they went anyway.

Once the soupy fog that shrouded early fall mornings finally burned through, Juliet felt like they were emerging from a damp cavern into the splendor of the open air. Brady pulled off the road along a deserted stretch of coastline, and they climbed a grassy knoll that rose above the surf where they could look out across the water. High above the desolate beauty of the land, the cries of the birds mixed with the whisper of the wind, nature's symphony underscored always by the dull roar of the ocean. How far away they seemed from San Francisco, Juliet thought, and how much farther still from the rest of her life.

Brady shaded his eyes and searched the vibrant blue expanse of water beyond the breaker line. "Too bad it's not a couple of months from now. We might really see some whales.'' He turned toward her. ''Have you ever watched them?''

''When I was a little girl,'' Juliet answered. ''I used to spend hours along the water when they were migrating.''

Taking her hand, Brady led her to a large flat rock, warmed by the sun, and watched with amusement as she unzipped her jacket and lay down flat on her stomach to soak up the heat. Slipping his hand beneath her loose jacket, he rubbed his palm lazily across her back. ''Juliet,'' he said thoughtfully, ''when you first came up with that hare-brained scheme to have a baby, did it ever occur to you that you might have—'' he searched for the right words ''—some problems?''

''What do you mean, 'problems'?'' Juliet responded sleepily.

''You know damn well what I mean.'' She didn't answer. He tried another approach. ''Did you ever consider the process of getting pregnant?''

Juliet opened her eyes, propped herself on one elbow, and looked at him. ''Well, sort of. I guess I didn't worry too much about the specifics.'' She shaded her eyes against the sunlight. ''What I wanted...what I *want* is to have a baby. I kind of thought we'd have some meetings, very carefully timed, of course, and then, well...I'd be pregnant.''

Brady frowned. ''That wouldn't have been much fun.''

Juliet eyed him curiously. ''It wasn't supposed to be fun. It was supposed to be productive.''

''Damn.'' Brady swore softly. ''Is that what you think about sex, Juliet?''

"Well..." Her eyes twinkled mischievously. "Maybe *thought* is a better word than think." Playfully, she pulled his head down and found his mouth. She teased his lips with the tip of her tongue until he kissed her back. He shifted his weight so that he was lying next to her and let his fingers trace the curves underneath her yellow knit shirt.

"Oh!" Juliet gasped in surprise. Those now familiar sensations, never far from the surface when she was with Brady, sprang to life again. "Let's go back to the inn," Juliet whispered. Her thighs were pressed against his hip.

"Why?" Brady asked, burying her answer beneath his lips.

Juliet pressed tighter against him. "Because what we're doing makes me want—" She gasped as his tongue blazed a trail down the side of her cheek and his breath, hot and moist, grazed her ear.

"And then again," Brady murmured, "we could stay right here." He slipped his hand under her shirt.

"Right here?" What he was suggesting suddenly sank in. Her whole body quivered. "Brady, stop," she pleaded. "We can't. What if someone—"

"No one will. It's just us and the seagulls," he assured her, his voice almost lost in the lone piercing cry of a bird.

"But, Brady..." Juliet struggled one last time, and then his fingers were stirring a throbbing, pulsing passion that blotted out her reservations. She heard the barking of the sea lions above the roaring surf and felt the wind brush across her bare skin. The sun's warmth became an intense heat all around her, and then, it seemed to be coming from inside her.

Afterward, she stayed a part of him, their bodies joined together even as they lay still. A long time later, Juliet felt the wind ruffle her hair and she shivered with cold as Brady moved away from her. "The sun's gone behind a cloud," he told her, rearranging her shirt and jeans.

She sat up. "Is that why it feels colder?"

"Not entirely." His lips brushed her cheek. "We were generating a lot of heat on our own." He took her hand and helped her to her feet, again wrapping his arms around her and holding her close. Then, hand in hand, they walked slowly down the steep slope, the whales forgotten, as they got in the car to head back toward Carmel.

On their last day they went back to bed after breakfast. It wasn't until noon, when Brady was drying Juliet's back after a long, luxurious shower, that he decided it was time for them to plan what came next. "I've been thinking...." He paused to kiss the back of her neck. "I'm not sure where the best place is for us to live." He soaked up the droplets of water clinging to her shoulder blades and then rubbed the towel across her hips. "My apartment in the city is a small studio—I only keep it for nights I can't get out to the beach. The house there is perfect, except for the commute. I don't know if you're going to want to drive that far. I suppose we could try your apartment—"

Juliet tensed, resisting the urge to clasp both hands over her ears to shut out his words. "Wait a minute," she said quietly. Then she took a towel and wrapped it firmly around her body. "What do you mean *we*?"

He drew back, frowning at her. "Just what I said. We. We—that's you and I—we have to figure out where we're going to live when we get back to the city.''

With her back toward him, Juliet slipped quickly into her robe. "I presume," she said without looking at him, "that 'we' will live where we've always lived— you in your house or apartment, or whatever you have, and me in my apartment."

The change in Juliet registered instantly with Brady as he followed her out of the bathroom. This was the lawyer talking. Not cold, exactly, but distant. Determined. Not at all like the woman who had spent the last week with him. "That's a rather unusual arrangement for two people who are married," he noted dryly.

"But we're not married," she countered, concentrating on the slacks and heavy cotton sweater she was removing from her suitcase. "We have an arrangement."

Brady paced across the room, walking past the unmade bed to sit in one of the wing chairs near the fireplace. "Ah, yes. An arrangement." He crossed his legs and sat back. "And if I recall correctly, your purpose in the whole affair is to get pregnant. That requires some contact."

His voice was controlled, but not sarcastic. Juliet wasn't quite sure what to do. It had never occurred to her that he would expect to live with her. That was carrying things too far. She had her own apartment, her own routine, her own way of doing things. Besides, her apartment wasn't big enough for two people. But that wasn't the only thing bothering her, and she knew it. Ever since they'd started getting ready to go home, Juliet had begun to feel differently. For the first time in a week she'd thought about the office, the work that was waiting for her, the life she'd left behind. She turned toward him, her clothes over her arm, her robe clutched tightly around her. "We can't live together, Brady. Neither apartment is big enough and the beach is too far."

"Then what's the alternative?" Brady kept all emotion out of his voice. She was obviously trying to be reasonable.

"We can see each other. Maybe spend the night together sometimes. I already know when I'm most likely to get pregnant." She reached down in the corner of her suitcase and produced a pink engagement calendar. "I've got it all charted in here."

Brady just stared at her.

"Is something wrong?" she asked.

"No, Juliet, I guess not. We just have two different pictures of the way we were going to proceed." He stood up slowly and walked toward the door, making no move toward her. "Why don't you get dressed while I go down to the office and settle with the inn?" he suggested.

"Wait, Brady," she stopped him. "Shouldn't we split the bill?" She hadn't really thought about the expenses all week when he automatically picked up the tabs. Suddenly she felt she needed to ask.

For a long moment Brady looked at her, silently. He couldn't figure out the unfamiliar and unpleasant tension between them. "No, Juliet, we don't need to split it. This one's on me." He closed the door firmly, leaving Juliet feeling very much alone. She walked into the bathroom, locking the door behind her.

They said very little during the drive home. Brady put a cassette of classical music on the tape deck, mostly to fill the silence. When they arrived at Juliet's apartment, he offered to carry her suitcases up for her. He wasn't surprised when she thanked him but refused. Before she got out of the car, she slipped the wedding ring off her finger and wordlessly handed it back to Brady. He took it without comment and put it into his jacket pocket. He didn't want it back, but there wasn't much point in making an issue of it.

Brady waited, the car still running, until her apartment light switched on, glowing along with hundreds of others in the early-evening darkness. He sat quietly for a long time, staring at that light, watching for shadows of movement. His fingers idly traced the gold band in his pocket. Finally he gunned the accelerator and headed for his apartment. He didn't have it in him to drive all the way to the beach.

# CHAPTER NINE

BRADY TOOK ANOTHER sip of coffee. He was damn sick of seeing Juliet by appointment only. It had been like that for weeks, ever since they got back from Carmel. If she wasn't busy, he was. She claimed she wasn't avoiding him. In fact she'd accused him of avoiding her.

He ran his finger down the listings in the real estate section of the morning paper. "Two bedroom, beautiful view.... Sublet, available immediately.... Dream pad near Golden Gate Park...." Occasionally he picked up the pencil that kept getting lost in the newspaper spread all across his kitchen table, and marked a likely-looking apartment. If he could find a couple of good ones, maybe he could persuade Juliet to go look at them. He checked his watch. He was picking her up at one. He would call ahead and arrange to see the few that looked like the best prospects, and if she refused to go look at them—well, then she refused.

But they were going to have to figure out something. She'd informed him that according to her pink book they'd totally missed out on prime time last month. He wasn't wasting any sympathy over that one. He didn't like scheduling his sex life by some woman's little pink book.

Disgusted, he went back to the listings, copying phone numbers and addresses on a separate sheet of paper. He barely looked up when the back door banged.

"You considering going into real estate?" Phil looked over Brady's shoulder at the real estate section.

"Hell, no," Brady growled. He kept writing. "Get yourself some coffee and have a seat."

Phil tossed his jacket on a chair and opened the cupboard to find a cup. Brady was in a lousy mood. Marriage obviously wasn't agreeing with him, although it wasn't much of a marriage with him out here and her in the city. Of course, Phil reminded himself as he poured the coffee, their union was only a paper agreement. From what he'd seen of Juliet Cavanaugh, a relationship with her would be damn hard to keep on paper.

"So what are you up to?" Phil prodded. He pushed the front section of the newspaper aside and sat down across from Brady. "Is the lease up on your apartment?"

Brady scowled. "No. I'm going to try to convince Juliet that we should rent an apartment together. I saw more of her before we got married."

"It would put you in a better position legally if you were living together," Phil observed. "This looks suspicious. But I thought you told me she refused to live with you."

"She did." Brady slammed down his pencil. "And she's never going to get pregnant this way."

Phil eyed Brady skeptically. He had the distinct impression that getting Juliet pregnant had very little to do with the real problem, at least from Brady's perspective. "I take it that's the excuse you plan to use," he needled his friend.

"Got any better suggestions?"

Phil started to give him a flip answer, and then he stopped. "Yes," he answered, "maybe I do."

Brady looked at him with renewed interest.

"Why don't you buy a house?"

"Don't be funny," Brady snapped. Sometimes Phil irritated him.

"No, wait a minute, I'm serious." Phil shifted in his chair. "I have a client who's got to unload one of those old Victorians up in Pacific Heights in a hurry. He bought the thing for investment, was planning to renovate it. Then the IRS caught up with him. If he doesn't get hold of some cash in a hurry, it's all over."

"Probably a good deal," Brady muttered. "But it doesn't solve my problems."

"Your brain's in neutral," Phil complained. "We're talking about an investment—you know, money to make money?" For someone with as much imagination as Brady, he sure wasn't picking up on this one.

"Huh?" Brady stared at him.

"If Juliet won't live with you, maybe she'll invest with you. If you'd live in the thing for a few months and get it decorated and furnished, you could sell it for a tidy profit. You could put your earnings in trust for the baby—that should appeal to her."

Brady wadded up the piece of paper he'd been writing on and pitched it at the wastebasket. "By God, she might go for it. When can we move in?"

"As soon as you can come up with the earnest money," Phil told him. "My client's about to list it with a realtor, but I've got the keys now if you want to go take a look at it."

"You're on!" Brady grinned. "I'm picking up Juliet at one. Say, how about coming with us? I could use an advocate. If you tell her what a good deal it is, maybe she'll bite."

"Sorry, Brady, I can't make it. Eileen's coming by to see the kids." Phil took a drink of coffee. The compassion in Brady's eyes was too close to pity. He didn't want it.

Brady sensed Phil's discomfort. He wished again he hadn't said some of the things he had after Eileen left. "Is she any better?" he asked cautiously. He knew how hard it was for Phil to talk about his wife.

"She seems to be." Phil's tone was noncommittal. "She claims she hasn't had a drink for a couple of weeks and she's got a new job."

"Still as a waitress?"

"This one's in a bar and grill—lousy neighborhood."

Brady winced. Eileen working in a bar sounded like a bad idea to him.

Phil finished his coffee and carried the cup to the sink, preoccupied. "She said there was something she wanted to talk to me about," he continued, putting on his jacket.

"Any clues as to what?" Brady asked.

"Not really. The build-up sounded like she wants the boys."

Brady shoved his chair back and stood up. Phil lived in constant fear that Eileen would take him to court and try to get at least partial custody. It would be wrong, all wrong. When she was drunk, there was no telling what might happen to Michael and Timmy. "You think she's considering legal action?" Brady asked.

Phil zipped his jacket, making a harsh, grating sound. "I don't know."

"Hell, Phil, even if she did, no court would—"

Phil cut him off, his eyes hard. "When you're dealing with a mother and children, you can't even start to predict what a court might do."

Brady backed off. He was right, and they both knew it. They could only hope Eileen had enough sense to let well enough alone. Brady wasn't betting on it. Any mother who would walk out on her children would do practically anything.

"Stop by on your way into the city and I'll give you those keys," Phil called over his shoulder. He vaulted lightly over the deck rail and took off at a dead run down the beach.

"Damn!" Brady muttered, slamming the back door.

BRADY PICKED JULIET UP at one on the dot, surprised that she was ready. "The last time I showed up here at this hour on a Saturday afternoon you were dressed in bubbles," he teased her, brushing his hand across her hair. Whenever he saw her, he wanted to touch her. Even hearing her voice on the phone unsettled him.

"The last time you came at one, you weren't due until eight," Juliet retorted, "and I practically set a speed record getting ready." The words weren't what she wanted to say to him. What she'd wanted to say was that she'd missed him terribly, and she'd been ready for an hour, and she'd hoped he'd be early.

Linda had been expecting her at the office to go over a new case, but as soon as Brady called, Juliet had postponed the meeting with Linda. They could do that anytime. What she really wanted was to see Brady.

Ever since they got back from the honeymoon, they'd had one problem after another getting together.

"I've got something I want you to look at," Brady said casually. He'd slipped his arms around her and was looking down into her eyes. Her invitation was blatant. She'd been waiting just like he had. Maybe just for a little while... God, he wanted her. He knew it was crazy. There wasn't going to be any little while. "We need to see it now, in the daylight," he told her.

"Need to see what?" Juliet asked. She ran her fingers along the line of his jaw, slowly, suggestively.

"I want us to go see..." He paused. He had to do this just right and it was so damn hard to concentrate with her so close to him. "I want us to look at an investment," he said finally.

Juliet took her hand away. "An investment?" The only investment she was interested in was right here.

"Yes," he continued speaking quickly. "Phil told me this morning about a great opportunity, and I thought you might be interested, too."

Juliet stepped back, feeling disappointed. "Exactly what kind of investment did you have in mind?"

Brady sucked in his breath. He hadn't meant to approach the subject like this. He'd wanted to ease her into it. But now he was going to have to level with her. "One of those old Victorian houses in Pacific Heights." He quickly added, "Phil says it'll go cheap."

"You're suggesting we buy an old Victorian house?"

"Right," Brady affirmed. "As an investment. We can fix it up, sell it in a few months, and make a good profit." Before Juliet could protest, Brady took her hand and started for the door. "We can at least look at it. Come on—we'll talk while we drive."

Juliet was irritated all the way to the car. Ever since she woke up, she'd been fantasizing about the afternoon with Brady. None of those fantasies included going to look at an old house. Her frustration mounting, she tried to discourage him. "Brady, this is an exercise in futility. In the first place, where are we . . . or at least, where am I going to get the money to buy a house? Up there, cheap costs a fortune. And besides that, we're so busy we can't even find time to get together. And you want to renovate a house in the spare time we don't have?"

Brady kept his eyes on the road. It was a little easier to think now, with her belted on her side of the car and him on his. So, she was concerned about the cost of the house. He could give her the money, but she'd never go for that. Then he remembered. "At the beginning you talked to me about a . . ." Damn! She'd said it was crass to call it a stud fee, but what else could you call it? "You talked about paying $25,000 to the baby's father." That sounded better. He glanced sideways at Juliet. She appeared to be listening attentively. "I told you I didn't want to be paid—and it's not in the contract—so maybe you could use that money as part of the purchase price of the house."

Juliet was floored. When she thought about it, she realized he was right. They'd signed his contract, not hers, and the fee wasn't mentioned. How had she overlooked that? She'd never intended to drop it. "I fully expect to pay you Brady," she insisted. "That's the only way to carry out this arrangement on a business basis—"

*She really is stubborn,* Brady thought. But he was on the right track presenting this as a business investment. Pulling up at a red light, he reached over and took her hand. "Tell you what," he proposed. "If this house looks good, you put the $25,000 into it, and I'll come up with the rest of the purchase price. When we sell it, we'll each take back our investment, and the profit can go into a trust fund for the baby."

The light changed, the car behind them honked, and Brady turned back to his driving, guiding the car carefully up the steep hills along narrow, winding streets. Juliet sat frozen, her mind racing. This was one more involvement with him. She could see herself getting in deeper and deeper. And yet it was such a reasonable offer. Not just reasonable but generous. She stole a sideways glance at Brady. Maybe he felt some obligation to the baby even though he would never see it. He was that kind of person. This might help him meet that obligation and make things easier later.

Brady drummed his fingers on the steering wheel. The silence meant she was at least thinking about it. "So, how does that sound?" he inquired.

"It's very unexpected." She hesitated. "But if you want to do it—"

"I do," he cut in quickly, then he pulled the scrap of paper with the address on it from his jacket pocket. "Should be just another block or so...." Brady hit the brakes and swerved forward into a large parking place. "There it is," he announced, checking the address once more.

Juliet stared out the window at a slate-gray house, its columned front porch outlined in wooden filigree. A witches' turret rose high on one side with a curved window outlined in white. The place looked like an expanded version of the gingerbread house in *Hansel and Gretel*, except for the candy. In its day it had no doubt been lovely, and beneath the peeling paint she could still see possibilities—and a lot of work.

"Not bad," Brady commented. He hoped the contractor who had checked out the house had been reliable, because from the outside the place looked like it had problems. Phil had shown him the estimates and there hadn't been anything major. If it weren't for the circumstances, he'd think long and hard about buying this one. He opened his car door. "Let's go in and take a look."

"Inside?" Juliet questioned. "I thought we were just driving by."

"I got the keys from Phil this morning," Brady explained. "It looks as though it could use a little paint," he observed as they climbed the steps to the front porch. One corner of the porch was sagging, he noted silently.

"Brady, renovating this house would be a major project," Juliet said dubiously.

Brady was concentrating on the lock, finally getting it to work after several attempts. "We can't tell for sure until we've looked inside." He quickly opened the door, not ready to discuss the details quite yet.

Juliet was pleasantly surprised when she walked in. The sun streamed through a fan window above the doorway, making a rainbow of color on the wooden floor of the foyer. The drab walls and dirty wallpaper couldn't hide the beauty of the dark-stained wood and the graceful arches that invited them from one room to the next. The kitchen was spacious, with natural wood cabinets and up-to-date appliances, and the bathrooms were in reasonable condition. They even had claw-footed bathtubs. Obviously, someone had begun work on the house, probably over a period of several years, and then been interrupted before the job could be finished.

Brady found himself looking more carefully at Juliet than at the house, which appeared to be in line with the contractor's estimates. But that wasn't important right now. What did matter was Juliet's opinion. As they climbed the stairs, their footsteps echoing through the empty rooms, Brady could feel her excitement. He said nothing until they climbed the final staircase to the rounded turret which looked out across the rising hills of San Francisco. Standing behind her, one arm around her waist, he asked casually, "Well, what do you think?"

When she looked up at him, her eyes were sparkling. "I really like it, Brady," she said softly. "I know that's no reason to go into an investment, but . . . but maybe if I like it, someone else will." She hesitated. "What do you think?"

He looked down at her, studying her eyes and the shape of her face in the late afternoon sunlight that filtered through the window. His hands ringed her waist and then slid down over her hips. "If you like it, I think it's perfect," he agreed.

"But, Brady, how will we ever have time to oversee all the work that has to be done?" She felt his hands moving back and forth, and her response, immediate now whenever he touched her.

"There's more to do than I'd expected." His voice was deliberately casual. "Probably the best approach would be for us to live here."

Juliet stiffened, but Brady didn't move his hands away. "You mean together?" she asked him.

"I mean together." He pressed her closer to him, his hands wandering up her back.

"Wait a minute!" She put her hands on her hips and pulled away. "Was that what you had in mind all along?"

A slow smile settled across his face. "It had occurred to me," he admitted. "Will you think it over?" He pulled her to him again, and she didn't resist. Privately, she knew she wasn't going to resist the house, either. It would be far better than the uncertainty about when they might see each other. She pressed her hips against him and felt his rising passion.

Brady tried to gather his thoughts. He knew there were other keys out for the house. When he'd picked up this set, Phil had said something about a realtor looking at the place today. But he didn't care. Right now they were alone. Then she tipped her head back and he saw her eyes. He didn't want to wait till they got back to her apartment to make love. He pushed up her sweater and kissed her.

Juliet felt like a volcano about to erupt. Her breath coming in short gasps, she opened her eyes. It was at that moment she saw the man in a business suit walking briskly up the front sidewalk.

"Brady," she cried, grabbing his shoulders. "Brady, someone's here to see the house."

"Oh, God," he groaned, his arms tightening around her. He mentally calculated how long it would take for someone to get in the house and find them up on the third floor. He felt her tremble. "We've got time, Juliet." His voice was tight, raspy.

"Brady, no..." she cried out. "I can't..." Then she felt her legs shake uncontrollably, and she sank slowly down to the bare wooden floor, aware of Brady's arms around her, breaking her fall.

Far below them a key rattled in the front door lock. "Brady, do you hear that?" she whispered. It rattled again.

"Ignore it," he whispered. He knew this was a damn fool chance he was taking, but he couldn't stop himself. He wanted her beyond all reason.

Trying to shut out the sounds, Brady pulled her to him. He heard the key again, and then nothing else. He was driven by a compelling need, desire pushing him beyond the razor's edge of reason.

Juliet gripped him tightly, listening, too. A sound, the click of the latch, broke the silence. She dug her fingernails into Brady's shoulders, struggling for control, but she was already too much a part of him. She began to soar outside herself and nothing else mattered anymore.

Almost as quickly as it had begun, it was over, and yet Juliet felt complete. Brady collapsed on top of her, his breathing deep and ragged and she lay beneath him, holding him in her arms. Once again she heard the sound of footsteps echoing through the house.

Jarred back to reality, Juliet opened her eyes. "Brady!" she whispered.

"It's okay," he reassured her. "He's just starting up to the second floor."

Brady got up quickly and Juliet scrambled to her feet. With trembling hands she adjusted her sweater and straightened her skirt while Brady stuffed his shirttail inside the waistband of his pants. They heard heavy footsteps on the stairs.

"We're about to have company." Brady grinned and put his arm around Juliet, drawing her closer.

"Are you ready?"

Juliet looked up at him, nodding. Now that she and Brady were safe, she could almost, but not quite, return his smile.

They were standing calmly by the stair rail when the man started up the last flight. "Who are you?" Brady demanded.

The man jumped, obviously startled. "I...I'm a realtor, preparing a listing on the house. I didn't realize anyone was here," he added apologetically.

Juliet suppressed a grin. Brady had him on the defensive. A few minutes sooner, and the situation would have been very different.

"That's quite all right," Brady told the man, at the same time making a mental note to call Phil right away with their decision before a realtor got in on the act. "We were just leaving," Brady added, taking Juliet's hand.

As they started down the stairs, Juliet saw the lace edge of her underpants peeking out of Brady's pocket. She started to reach for them, and then thought the better of it. She'd just hope they didn't fall out and land right in front of the realtor.

Once in the car, both Brady and Juliet burst out laughing. "That was really dumb," she told him. "I can't imagine what ever made you—"

"Made me?" he asked. His eyes crinkled, and his mouth formed a broad, mischievous grin. "Just exactly who was it who didn't want to go home first?"

Juliet's cheeks flamed. "Oh," she said softly, and contritely folded her hands in her lap. Before Brady, she could never have done anything like that. But now . . . now a lot of things were different.

Brady made a quick call from Juliet's apartment to tell Phil they wanted the house, and then he and Juliet spent the next several hours planning. They decided not to sublet their apartments, because their time in the house wouldn't be long enough to really make it worthwhile. Brady suggested Juliet try to find someone to house sit, as though she were going on a long vacation. She smiled, quietly, and snuggled into his shoulder. That, she decided, was an extraordinarily good description of what was about to occur.

By the time Brady returned the keys to Phil on Sunday night, he and Juliet had decided to move in the following weekend if the arrangements could be made. The bell was still chiming when Phil opened the door. "Come in," he urged, "and tell me about the house."

"I owe you one for this," Brady said, dropping the keys on the table.

Phil took a closer look at him. "You look a hell of a lot more relaxed then you did yesterday morning," he observed pointedly.

"Weekends can do that for you," Brady answered with a smug expression on his face as he thought back over the last two days with Juliet. Before Phil could follow it up, he added, "Did you get any word on exactly when we can move into the house?"

Phil got the message. Apparently their sex life was good, and Brady didn't want to discuss it. "You should be able to move within a week," Phil answered. "We'll work out a temporary rental agreement until you close. All you need is some up-front money."

"No problem," Brady assured him. He turned to leave.

"I'll keep an eye on things out here while you're gone," Phil offered.

There was a crash as Timmy appeared in the doorway and an armload of cars clattered to the floor. "Where's Brady going?" he demanded. "He's got to fix my racer." He held up the black car, which was minus one headlight and three of its four wheels.

Brady took the car and gave Timmy a rough pat on the head. "If I can make one that survives you, we can advertise it as indestructible."

Timmy picked up the rest of his cars. "My mommy was here yesterday," he told Brady. "She said we should tell you hello." Cars in hand, he disappeared up the stairs.

Brady had been so caught up with Juliet and the house that he'd forgotten about Eileen coming. "How'd she look?" he asked Phil.

"If you mean had she been drinking, the answer's no." Phil shoved his hands in his pockets. He'd only seen Eileen a few times since she left and it got harder every time. The woman she was now didn't match his memories of his wife.

Brady proceeded cautiously. "Did it go all right?"

"A little strained." Phil paced slowly across the hallway as he talked. "The kids aren't sure how to react to her anymore and she doesn't quite know what to do either. I talked to her alone before she left. She wants the kids, Brady. A weekend for starters, and then . . ."

"What did you tell her?" Brady prodded.

Phil paced faster. "I told her no. What the hell was I supposed to say? I'm not going to give them up,

Brady. She can come here and see them and if she stays on the wagon, maybe after a while she can take them for a day." Anger glinted in his eyes. "But, dammit, she's the one who walked out."

"Yeah, I know," Brady muttered. "Do you think she'll do anything?"

Phil stopped pacing and leaned against the staircase. "I don't know. She was pretty angry when she left."

Brady knew that meant the answer was probably yes. "Do you think you ought to see a lawyer, Phil?" It wasn't the first time he'd made the suggestion, but this time he went farther. "Maybe you could talk to Juliet."

For a long moment, Phil didn't answer. He wondered if Brady thought he had his head in the sand. The fact was, he didn't want to talk to a divorce lawyer, because he didn't want a divorce. He didn't want to get the courts involved at all. And he kept hoping against hope that Eileen wouldn't either. Maybe eventually, one way or another they could work out something themselves. Maybe she'd finally agree to get help. "Thanks, Brady," he answered. "I think I'm going to let it ride a little longer."

The response didn't surprise Brady. He only hoped Phil wouldn't wait too long. "Let me know if there's anything we can do," he offered, reaching for the door. "I'll come by your office and sign the papers on the house whenever they're ready."

"If this is going to be joint ownership, you'll have to bring Juliet," Phil reminded him.

Brady grinned sheepishly. "Yeah. I completely forgot."

ONCE THE PAPERS had been signed the next week, Juliet spent most of her free time getting her apartment in shape to leave it. Linda offered to come over and help her, but she declined. She had already decided not to take much with her, other than her clothes. She and Brady would be basically camping out while they got the house fixed up.

Until she'd realized that fact, Juliet had had serious second thoughts about buying the place with Brady. The possible ramifications of what she was doing hit her hard one afternoon after she'd had three appointments in a row with new clients who broke down and cried when they talked about starting out full of dreams, only to have their lives crash down around them when the marriages soured. Two of them had lived with their husbands before marriage. They said they'd been so sure of their long-term commitments and they simply couldn't understand what had happened.

When the last client left, Juliet stood up and paced over to the window to stare out at the gray rainy day. She knew that her relationship with Brady had advanced well beyond the "purely business" arrangement she had once envisioned. And there was nothing wrong with that, she supposed. It was probably better that the baby's father be someone she liked because, after all, he was going to pass his genes on to the baby. She even wondered sometimes what it would be like to be really married to him, not just on paper but really married. What would it be like to plan a future with someone, to watch a child grow together, to furnish a house and plant a garden, and grow old together?

A knock on the door interrupted her thoughts, and Linda walked in, pulling on her coat. "Think I'll call it a day," she told Juliet. "I seem to be spending more time here than I do at home."

"I've about had it, too," Juliet agreed. "Hold on a minute and I'll go downstairs with you."

Linda looked surprised. "You have another client waiting. Didn't you know?"

"I thought Mrs. McDowell was the last one." Juliet quickly checked her calendar. "Who's here now?"

"That blond woman, you know the one who always refuses to give her name," Linda said. "I forgot to tell you—she came in again while you were in Carmel. She refused to talk to me—said you knew all about her problem and she'd wait till you got back."

Juliet shook her head. "Alice says she's been back a couple of other times, too. Apparently she sat here most of Monday morning while I was in court. Alice offered to make an appointment for her, but she said no."

"She obviously needs help...I see what you mean," Linda said. "What are you going to do about her?"

"Talk to her, I suppose." Juliet sighed. She was tired. It already had been a very long week. And it was unlikely she could do much for this woman, anyway.

Linda smiled sympathetically. "Don't stay too late," she said, partially closing the door behind her.

THE WOMAN HELD herself perfectly straight as she walked into the lawyer's office. She wasn't drinking much at all now, and she was tired of her husband always using that as an excuse. And she had followed the lawyer's advice. She had tried to talk to her husband, but he had shut her out. Again. Even when she told him she wasn't drinking, he kept talking about her going away to a hospital for some sort of rehabilitation program. That wasn't what she needed. What she needed was her babies, and it was the lawyer's job to figure out how to get them for her.

"Won't you sit down?" Juliet motioned to a chair near the desk. The woman looked better than when she'd been there before. She was wearing a soft peach-colored dress, and Juliet saw a spark of life in the pale blue eyes. "What can I do for you?" Juliet asked.

The woman sat on the very edge of the chair. "I followed your advice." Her eyes were almost accusing. "It didn't work."

"I don't understand." Juliet tried to remember what advice she had given the woman. She had no notes to jog her memory.

"I went to see my husband and talked to him about taking the babies, just for a weekend at first. He said no." The woman fidgeted as she talked, twisting and untwisting a handkerchief around her fingers. It wasn't as hard as it had been the first time, but she wanted to make sure the lawyer understood she'd done everything she was supposed to.

"Did he give you a reason?" Juliet inquired.

"He said it was because I drink. I told him it wasn't a problem, but he still said I need to get help. He always uses that as an excuse...like a drink now and then was going to make me an unfit mother."

Something about the way she said the words put Juliet on guard. If the woman had a serious drinking problem, she probably did need help to stop completely. But at least she was trying. "You say you have two babies?" Juliet began.

The woman nodded.

Juliet picked up her pencil and began to write. It was almost time to get the woman's name, but she'd let her talk a little more about the children first. "How old are they?"

"Four and seven." The woman brightened. "They gave me pictures when I was there. Would you like to see them?"

"Of course," Juliet answered politely.

The woman already was digging in her purse. She produced two slightly bent pictures.

Juliet stared at the images on the film, a towhead with a huge grin on his face, and his little brother with dark hair, clutching a tattered blanket. "My God!" Juliet blurted out. "You're Eileen Gentry!" She was immediately sorry. It was the most unprofessional thing she could ever remember doing.

The woman drew back, a hostile uncertainty in her eyes. "How do you know that?"

Juliet tried to placate her. "I know your sons. They're very nice boys."

The woman was still suspicious. "How do you know them?"

Juliet hesitated, searching for the best explanation that still was true. "I know them through Brady Talcott."

"Then you know their father."

Juliet could see the anger building. "Well, yes, but only professionally... and as a friend of Brady's."

Enraged, the woman stood up. "You lied to me," she accused Juliet. "You're on his side too."

"That's not true, Mrs. Gentry," Juliet protested. "I didn't even know who you were until right now."

Her words made no impression on the woman, who was shouting now. "You're just like all the rest of them. You want to keep my babies from me.'' She snatched the pictures off Juliet's desk and clutched them in her hand. ''I thought you might understand because you're a woman, but you don't either.'' She glowered at Juliet with a frightening intensity. ''I just want you to know I'm going to have my babies—and there is nothing you can do to stop me.''

Eileen ran out of the office, slamming the door behind her. She was down the hall and into the elevator before she stopped to think. She shouldn't have gotten so angry. The lawyer was probably telling the truth when she said she didn't know her. But it wasn't fair that everywhere she turned, everyone was against her.

She looked down at the pictures she still held in her hand. She felt so awkward with Michael and Timmy now. Timmy had given her a big hug before she left, but Michael... He seemed so grown-up now, and so shy with her. She didn't know what he liked to do or even what to talk to him about. She watched the lighted numbers on the elevator panel descend toward one. Obviously this lawyer wasn't going to be any help, and she wasn't sure any of the others would be any better. They probably all knew Phil.

The doors opened, and she walked past a faceless crowd waiting to enter the elevator, and on through the lobby to the street. It was still drizzling. She pulled up the collar of her raincoat. She didn't have any umbrella. For several blocks, she walked aimlessly, obsessed with the idea of having the children with her but without any notion of how to accomplish it. She slowed as she passed a bar where she used to go after work. She knew the bartender and all the regulars. Now that she didn't go in anymore, she missed the company. It looked warm in there, and dry. On impulse, she turned and walked inside.

For the next several days, Eileen's agonized face haunted Juliet. It had never occurred to her that the woman was Phil Gentry's wife—until she saw the boys' pictures. And then she had handled the situation badly. Eileen was obviously trying very hard to fight the drinking and the loneliness. She needed help, and frightening her off had probably only made things worse. Eileen was desperate. Juliet wished she knew enough about her to be able to guess what she might do next. She considered talking to Brady about it, or even to Phil, but immediately rejected the idea.

Juliet found herself thinking about Eileen and Phil as she sorted through her closet to choose the clothes she would take to the new house. People made such a mess of their lives. She hoped she wasn't making a mistake by living with Brady. But the more she thought about it, the more it was something she wanted to do.

Moving into the house turned out to require no more than one carload and a few trips in and out. Juliet and Brady had agreed they wouldn't need furniture, except for a kitchen table and chairs and a bed which Brady had promised to take care of. When the bed arrived, it turned out to be a massive four-poster from an antique store. As they watched the workmen assemble it, Juliet felt Brady's hand wander across her back until his fingers slipped ever so slightly under her sweater and settled just inside the waistband of her jeans. She knew that as soon as the workmen left they were going to try it out. The longer she stood next to Brady, the better an idea that seemed.

Once they were settled, the weeks slipped by quickly. Juliet liked sharing the house with Brady, and overall, things were going very well except for one problem. She still wasn't pregnant. Juliet was temporarily hopeful, and she even bought a home pregnancy test. But her optimism turned out to be premature. She got more and more impatient. One night while Brady sat tinkering with a toy bulldozer, Juliet flipped through her pink datebook, studying the careful markings she had made. She looked up to find him watching her.

"Is something the matter, Juliet?" he asked.

"Sort of." She marked her place on the page with her finger. "Brady, I really ought to be pregnant by now." She'd talked to Cass about it, and her mother had told her to be patient. But she had been patient. By now her approach should have worked.

Brady grinned. "Is that all? Sometimes getting pregnant takes time."

"But after that first month, we've been right on schedule—"

Brady jumped to his feet. "Wait a minute! You mean to tell me you've kept track of every time..." His voice rose as he snatched the book from her.

"But how else are we going to know—"

"Damn!" Brady exclaimed, scowling at Juliet's neat entries. He stalked over to the fireplace and pitched the book into the flames.

"Brady! Stop! You can't do that." Juliet reached him just as the paper caught fire.

Brady's jaw was set. "The hell I can't." He turned to Juliet, his eyes blazing. "There are some things you don't do on schedule, and this is one of them." He took her roughly in his arms, and kissed her hard.

Meshed with hers, his lips softened, and his irritation melted into desire.

Juliet never mentioned the book again. Secretly she knew that what Brady had said, and what her mother had told her, was true. There were some things that shouldn't be scheduled, and now that she and Brady were living together, scheduling had actually turned out to be totally unnecessary. Spontaneity covered all the bases.

She found that both of them were beginning to spend more time at home. It was something that had happened gradually, but it had happened. There seemed to be fewer night meetings and less work that was important enough to keep either of them late at the office. Juliet liked the evenings in front of the fire, curled up in the beanbag chairs Brady had brought from his beach house when he got tired of sitting on the floor. Despite its lack of other furnishings, the living room felt like someone lived there. But the rest of the house was still drab and shabby, which had started to bother Juliet.

"You know, we're not moving along very fast with this house," Juliet observed one night, as she eyed the cracked plaster on the living room ceiling.

Brady closed the wallpaper book he had been studying. "You're right and I haven't told you the latest. That guy Simmons who was supposed to show up next week? He fell off a ladder yesterday and broke his leg."

"Fantastic," Juliet muttered. "Of course the people I lined up didn't work out any better. You know," she mused, "I've been thinking about it. Maybe we ought to do some of it ourselves."

Brady shot her a skeptical look. "You mean decorate the house? Have you ever painted?" He surveyed the ten-foot walls.

"Well, no," Juliet admitted. "Except I did help Cass with a bathroom once." She sat down and picked up a strip of paint samples. "How about you?"

"Not for a long time. I worked for a painter one summer when I was in high school." Brady sat down cross-legged on the floor facing her. "But that doesn't make sense, Juliet. Any work we have done by professionals will be a tax write-off when we sell the place."

"We can't write it off if we can't get anyone to do it," she noted pragmatically. "Besides, it might be kind of fun."

Brady had never thought of painting walls as much fun, but it might be with Juliet. "Maybe you're right," he agreed. "We can at least give it a try."

Juliet's eyes sparkled with anticipation. She'd always thought it would be fun to fix up an old house, or any house. "Who do you suppose we might get to help us?" she asked.

"Any number of people," Brady answered. "Steve and Linda, Cass, Phil . . ."

"Cass would be super at selecting the paint colors, but I think Steve and Linda are out. Their enthusiasm for decorating is definitely lacking since they remodeled their kitchen last summer. They were knee-deep in plaster dust for weeks." Juliet laughed at the memory.

"Phil's probably the answer then, at least for the big jobs like wallpapering." Brady shoved the book of wallpaper samples over toward Juliet. "What do you think about these stripes for the hallway?"

Juliet barely glanced at them. "Phil does know that our marriage and living together in this house is nothing more than an arrangement, doesn't he?"

"Of course. He drew up the contract. Does that bother you?"

"No," Juliet answered slowly.

"What's the problem then?"

Juliet hesitated. She wanted to tell Brady that ever since she'd discovered it was Eileen Gentry who had come to her office seeking help she had been uncomfortable around Phil and the boys. But she couldn't talk about it without breaking a client's confidence. And she never did that. "There's no problem," she answered.

Brady looked at her carefully. There was something Juliet wasn't telling him. "Are you sure?" he asked.

"Absolutely positive," she replied. She slid the heavy wallpaper book between them. "Now, show me again which stripes you want to put in the hall."

# CHAPTER TEN

PHIL HAD BEEN genuinely glad to help Brad and Juliet with the house. He had missed the casual camaraderie of such projects. Since Eileen had left, he hadn't done much of that sort of thing at home, because working alone was sheer drudgery.

But as he hung up the phone, he wished he weren't going. Eileen's anger echoed in the silence. "They're my babies, too, and I have a right to be with them," she'd shouted. "You're just using them to get back at me."

It was the third call he'd had from her in a week, all of them emotional confrontations. He'd told her he wasn't going to be home today, that he'd be glad to have her come tomorrow. But that wasn't good enough. She didn't want to wait. She wanted the children while he was gone. No, he'd said, that wouldn't work out. The hell of it was that would have been a better plan all the way around. He'd be able to do a lot more at Brady's if the kids weren't along.

He'd been tempted, but only briefly. Eileen's voice hadn't sounded right. Maybe it was his imagination. Or maybe he did want to hurt her because she'd made such a mess of all their lives. But if she drank, and something were to happen to the boys...

"Daddy, I'm hungry," a small voice whined. Timmy was standing in the middle of the kitchen floor in his pajama bottoms and bare feet.

Simultaneously Phil smelled the oatmeal, and it was too late. He snatched the burned pan from the stove. "Timmy!" he roared. "I told you to get dressed."

Frightened by the unexpected anger, Timmy dropped his glass of grape juice, splattering the floor with purple. He ran out of the room sobbing.

Phil leaned back against the stove and covered his face with his hands. He didn't know how much longer he could go on, how much longer he could do it all alone. He was juggling the boys and his law practice, and now, with Eileen calling all the time, it was too much. Slowly he took the roll of paper towels out of the holder and began to soak up the purple puddles and gather up the shards of glass. The mess looked endless, just like the rest of his life.

By the time he rang the doorbell at the old Victorian, Phil felt slightly better. It was a cloudless blue December day, and the boys were excited about visiting Brady. Michael had brought his newest C. S. Lewis book along, in hopes that Juliet might read some of it to him. Whatever she'd done that day in Brady's office when Michael had had the chicken pox, she'd won him over. He was always trying to think of some reason to see her.

Juliet answered the door, dressed in paint-spattered jeans and one of Brady's old shirts. She looked radiant, Phil thought. There wasn't a hint of that cool lady lawyer he sometimes saw striding down the corridors at the courthouse.

"You're just in time," she told them. "I'm painting trim, and Brady is trying to build a scaffolding. From the sound of it, he could use some help."

"I'm ready," announced Timmy, holding up a hammer half as big as he was.

"You're too little to do anything," Michael scoffed. "You'd get the nails all mixed up in your dumb blanket."

"Michael!" Phil took the boy firmly by the shoulder.

Juliet tried not to smile. "Why don't you go on in, Phil, and let me show the boys what Brady brought home from the office last night." She knew the surprise was going to solve a lot of the problem. She and Brady had hauled in half a dozen cartons and set them in one of the empty bedrooms, purposely leaving them packed so the boys could have the fun of discovering what was inside. Except for one. Brady had shown her a new building system he was working on with large-size nuts and bolts and color-coded wrenches, and she had pulled the whole thing out and spent more than an hour building a fort.

As she had expected, the boys were equally fascinated. "I'm still going to help you paint," Michael promised, "but maybe I'll play here for a while first."

Juliet laughed and gave his shoulder a squeeze. "Stay as long as you want," she told him. "We'll be painting all day."

The scaffolding went together quickly under Phil's direction, and with the men wielding paint rollers and Juliet using a brush on the trim, the dining room was quickly being transformed. Juliet's choice of a light-colored paint with just a hint of peach turned out to be perfect. Even Brady gave his approval. "This color was grotesque in the can but it isn't too bad on the walls.''

"Told you so," Juliet answered smugly.

"Women must all be alike," Phil sighed. "That's what Eileen said when we had a big fight over painting the bathroom pink, and it didn't look half bad."

Brady watched Phil soak his roller and swipe it across the wall. Something had been bothering his friend all day, and it was a good bet that Eileen was behind it. Maybe if he could get Phil talking about it, Phil would ultimately ask Juliet for legal help. That wasn't going to solve the problem, but at least it would give him some protection if Eileen went to court. "Did Eileen call again?" Brady asked innocently.

"This morning." Phil's words were clipped. "She wanted to see the boys today."

Juliet flinched, painting furiously. She didn't want to hear about it. She wanted to keep as much distance between herself and the Gentrys' problems as possible.

"What did you tell her?" Brady prodded.

"That we couldn't do it today. I told her tomorrow, any time, but she wasn't interested. She got mad and hung up on me again."

Juliet could almost see Eileen's face, and pale blue eyes so full of pain, boiling over with frustration and loneliness. Phil laid down his paint roller and continued almost as though he had forgotten she were there. "Dammit, Brady, I was tempted to just tell her to take them for the day. But they're still little kids. If she's drinking, anything could happen to them."

Brady continued to paint, slowly, methodically. This was the time to bring in Juliet. "You know, Phil, we've hashed this over a hundred times and we never get anywhere. Maybe we need another opinion.'' Phil didn't answer. Brady knew he was treading on dangerous territory. ''Maybe Juliet can come up with an approach—she's a woman.'' He purposely didn't point out that she could also provide specialized legal advice. One step at a time.

Juliet kept painting. The less she said, the better. ''I don't know that being a woman gives me any special insight,'' she commented.

Brady frowned. He had expected her to cooperate. ''Well, give us an opinion anyway. What do you do with a wife who walks out, has a drinking problem and wants to see the kids?''

There it was, in a few short phrases, the anatomy of one more marriage that had fallen apart. Tucking a stray lock of hair under her bandana, Juliet searched for an appropriate nonresponse. She knew what Eileen Gentry wanted, and she knew what Phil wanted. She didn't know what was right. ''It sounds to me like Eileen needs help,'' she suggested cautiously.

Phil turned toward Juliet, his interest piqued. She'd gone right to the guts of the problem. Maybe it was worth talking to her. ''But how do you persuade somebody to find help when she won't listen, when all she can say is you don't understand? She says I'm using the children to hurt her.''

Juliet couldn't find any way at all to change the subject. ''Has she tried Alcoholics Anonymous?''

''I don't think so. I've brought it up, but she says she isn't like those people.''

For the first time, Juliet noticed the deep lines etched on Phil's face. They formed a pattern of disillusionment that made him look far older than his years. It was such a stupid waste. He'd done a fantastic job with the boys. He should be pleased with his life, but instead he was bitter and discouraged. On the other side of the fence stood Eileen, lonely, afraid, seeking comfort from a bottle. In the middle were the boys, the innocent victims, who could ultimately bear the brunt of it all.

Phil wiped his sleeve across his forehead, streaking the paint that had splattered. "I've tried so damn hard to figure this thing out. She claims she has a right to the boys, and I suppose in a way she does. She is their mother. But what if she gets drunk? She's already totaled one car and now she's got her license back and she's driving again. I'm afraid to let them go with her."

Brady broke the ensuing silence. "I don't know much about the legalities of this, but it looks to me like Phil needs a lawyer who specializes in family law. Do you suppose you could help him out, Juliet?"

Juliet froze, her paintbrush dripping on the drop cloth under the window. Brady was right, of course. Phil probably was going to need a lawyer, eventually if not right now. And she wasn't a candidate. Even though she wasn't representing Eileen, she was far too emotionally involved.

"I don't think so," she mumbled. "I always try to keep business and friendship separate." It was a lame excuse, but the only one she could think of. She scraped the paint off her brush on the side of the paint can and covered the bristles with plastic wrap to keep them from drying out. "I think maybe I'll go check on Michael and Timmy. They're probably getting hungry, and I bought some peanut butter yesterday."

Juliet spent the rest of the afternoon with the boys, avoiding Phil and Brady, who had moved the painting operation to the living room. It wasn't until after Phil left that she saw the anger glinting in Brady's eyes.

"What the hell was your problem this afternoon?" he confronted her.

"My problem?" Juliet hedged. She took the remains of their Chinese carry-out dinner out of the living room and dumped them in the kitchen wastebasket. She knew exactly what he meant.

"I've tried for months to get Phil to go to a lawyer. I finally got him talking...he was receptive to you. You could have helped him and you refused. Why, Juliet?" he demanded.

"I told you. I keep business and friendship separate." Juliet busied herself putting away the peanut butter and jelly she'd left on the kitchen counter.

Brady scowled, towering in the doorway. "That's a bunch of bull and you know it. Phil's been my lawyer ever since I needed one and he's also my best friend. Lawyers always represent their friends."

Not saying anything, Juliet closed the refrigerator.

"Answer me, Juliet!" Brady demanded. "What's the problem? Is it because he's a man and in your book the man's always wrong?"

Juliet spun around. "That's not true and you know it," she snapped.

His voice rose. "Then what is it, Juliet?"

She took a deep breath. "I can't represent Phil Gentry. I've already been contacted by his wife."

The heavy silence between them had a texture of its own. Brady stared at her, unmoving. Slowly, she crossed the kitchen and sat down at the table. She hadn't wanted to tell him, but there wasn't any choice.

Brady sat down across from her, his face grim. "Then you're representing Eileen?"

Juliet shook her head. "No, I'm not representing anyone. She's so frightened and upset that she refused to tell me her name. When she showed me pictures of the boys, and she found out I knew them, she walked out." Juliet stared out the window at the city lights far below. "Brady, there's no way I can represent Phil after his wife talked to me. And in good conscience I can't tell him why."

Brady picked up a napkin and methodically folded it into triangles. This meant Eileen had sought legal advice. He'd been right. Phil did need a lawyer. "Is she going to do something immediately?" he asked Juliet.

"I don't know what she's going to do." Juliet found herself relieved to finally be able to talk about it. "She really needs help. She thinks that the whole world is against her, conspiring to keep her from having her children."

"But she's drinking..." Brady interjected.

"Probably," Juliet agreed. "I don't know the answer. I'm not sure there is one." She looked up at him and found him no longer angry with her. "She's desperate, Brady," Juliet added. "I don't have a good feeling about her."

Brady thought about the boys and about the agony Phil had already endured. "I don't have a good feeling about the whole damn thing." He stood up abruptly and walked out of the kitchen.

JULIET AND BRADY didn't discuss Eileen and Phil again. One drizzly Sunday afternoon, nestled in a beanbag chair in front of the fire, Juliet considered asking Brady if Eileen had called Phil or tried to see the boys. But she didn't ask. It would have created discord, and they didn't need that. They were simply too happy just the way they were.

They were not, she noted, making love at the moment. Nor had they been all afternoon. When they first moved into the house, they'd wound up in bed at every available opportunity. But sometimes now, just being close was enough. Juliet had never been able to share her innermost thoughts with anyone, but with Brady, it was easy. She watched the orange flames dance in the fireplace, wondering if Brady ever imagined pictures in the fire the way she did. She thought about asking him, but he was engrossed in a book. Instead, she laid her head on his chest, rubbing her cheek against the scratchy wool of his shirt. She was very content.

Lazily, Brady reached around Juliet and stroked her hair. He liked the quiet times with her. Usually they didn't do much of anything. Sometimes, like now, they didn't even talk. But the silence was comfortable. He supposed that was an outgrowth of living together. A man and woman were bound to grow close when they spent a lot of time under the same roof. Brady laid his book down on the floor beside him.

"Juliet," he whispered. Her eyes were closed, and he didn't want to wake her if she was asleep.

"Mmm." Her head stirred on his chest, and her eyes fluttered open. In the glow from the fire, their brilliant emerald color softened to a subtle jade.

"I've been thinking about Christmas," Brady began. Actually, the subject had been bothering him for several days and he knew he had to deal with it soon.

His mother was expecting him in Boston for the holidays.

"Christmas?" Juliet asked in a sleepy voice. "That's a long time away."

"Less than two weeks," Brady pointed out. "How do you celebrate Christmas?"

Juliet yawned. "No particular way. Last year I went to the ballet and saw *The Nutcracker Suite*. Sometimes I go to Linda's, except this year she and Steve and the kids are going to her parents' Christmas day."

Looking at her curiously, Brady asked, "What about your family? And the presents and the tree and all that?"

Juliet sat up and laughed. "Cass is my only family, and she's gone to Yosemite skiing the last few years. When I was little we had a special dinner and a few presents—but a Christmas tree?" Juliet shook her head. "That was out of the question."

"You've never had a Christmas tree?" Brady hadn't known anyone who celebrated Christmas without a tree.

Juliet wrapped her arms around her knees and looked up at him with a serious expression. "I know this is going to sound strange, but Cass thinks that killing trees to celebrate the season of eternal life is insane. She won't have a Christmas tree in the house."

"Didn't you miss it?"

Juliet shrugged. "How can you miss what you've never had?" Then she grinned at Brady. "But I don't even have to ask you. I'll bet your mother always has an enormous tree and piles of presents and a traditional family dinner with enough food for an army."

"You've got it," Brady answered. "And don't forget my sister, her husband and kids, my Aunt Elinor, her yapping schnauzer, and usually a stray cousin or two.''

Juliet's eyes sparkled. "You make it sound like a lot of fun.''

She paused, and Brady realized he'd just made a major mistake. She was waiting to be invited, but there was no way he could possibly take her to Boston. His family didn't even know they were married. He'd always figured there wasn't any point in bringing it up since the marriage was going to be so brief. But it was awkward not having explained all that to Juliet. "I don't think I'll go to Boston this year, though,'' he said nonchalantly.

Juliet frowned. That didn't sound quite right. "I thought you always went.''

"I do,'' he admitted. "It might be fun to do something different for a change.''

Juliet had talked to enough people about family Christmases to know that tradition ran strong. Brady didn't seem to have any reason at all for not going home. Unless... "Brady, if you're not going to Boston because you don't think I'd want to—''

"Oh, no, nothing like that,'' he cut her off. "There's a lot of noise and confusion....'' That didn't sound very convincing, he realized. He held his breath, hoping Juliet would make an alternative suggestion which meant she'd accepted his explanation. But she didn't say anything. The silence deepened. He shot a sidelong glance at her, and saw she was staring into the fire. He had the distinct impression she didn't believe him, and if she'd say so, he could at least defend himself. Brady picked up his book, but he couldn't focus on the page. He felt rotten. He was lying to Juliet and it hurt her.

"This is no good, Juliet," he muttered. "It's time I told you the truth."

Apprehensive, Juliet watched him. But she didn't say anything.

"We can't go to Boston for Christmas because my family doesn't know we're married," he announced flatly.

Juliet dropped her eyes. After thinking about his flimsy excuses, she'd suspected as much. "I see," she responded quietly.

Brady stood up and shoved his hands into his pockets. "It seemed easier not to tell them under the circumstances," he continued. "Except now...now I wish I had." He knelt down beside Juliet, taking both her hands in his. "Things have changed between us, Juliet. It's not like it was at the beginning."

Juliet met his eyes, not needing any more explanation. She'd felt them growing closer, just as he had. Sometimes, when she woke up early and lay beside him, she wondered what it would be like if they were really married, whether anything would change.

"Do you ever think about the future?" Brady asked her.

"Not very often anymore," Juliet answered truthfully. The future used to be almost all she thought about—the time after she got pregnant and then had the baby. But that had changed, too. "I guess I've been too caught up in the present," she continued slowly. "I don't think I'm ready to look ahead right now."

Gently, Brady touched her cheek. He understood, and he was willing to wait.

"If you want to go to Boston for Christmas—" Juliet started to suggest.

"We can both go to Boston," Brady interrupted, "but it may be awkward. Instead let's stay here together, and we'll create our own traditions."

"I'd like that, Brady," Juliet answered softly. "I'd like that very much." Lying back on the beanbag chair, Juliet reached for him. She sensed a bonding between them that had grown out of the words that were spoken and those that weren't.

Something very special had happened between them that December afternoon, but Juliet mused about it only briefly before Brady's mouth was on hers. She might have suggested they go upstairs, but she didn't. The late afternoon darkness was gathering rapidly, and the only light in the living room came from the glowing embers of the fire. She knew he wanted her, and her whole being was alive with desire for him. They came together quickly and in the fading light their passion burned with a brilliance that left an indelible imprint on them both. They stayed there together long after the fire burned away and the last of the daylight was gone.

FOR THE FIRST TIME since she could remember, Juliet was counting the days until Christmas. Ever since they had decided to stay home together for the holiday, she'd been excited. She'd made a wreath for the front door and had spent an entire Saturday baking cookies. She had to admit you couldn't tell the angels from the stars, but Brady assured her they tasted wonderful and the shape didn't matter.

"Maybe we can give Phil some cookies to take home to Timmy and Michael when he comes tonight for eggnog," Juliet suggested.

"Terrible idea," Brady answered immediately.

Juliet put both hands on her hips. "Now wait just a minute. I thought you liked my cookies."

"That's the problem," Brady admitted, still crunching. "I just ate the last one."

"The last one?" Juliet was outraged. "I baked six dozen only a few days ago. Now what are we going to give Phil with his eggnog?"

Brady kissed her lightly on the tip of her nose. "Slice up some of that vile fruitcake your secretary gave you. Phil says anything is better than his own cooking. Let's call his bluff."

"We can't do that!" Juliet argued. "Maybe I'll bake one of those loaves of cinnamon bread we bought."

"Suit yourself." Brady pulled on his jacket.

"Where are you going?" Juliet asked.

"Out to run a couple of errands," he answered nonchalantly.

"Good." Juliet started for the closet. "I'll come with you instead of baking cinnamon bread. I need some sage for tomorrow anyway."

Gently, but firmly, Brady took hold of Juliet's shoulders and stopped her. "I'll get the sage for you. Why don't you stay here and bake?"

"Wait a minute!" Juliet called as he hurried out the kitchen door. "That's not fair." Brady obviously had plans that didn't include her. That was odd, because they'd agreed not to give each other presents, so he couldn't be doing last-minute shopping. She hoped he was going to stick to his word, because she had.

She took a cookbook out of the kitchen drawer and turned to the section on poultry. It was funny—they'd also decided to keep the entire holiday season spon-taneous and just do whatever they felt like doing at the moment. But they seemed to be doing most of the same things everyone else did, including cooking a turkey, which was ridiculous, considering it was for two people. They'd be eating leftovers for a month.

Juliet flipped the pages in the cookbook to the section entitled "Creative Uses of Turkey." Running her finger down the recipes gave her a pretty good idea why Cass didn't ever cook turkeys. She wondered if Eileen was going to fix dinner for Phil and the boys—he'd said she was going to come for Christmas. Phil would probably take care of it himself, Juliet decided. He was actually a pretty good cook.

Her eyes wandered to the refrigerator door which was almost entirely covered with the painting Michael had done of himself for Juliet. His hair was bright yellow and standing straight up on the top of his very round head. He had a big red grin on his face, probably because he was happy about the kite he was flying. In fact, Michael generally seemed like a pretty happy little kid. So did Timmy. Juliet wondered how it would affect them if their mother ever moved back into the house.

A heavy pounding on the front door interrupted her thoughts. "Hey, Juliet," Brady shouted. "Come open the door for me."

Juliet didn't rush. "What happened to your key?" she asked as she pulled open the heavy oak door.

Brady's face was red, and beads of perspiration stood out on his forehead. "Couldn't get to it." He gasped for breath between the words.

"Are you all right?" Juliet stepped out on the porch.

"Don't come out here," Brady warned sharply, and Juliet immediately retreated. "I'm fine. Just prop the door open, and go wait in the living room."

"Are you sure?" Juliet questioned. He didn't look fine, leaning against the door frame in a definitely unnatural position. But he didn't look sick, either.

"I'm positive," Brady panted. "And close your eyes when you get there."

*Aha,* thought Juliet, *he's playing a game.* She had no idea what it was, but she was willing to go along. Walking to the exact center of the living room, she closed her eyes and listened carefully. Whatever he was doing, he was making a lot of noise, thumping and bumping and dragging something in the hallway. "Brady," she called out, "be careful of the new wallpaper." There was no answer, only more bumping. As the sound came closer, a pungent fragrance filled the room. It was very familiar, something like—no, exactly like pine.

Cautiously, Juliet opened her eyes. There, in front of the bay window stood the most beautiful evergreen tree she'd ever seen. "A Christmas tree," she breathed. "You got me a Christmas tree!" She stood absolutely motionless in front of the tree, just staring at it.

"Yep," Brady said proudly. "That's exactly what I did, and it's not dead, either." He patted the burlap-covered dirt ball around the roots of the tree and grinned. "I remembered what you said about Cass not wanting to kill a tree to celebrate the season of life. She may be a little eccentric, but some of her ideas aren't all that bad."

He looked expectantly at Juliet. She hadn't said a word, and she still hadn't moved, except to cover her mouth with her hands. That wasn't exactly the reaction he'd expected from her. Maybe she really didn't like Christmas trees. "Juliet?" he said apprehensively. "It's all right to have a tree, isn't it? It's alive, and we can plant it in the backyard after Christmas."

Juliet never took her eyes off the tree. She couldn't believe Brady had thought of getting her a live Christmas tree. All at once she threw her arms around him. "It's perfect," she whispered, burying her face in his neck, "absolutely perfect. I've never had such a wonderful present."

"You're sure?"

She hugged him tightly. "Oh, yes, Brady, thank you."

Brady heaved a great sigh of relief. She liked it. That was all he cared about. He wanted to get her something special for a present, something she would never dream of getting, and he'd done it. He kissed her tousled hair and held her close. "Next comes my favorite part," he told her. "We get to decorate it."

Juliet looked up at him in amazement. "Did you buy ornaments, too?"

Brady let go of her and went out into the hall. He returned carrying three large boxes. "I only have lights," he answered. "We'll have to use our imagination for the ornaments." He opened the first box and, while Juliet watched, he clipped dozens of tiny white electric candles to the branches. "They are imported from Germany," he explained. "I thought you should have very special lights for your first Christmas tree."

"Then you've been planning this!" Juliet exclaimed.

"I guess you could say that," Brady admitted. He finished clipping on the last string of lights and plugged them in, bathing the whole room in a mellow glow.

Juliet was enchanted. "It's lovely, Brady," she told him. Her eyes swept up the perfect symmetry of the tree. Now all it needed was ornaments. "I know!" Her voice was full of excitement. "We can put a star on top and some little red birds nesting in the branches." She disappeared into the hall closet and returned dragging a carton of art supplies Cass had given her to keep Michael and Timmy busy when they came to visit.

"I'm sure there's some silver paper in here somewhere," she muttered to herself as she dug around in the box. "Here it is," she called out triumphantly. Within moments she had cut and folded a multipointed star which Brady attached to the very top of the tree.

Next, she found some origami paper and spent a considerable amount of time trying to teach Brady to fold the delicate Japanese animals. "That's not bad," she said when he pulled his bird's tail to make the wings flap. She finished her pink turtle, strung some translucent fishing line through it, and hung it on the tree.

"These origami animals are for graduate students in fine arts," Brady grumbled good-naturedly. "I'm going back to the kindergarten level where it's easy." Before long, he had constructed a chain of thin strips of gold paper and looped it around the tree. "Not bad, at all," he remarked, as much to himself as to Juliet. "But next year we're going to—"

Brady stopped in mid-sentence. There might not be a next year for them. He kept forgetting that. The only thing that was certain was now, this moment.

A heavy silence settled in the room. Juliet had heard Brady and noticed the meaningful pause, but it was easier to pretend she hadn't. She picked up the last scraps of paper from the floor and dropped the scissors into the carton. She didn't want to think about next year. She stood up, her eyes resting on the shimmering Christmas tree. She'd wanted a baby by next Christmas, but now... She wasn't sure anymore that a baby would make her life complete.

"Why don't you build a fire before Phil comes, and I'll go put some cinnamon bread in the oven," she said to Brady. It was as good an excuse as any to escape the thoughts of the future. All she wanted was to go ahead with this Christmas, right now, just the way it was.

# CHAPTER ELEVEN

EILEEN GENTRY HAD been driving aimlessly for hours, thinking about why she was alone on Christmas Eve. The car was dark and quiet. There was nothing on the radio but Christmas carols. She'd turned it off right in the middle of Perry Como singing ''I'll Be Home for Christmas.'' She used to love that song. This year it was depressing.

Home. That's where she should be. At home with Phil and the boys helping them hang the stockings and fix a plate of cookies for Santa Claus. But she wasn't. She was all alone, driving around in her car. And it was rotten.

She drove past a bar, watching its pink neon light flash on and off, and thought about stopping for a drink. A bar was always a good place to find someone to talk to, especially tonight. There would probably be a spillover from office parties, people who wanted to do a little more celebrating. She glanced at the bottle of wine in the brown paper bag next to her on the seat and decided not to bother. Instead, she turned her car south and headed down the coast.

When Eileen swung onto the beach road, she wasn't sure what her intentions were. All the homes along the road glowed with the warmth of Christmas. Tree lights sparkled in every window, and she could see people inside, some still decorating their trees. In almost every home there were children.

Eileen stopped the car alongside the curb down the street from her house. Like the others, it had a sparkling Christmas tree in the window. She could see Michael inside, already in his pajamas, sitting next to Phil on the couch. She watched as Timmy appeared, dragging his blanket, and climbed up on Phil's lap. An ample woman was hovering in the background, probably Mrs. Campanelli from down the street. Eileen wondered if she'd come in just to be with the boys on Christmas Eve or if Phil was planning to go out somewhere.

Eileen reached for the bottle of wine and unscrewed the plastic top. One thing about cheap wine. It was easy to open. She should be in the living room with the boys. They were hers, and another woman was taking care of them. She took several swallows of wine, savoring the warm, almost burning sensation in her throat, and continued watching the scene before her.

Phil was reading to the boys now from a big, flat book. There was a catch in Eileen's throat and she drank some wine to get rid of it. She knew what Phil was reading. It was "The Night before Christmas." He read it every year, even the first year they were married, before there were any babies. It was a custom in his family. She could imagine his deep, resonant voice, but she ached to really hear it.

The wine was nearly gone. Phil had finished the story and Eileen watched him kiss her babies good night and send them off with Mrs. Campanelli. Eileen felt the first flickers of anger. She wanted to be the one to hold them close and kiss them good night. They were hers. That was her right.

She finished the last drops of wine. Phil had his coat on now and was checking for his keys, the way he always did before he went out. She watched him hurry down the stairs and drive away in his car. Eileen clutched the steering wheel until the taillights of Phil's car disappeared around the curve at the end of the street. The anger inside her grew. He had no right to keep her away from her babies. It was her house, too. She fumbled in her purse for the key to the back door, the one nobody knew she had.

Unsteadily she approached the house and walked to the back. She'd thank Mrs. Campanelli and send her on her way. Then there would be no one to keep her from her babies. Popping a mint in her mouth, Eileen turned her key in the lock and the door opened easily. Silently she slipped inside.

PHIL PARKED HIS CAR and climbed the steps to the porch of Brady and Juliet's house. Even as his hand reached for the doorbell, he had reservations about being there at all. It was a long-standing tradition, having eggnog together on Christmas Eve. But it had always been Brady who came to his house, bringing the toys he'd kept for Phil from the time Michael got old enough to dig through the closets. This year Brady had been adamant about his coming to see their tree, wanting him to share Christmas Eve with them.

Phil hadn't minded, except he wished Mrs. Campanelli had told him earlier that she was going to midnight mass. He checked his watch. He couldn't stay very long. He'd promised her he'd be back home by ten-thirty.

"Merry Christmas," Brady greeted him, opening the door. A wide arc of light beckoned Phil inside. Christmas music played softly in the background and the smell of something baking wafted out of the kitchen.

Juliet gave him an exuberant hug. "Come in and see our tree," she urged, leading the way into the living room. "We just finished decorating it."

An aching loneliness swept through Phil when he looked at the tree sitting proudly in the front bay window, its limbs cradling homemade ornaments and twinkling with tiny lights. Phil knew it wasn't only the tree itself that made him feel wistful, but also the love and sharing that had created it. Objectively it wasn't nearly so impressive as his huge tree with its ten-year accumulation of ornaments, but there was a different feeling about this one. "You did this?" he asked.

"Yep." Phil could hear the pride in Brady's voice. "All tonight."

"It's really beautiful." Phil coughed to get rid of the catch in his voice. "I'd say you two make a pretty good team."

Smiling, Brady handed him a glass of eggnog with a touch of rum, and gestured toward the beanbag chair next to a small table where Juliet had placed a plate of hot cinnamon bread. He wanted to tell Phil what was happening, how he felt about Juliet now. But he hadn't even really told her, and he wasn't sure it was quite time. Instead he asked, "Are the boys asleep?"

"Probably, by now. Mrs. Campanelli is very firm," Phil replied, sitting down. "We read 'The Night before Christmas' three times, and I issued the warning about Santa stopping only at houses with sleeping children." He sipped his eggnog and took a piece of bread. "I can't stay long," he added. "Mrs. Campanelli wants to leave at ten-thirty for mass."

Juliet listened with an odd sense of longing. Cass had already explained to her about Santa Claus when she was Timmy's age. "I'll bet they're really excited—we've got the toys all ready and Brady added a few more."

"All of which Juliet wrapped," Brady added, squeezing her hand.

"Thanks ... to both of you," Phil told them gratefully. He took another drink of eggnog. It made no sense, but he felt uncomfortable, as though he shouldn't be there. Maybe it was because he knew too much about Brady and Juliet. He could see what was happening. Without expecting to, without wanting to, they were creating a marriage. A real marriage.

Brady turned over the cassette tape in the portable tape deck and Bing Crosby's voice, smooth as honey, crooned "White Christmas." "Is Eileen still coming tomorrow?" he inquired.

Phil shifted in his chair. "As far as I know. She told me on the phone that she had presents for the boys. Timmy is really happy about it. Michael isn't so sure." He hesitated, wanting to stop and yet needing to talk about it. "Michael says he wants her to come back when she isn't going to leave again."

"That's a tough one," Brady sympathized. "There's not much you can say to him. He's too young to understand."

It wasn't just Michael who didn't understand, Phil thought, staring into the fire. "I've been thinking about it a lot lately," he told Brady. "For a while I thought I wanted to talk to her, maybe try it again, but

I can't handle the drinking anymore. It's too hard on the kids, on all of us."

They lapsed into silence, with only the crackling of the flames punctuating the soft Christmas music from the tape deck. Juliet wished she knew some way to help ease Phil's pain. At least he recognized the folly of starting over again. The sooner he and Eileen could make a clean break, the better off they'd all be.

"How about some more eggnog?" Brady offered, picking up the pitcher.

Phil stood up. "No thanks," he declined. "I have the feeling I need to go home."

Brady and Juliet helped him carry sacks of brightly wrapped packages until the trunk and the back seat of the car were overflowing. Phil said goodbye quickly. He was in a hurry to be home.

When he arrived there, the outside lights were blazing but the front window was dark. He wondered why Mrs. Campanelli had turned off the tree. He grabbed one sack of presents and found his house key to unlock the front door. Dropping the sack on the hall bench, he called to Mrs. Campanelli.

There was no answer. He checked his watch. Ten thirty-eight. He was late, but not that late. Irritated, he called her name again. He knew she was anxious to get to mass before the church got crowded, but to leave the boys alone...

He tiptoed noiselessly up the carpeted stairs. Everything was quiet, and their bedrooms were dark. He peeked inside cautiously, smiling when he saw the familiar lumps under the blankets. They slept in some of the strangest positions. He wanted to go in and kiss them good night, but children slept so lightly on Christmas Eve. He was afraid he would wake them, and then it might be an hour or more before it would be safe to put the presents under the tree.

He hesitated a moment more and then tiptoed back downstairs. Things seemed to be all right, but he still couldn't understand Mrs. Campanelli leaving Michael and Timmy alone. Flipping on the Christmas tree lights as he passed through the living room, Phil walked to the car to get the rest of the presents. They were all wrapped but Timmy's rocking horse and the dirt bike for Michael. He arranged the presents carefully around the tree, and then stood back to admire his work. His eyes traveled upward to the star that glowed softly at the top of the tree. He and Eileen had bought that star the first year they were married. It had been outlandishly expensive, but she had fallen in love with it. They would keep it forever, she'd said, and a hundred Christmases down the road it would still be shining for their children's children.

Phil felt sudden rage. He wanted to tear down that star and smash it in a million pieces, the same way she had smashed his life. He stood perfectly still, his jaw clenched, his hands in tight fists. The fury passed, and he turned off the lights. It was a long time before he slept that night. He tossed restlessly, kicking off the blanket and then pulling it back again, slipping in and out of an uneasy sleep. Christmas was a hell of a time to have to celebrate by yourself, he thought bitterly.

Sunlight was streaming in the bedroom window when Phil awoke. He lay quiet, listening. An eerie silence filled the house. He checked the clock on his nightstand. Nine o'clock. Michael was always up at dawn on Christmas. The routine was the same every year. He'd peek downstairs and then come racing in and bounce on the end of the bed, yelling that Santa had really come. Phil shoved his feet into his slippers with an odd sense of urgency. Halfway down the stairs he leaned over the railing. The presents hadn't been touched.

He opened the door to Michael's bedroom and saw the lumps still under the covers, but in the bright morning light the bed didn't look right. Fear gripped him, and he crossed the room in two strides and tore back the blankets. Except for wadded up pillows, the bed was empty. Phil froze, his palms clammy, his breath coming in short, hard spurts. "Michael," he shouted, "Michael where are you?"

With a sick feeling in his stomach, he raced into Timmy's room. Before he even touched the bed covers, he knew. He sank to his knees beside the bed, his face in his hands, dry sobs wracking his body. "My God," he whispered into the silence. "They're gone."

He had to think. He had to do something immediately. He dropped his face into the crook of his arm and lay against the bed, paralyzed with fear. They'd been gone for hours. But where? And why? He lifted his head and something cold and hard raked against his cheek. He tried to pick it up but it was hooked under the blanket. Frowning, he looked at it more carefully. It was the bracelet, the gold bracelet he'd given Eileen when Timmy was born. Then he knew. The fear mixed with a helpless rage. Eileen had taken the boys.

Phil raced downstairs and snatched the telephone receiver, hurriedly running his finger down the list of numbers by the kitchen phone until he found Mrs. Campanelli's name. The phone rang three times and then four. "Answer it, dammit," he muttered. When she came on the line, he could barely hear her over the excited shouts of children in the background. "It's

Phil Gentry," he said, trying to fight the note of panic in his voice.

"Merry Christmas! And to the boys, too," she exclaimed joyfully.

"Mrs. Campanelli." Phil's voice was grim. "Were Timmy and Michael all right when you left?"

There was a pause and more shouting in the background, and then Mrs. Campanelli's voice yelling for everyone to be quiet. "They were sound asleep," Mrs. Campanelli told him. "Mrs. Gentry came in just before I left and said she was going to be with you for Christmas. Mr. Gentry, is something wrong?"

He wanted to shout at her. How could she have been such a fool? But he realized it wasn't her fault. She couldn't possibly have known. "I'm sure everything is all right." Phil forced himself to be calm. "Mrs. Gentry has apparently taken the boys out for a little while."

"Oh, Mr. Gentry—"

The noise level in the background was building again, but he could hear the concern in her voice. He didn't need her showing up with half a dozen relatives and lots of advice. "You go back to your Christmas, Mrs. Campanelli." He tried to sound cheerful. "I'm sure everything will be just fine."

Phil hung up the phone, trying to decide what to do next. At least he knew where Michael and Timmy were. Actually, he didn't know at all. He knew who they were with, but Eileen had refused to tell him where she lived and she didn't have a telephone.

He started to dial the police emergency number and then put down the phone. That wasn't going to work. Eileen was their mother. And even if he could persuade some sympathetic cop that the children might be in danger, it still probably wasn't the answer. At least not yet.

He stared through the archway at the Christmas tree, still surrounded by mounds of presents. The bicycle, all glistening chrome and knobby tires, stood to one side, blatantly alone and unused. Michael had wanted it more than anything. He had talked about that particular bike for weeks, persuading Phil to detour past the sports store every time they were in the neighborhood so he could look at it again. What had Eileen told Michael when he woke up this morning? That Santa Claus had forgotten?

Phil felt sick to his stomach. In desperation, he dialed Brady's number. His friend's sleepy voice answered.

"Brady, wake up!" Phil commanded. "She took them. Eileen took the boys."

Brady sat bolt upright in bed, jarring Juliet out of a sound sleep. "When?"

"Last night, after Mrs. Campanelli left. I didn't know they were gone till this morning."

Brady let out a long, slow breath. "Jesus Christ," he muttered. "We'll be right there."

Juliet grabbed his arm. "What's happened, Brady?" When he told her, she closed her eyes, bombarded by images of Michael and Timmy, their faces open and innocent, of Eileen driven by loneliness and frustration, and of Phil who must be frantic with worry and guilt. "Has he called the police?" she asked Brady, who was already pulling on his jeans.

"I don't know. I just told him we'd come."

Juliet dressed quickly and then fumbled through her purse, which was hanging on the doorknob. "The police won't help anyway," she muttered. She found

Linda Burke's unlisted number and picked up the phone. "The police would tell Phil to sit tight and see what happens. After all, Eileen's their mother and there's been no court action."

"What are you doing?" Brady asked as she dialed the number.

"Calling Linda Burke. Eileen talked to her once. I doubt that she knows anything, but just in case..."

When Linda answered with a cheery "Merry Christmas," Juliet told her briefly what had happened. The only thing Linda could remember was Eileen saying she wanted her boys more than anything in the world and she'd do anything to have them. At the time Linda had assumed she was referring to her efforts to quit drinking. Later she'd wondered briefly if the woman had meant something else, and then she had forgotten all about it.

Juliet thanked her and wished her a Merry Christmas. She hung up the phone slowly. Eileen had made virtually the same threat to her. She wished all of them had paid more attention to the warning signs.

"Linda doesn't have any information that will help," Juliet told Brady. "I knew Eileen was desperate," she added, "but I never expected anything like this."

"Nobody did." Brady tied his shoes, his mouth set in a firm, straight line.

Juliet grabbed her coat and followed him down the stairs. The only thing left to do was go to Phil and wait with him. On Christmas Day, there weren't any other options.

## CHAPTER TWELVE

MICHAEL WASN'T SURE where he was at first. He stared at the patterns in the cracked plaster ceiling. Without moving his head, he could tell that Timmy was beside him, wadded up in a ball around his blanket. There didn't seem to be anyone else around. Tentatively, he raised up slightly, his hands clutching a rough green blanket against his chin. The room was old and kind of dirty. It had a window, but there was nothing except a brick wall on the other side. He was sure he'd never been there before.

Timmy stirred beside him. "Did Santa Claus come?" He rubbed his eyes sleepily.

"I don't know," Michael answered, his voice barely more than a whisper.

"Isn't it Christmas?" Timmy looked around. His eyes widened and he clutched his blanket. "Where are we?"

"I think we're at Mommy's," Michael answered. Feeling braver, he sat up all the way. "She came last night, remember?"

"No she didn't," Timmy asserted. "She's coming today. Santa Claus was supposed to come last night."

"No, stupid. You were asleep, and she was carrying you. I don't think Santa Claus came, because there wasn't anything under the tree. You probably don't remember."

Timmy put his thumb in his mouth. "I don't like this place," he announced.

Neither did Michael, and he was the oldest so it was up to him to figure out what to do about it. "Come on," he said. "We're going to phone Daddy." He grabbed Timmy's free hand and led him down a short, dark hallway into a tiny kitchen barely big enough for the two of them to stand between the sink and the refrigerator. He didn't see a phone anywhere, but there was a door at the end of the kitchen. Still barefoot, they tiptoed out onto a wooden porch with stairs leading up to the floors above them and down to the alley below.

"I don't think there's a phone out here," Timmy said, shivering in the cold air.

"No, I guess not," Michael agreed, peering through the broken slats of the railing. The porch smelled bad from all the garbage spilling out of the old, rusty can. He chipped at the peeling paint with his thumbnail. "Let's go back inside, Timmy. We really need to call Daddy."

Michael led his brother back through the kitchen and past the bedroom where they'd slept. Moving cautiously, they approached an open doorway a few steps farther on. "There's Mommy," Timmy announced, pointing to the woman lying on a lumpy flowered couch. "She's still sleeping."

"Sh-h-h." Michael put his hand over his brother's mouth. Their mother didn't move. He stared at the empty bottle on the table beside her. He could remember her at night sometimes when she used to be at home, sleeping so he couldn't wake her up. His father had told him once it was because she drank too much.

"Santa Claus didn't come here," Timmy whispered. "I want to go home."

Michael looked around for a telephone, but there wasn't one. He turned toward his brother. "Why don't you see if you can wake up Mom?" he suggested.

Timmy looked terrified. "What if she gets mad?"

That was the same thing that had been worrying Michael. "She won't get mad if you wake her," he assured Timmy. "I'll give you a jawbreaker when we get home if you do it."

"Give me two," Timmy negotiated.

"Okay, two," Michael agreed grudgingly.

Timmy tiptoed hesitantly toward the sleeping form. "Mommy," he whispered. "Mommy." He put his hand on her shoulder and shook gently. She groaned and he jumped back.

"Three jawbreakers," Michael promised.

Timmy tried again. This time his mother opened her eyes and stared at him with a dazed expression. "Timmy! What are you doing here?"

Confused, Timmy blurted out, "But Michael said you brought us here."

Eileen rubbed the palms of her hands hard against her temples to dull the throbbing. "That's right, I did bring you home with me." It was Christmas and her babies were going to spend Christmas with her.

She looked at them standing there, shivering in their thin pajamas. They looked alone and frightened, like she was, and they didn't look much like babies any more. "We can spend Christmas together." She tried to sound reassuring, but her head was pounding and nothing was very clear.

Michael studied his mother carefully. She was still wearing her clothes, the same ones she'd had on the

night before when she came to their house. She had
black smudges under her eyes. Michael wasn't sure
what to say to her, so he didn't say anything. His
mother sat up and smiled, but it was a funny, crooked
smile.

"Did you guys just wake up?"

Timmy looked helplessly at his brother.

"Yes," Michael said firmly.

"Then, if you'll wait just a minute..." Eileen stood
up unsteadily and walked to the bathroom, closing the
door behind her.

Timmy looked at Michael, his eyes wide with fright.
"She's not going to take us home. She said we have to
stay here and spend Christmas. I want to go home."

"Daddy will know what to do," Michael said, still
looking around for a phone. "Maybe there's a telephone outside." he crossed the room to the front door
and turned the knob as quietly as he could.

Timmy scurried up behind him. "I'm coming, too."
They leaned out the open doorway, and saw a long,
dark hallway dotted with doors. Timmy jerked back.
"But I'm not going out there." He grabbed the bottom of Michael's pajama shirt and pulled his brother
back inside. Michael quickly closed and latched the
door.

"Then we're going to have to figure something else
out," Michael told him, "because we can't stay here.
You tell her we want to go home and I'll give you the
whole bag of jawbreakers. Deal?"

Before Timmy could answer, the bathroom door
opened, startling them both. "You must be hungry,"
Eileen said, feeling more in control of herself. "I think
I have some orange juice." She led the way to the
kitchen and both boys reluctantly followed, watching

as she took a pitcher of orange juice from the nearly empty refrigerator. She poured three glasses and handed one to each boy before she opened the cabinet and reached for the bottle of vodka.

Her hand gripping the neck of the bottle, she stopped and looked at the boys. They were holding their glasses, watching her. Methodically, she unscrewed the cap from the bottle. Then she looked at the boys again. A drink would make her feel so much better. Turning away from them, Eileen wrapped her fingers around the edge of the kitchen counter and closed her eyes. She'd promised to stop drinking a hundred times, but this was different. This time it wasn't for her. It was for them, because she loved them—and because she didn't want to lose them.

With a shaking hand, Eileen poured the liquor down the sink, holding the bottle upside down until the last drops were gone. Then she threw the empty bottle into the trash. It was one of the hardest things she'd ever done. Both boys' eyes were wide, but for a long minute neither of them said a word.

Hesitantly, Timmy broke the silence. "Mommy?"

Eileen turned around.

"We want to go home." Timmy wasn't looking at her. "Michael said he'd give me a whole bag of jawbreakers if I told you."

"I did not," Michael protested.

"Yes, you did. You said—"

"Is it true that you want to go home, too, Michael?" Eileen questioned.

Michael stared at his feet.

"I want to," Timmy piped up, "because Santa Claus didn't come here."

"No," Eileen admitted, "but I have presents for you—"

"You're not Santa Claus," Timmy interrupted.

"But I'm your mother," Eileen said gently, "and I love you very much, and I'd like to spend Christmas with you just like we used to."

Michael looked up, his eyes full of hostility. "If you want to be with us so much then why don't you come home and live there like you used to?"

Eileen could feel the anger pouring out from deep inside him. "I . . . I can't right now, Michael—"

"Then it's not fair to take us away and make us come here. You don't love us, or you wouldn't do that." Michael turned his back to her and stood perfectly straight, staring at the wall.

She looked down at Timmy. "Please take us back to Daddy," he whimpered, large tears rolling down his cheeks.

"But I'd hoped . . ." she began to explain, and then she stopped because she could see it was another dream gone wrong. They weren't babies any more. She couldn't just take them and have them like she did when they were little. She looked back at Timmy's tear-streaked face. He was standing there crying for his daddy and there was nothing she could say. And Michael. She walked over to him and put her hand on his shoulder but he jerked out of her grasp. She wanted to tell him not to hate her, that she couldn't help what had happened. But there was no way to make him understand.

"I guess," she said slowly, "if you both want to go home, that's what we need to do. We can see if Santa Claus came."

Timmy brightened substantially, but Michael didn't turn around. "Does that make you happy, Michael?" Eileen asked him. She thought about the vodka. She was glad she had poured it out.

"I guess," Michael answered grudgingly. "Are you going to stay?"

Eileen hadn't thought about that. She had been supposed to spend Christmas with them. "Do you want me to?" she asked Michael.

Slowly, he turned around. "I guess," he said.

Eileen looked down at her wrinkled skirt and the blouse she'd worn for two days. She couldn't go looking so disheveled. She wanted to look nice, nice like she used to look when she had a whole closet full of clothes and could shop at any store. There was one dress, the green one, that she'd kept hidden away. It would be all right. She didn't have the necklace that went with it anymore. She'd sold that. But she did have the pair of plain gold earrings and the bracelet— she looked down at her wrist. She always wore the bracelet, but it was gone, too. So much was gone.

Eileen opened a door to one of the lower cabinets which was empty except for two brightly wrapped packages. "You can open your presents now, and then I'll go get ready." She handed one package to each boy.

Timmy's face broke into a wide grin. Michael remained more skeptical. She watched them untie the ribbons with a queasy feeling in her stomach. She had bought the presents at the dime store a week ago, one night when she was working and got a lot of tips. She'd been really excited at the time and had come home the same night and carefully wrapped each box. But now she wasn't even sure the boys would like the things she'd bought them. She barely knew them any-more.

Timmy ripped into the paper with a vengeance, and his present was open in seconds. He took out the brightly painted metal box inside and looked at it cur-iously. Finding the small handle on the side, he turned it, and the box played "London Bridge Is Falling Down." The faster he turned, the faster the music played. All of a sudden the top popped open and a grinning clown head popped out with a bang. "Yikes!" yelled Timmy, jumping backward. Even Michael laughed.

"Let me try," Michael demanded, reaching for the jack-in-the-box.

"Open your own," Timmy retorted, hugging the present to him.

Michael jerked at the ribbon he had been meticu-lously untying and opened the box. Inside was a min-iature fort and a bag filled with tiny plastic figures of soldiers, Indians, and horses. "Wow!" he exclaimed, and for the first time since Eileen could remember, she saw the light in his eyes that had once brought her such joy. He ripped open the bag and dumped the figures in a heap in front of him. "This is neat. I never saw one of these."

Timmy stopped cranking. "Lemme see." He leaned over Michael.

"Go play with you own toy." Michael covered the figures protectively with his hands. "This is mine. Mommy gave it to *me*."

With tears in her eyes, Eileen knelt down behind the boys, putting one arm around each of them. "Merry Christmas," she whispered.

Both boys looked up at her, and for just a moment Timmy rested his head against her shoulder.

"Merry Christmas, Mommy," Michael said quietly. He didn't pull away.

Joy flooded Eileen, sweeping through her to fill the emptiness. How long she'd waited for this moment. Her babies, her boys, were with her, and a halo of happiness surrounded them all. She'd missed them so desperately, and she wanted to be with them so much. "Do you two think you could share your toys for just a few minutes while I change my clothes?" she asked as she stood up.

The brothers glared at each other. "I guess," Michael said.

Eileen took a quick shower, humming all the while. She wished she had dusting powder or perfume, but there wasn't any. She rubbed the bathroom mirror with her towel to wipe away the steam and then brushed her hair hard until it seemed to take on a new luster. She wanted to look her very best today. The green dress was loose when she zipped it, and she pulled the belt a notch tighter than usual to gather it in at her waist. She was relieved to find the dress was long enough to cover the run in her only pair of pantyhose. Wishing she had a full-length mirror, she studied her image again in the small mirror in the bathroom. She didn't look perfect, Eileen decided, brushing her hair one more time, but it was the best she could do.

"Mommy you look different," Michael observed, when she reappeared in the kitchen where the boys were apparently waging war with Michael's new fort.

"Yeah, you look pretty," Timmy seconded.

It wasn't just their words, but the way they looked at her that filled Eileen with a new kind of courage. She'd lost so much, but maybe all of it wasn't gone forever. "How about calling a temporary truce and putting all your men into the fort?" she suggested. "We're going to..." She paused, and then she said simply, "We're going home."

The boys followed her down to the car, each with a blanket wrapped around his shoulders and his present clutched in his hand. Eileen shook her head. It had been stupid to bring them without clothes or even shoes. She hadn't been thinking. For a long time she hadn't been thinking. It was time she started.

She buckled Timmy firmly in the front seat beside her, and let Michael get in the back where he promptly began to set up his fort. The street was empty. Everyone was inside, celebrating Christmas. She considered calling Phil to let him know they were coming. He was probably worried. But the phone she usually used was in the bar down the street, and she didn't want to go in there this morning.

"Do you think Santa Claus has really come to our house?" Timmy asked as they started out.

"It won't be long till we find out," Eileen promised, knowing that he had indeed come. Phil would have seen to that, just like he'd always taken care of everything. Maybe that was part of the problem, she realized suddenly. She'd always seemed so unnecessary. Nothing she did was ever very important.

"I hope he brings me a whole lot of neat stuff." Timmy began cranking out "London Bridge."

"What do you want most?" Eileen asked.

"I know what I want," Michael interrupted. "I want this really neat dirt bike. It's silver and blue and it's really fast."

"You don't know it's fast. You just think so," Timmy countered smugly.

"Mommy! My soldier got lost down in the seat!" Michael exclaimed.

Eileen took a quick look over her shoulder. "I'll help you get him as soon as we stop—"

"Mommy!" Timmy shrieked.

Eileen turned her attention back to the road quickly and for an instant she froze in fear. An enormous truck was hurtling backward down the hill ahead. They were directly in its path.

"Stop!" Timmy shrieked again.

Eileen slammed on the brakes and spun the steering wheel. The car lurched to the left. Everything moved in slow motion, the truck bearing down on them, getting bigger and bigger until there was nothing else. Then came the sickening crash. Eileen felt the car begin to spin and from somewhere behind her she heard a long, piercing scream.

THERE WERE QUIET sounds, voices talking, dishes clattering in the distance. And an odd smell, like the school room after the janitor leaves with his bucket and mop. Her head was pounding, an incessant throbbing pain. The voices got louder. She opened her eyes, just a flicker, to find a bright light glaring down at her. Then she heard his voice.

"Eileen? Eileen, can you hear me?"

It was too much effort to answer. She wanted to go away again to somewhere that her head wouldn't hurt so much.

"Eileen? Please answer me, Eileen," the voice repeated.

He was calling to her. He wanted her. She had to answer. Using all her energy, she forced her eyes open, squinting against the brilliant light overhead. "Yes?" she said, her voice barely audible.

The pounding inside her head increased when she turned slightly. A hazy image of Phil's face bending over her came into focus.

"Eileen, are you all right?'

She knew he must be talking because his lips were moving, but his voice sounded hollow and far away. She thought about his question. Why was he asking her that? "I don't know," she murmured.

"Do you remember what happened?" he questioned. "You were in an accident, Eileen, in the car. You and the boys."

It began to come back. They'd been riding in the car, going somewhere, and then— She closed her eyes again, trying to shut out the image of the truck. It kept coming and coming at them and then the noise— Letting out a low moan, she clamped her hands over her ears.

She felt Phil touch her arm and slowly she opened her eyes and moved her hands back down to her sides. She was awake now, and she felt like she might throw up. Suddenly she grabbed Phil's hand and clutched it hard. "The boys," she whispered. "Are the boys all right?"

Phil nodded, squeezing her hand. "Yes," he nodded. "The doctor is checking Michael now, but he seems fine. Timmy has a broken arm and a nasty cut across his forehead. They want to keep him for a few days to make sure it doesn't get infected, but it's not too serious."

"Thank God," she breathed. She looked up at Phil, tears welling up in her eyes. "I didn't mean for it to happen. I didn't mean to hurt them." She could hear him telling her not to take the boys in the car. He'd told her when she was drinking it was so dangerous. Suddenly she had to make him understand. "I didn't have anything to drink, Phil. I didn't—"

He stroked her hand. "It wasn't your fault, Eileen. It was that damn truck. Some idiot didn't set the brakes. You did everything you could. The ambulance driver told me about the tire tracks. He said they were almost at a right angle." His voice broke, but he went on, having difficulty with the words. "When you swerved like that, it saved your lives."

Eileen remembered looking back at Michael and then Timmy's scream and the truck— She shut her eyes. "Oh, Phil, I've made such a mess of everything. All I wanted was for them to be happy," she sobbed softly. "All I wanted—"

"Sh-h-h," he whispered. "I know."

"No," she protested, her voice stronger, "you don't know. You don't know how close I came to taking a drink. I could have killed Timmy and Michael." The tears rolled freely down her cheeks and she didn't try to stop them. Her words came pouring out. "I shouldn't have taken them. I know I shouldn't. I hadn't had anything to drink for so long and then when it was almost Christmas I felt so bad. I saw you leave the house and I wanted my babies more than anything in the world. But then, this morning, I realized they weren't babies any more. They've grown up and I haven't been a part of it."

"Eileen," Phil interrupted her. "Don't do this to yourself. We'll have time to talk when you feel better."

She tried to sit up, but the pain in her head was too intense. "I don't want to wait, Phil. I've already waited too long." Her voice was choked with sobs. "I've lost everything that really mattered. I left because I was so lonely. You were never home anymore, and you didn't care. Nothing I did was right, and then you wanted another baby and I just couldn't do it anymore.... I thought if I went away you'd realize how much you needed me." She closed her eyes against the pain. "Except it didn't work that way."

Phil stared at her, stunned by the barrage of emotion. "I did need you, Eileen," he answered softly. "We all did. We thought you didn't want us anymore."

Her body was still, the crying over. "I guess I didn't, at least not like that. And now you don't want me."

Phil didn't know how to answer her. He remembered the months before she left, the hostility and the screaming rages. They couldn't go through that again. And yet the boys needed a mother. And he needed a wife. There had been too many lonely times. But he wanted the woman he'd married, not the stranger she'd become.

When he didn't answer, Eileen went on, speaking slowly and painfully. "I thought I had the drinking licked. I'd done really well until the last few days. I need help."

Those were the words Phil had hoped to hear for so long, but he wondered now whether it was too late. He reached out and gently took her hand again. "I don't know whether we could make it work again, Eileen."

He paused, thoughtful, tracing the pattern on the back of her hand as he'd done so many times before. "I don't know if there's anything left for us."

She looked up at him and met his eyes, searching with an understanding beyond words. "I don't know either, Phil," she answered.

"Maybe we could try," Phil said softly. He looked toward the window where the sun was slowly sinking toward the horizon, signaling the end to a long midwinter afternoon. "And maybe, when you're better, you could come home to recuperate for a while." He stopped, knowing what he was saying, not knowing if it was right or wrong. "After that, I don't know. We'll just have to take it a little at a time."

Eileen closed her eyes, trying to shut out the intense throbbing in her head. "Let me think about it, Phil."

He took her hand once more and held it gently, but her eyes were still closed and her breathing was slow and regular. He turned and walked quietly out of the room.

Juliet stood up when she saw him approach. "Phil, is she all right?"

"I think so." He sank heavily on a bench, and she sat next to him. It seemed to Juliet as though she'd been waiting to hear about Eileen forever. "She's kind of groggy from the blow on the head, but she seems all right," Phil said. " She's sleeping now."

"At least none of them is badly hurt. From what the police said—" Juliet knew it was better not to go on. The policeman she'd talked to while she was waiting for Phil had bluntly told her it was a miracle they all weren't killed. If the truck had hit the passenger door instead of the rear fender, the car would have been crushed and no one could have survived. "Will she be hospitalized for long?" Juliet asked.

"Probably not." Phil hesitated. "I think she may come home for a while when she's released."

Juliet frowned. "Are you sure that's wise?" She was immediately sorry she'd asked. It was absolutely none of her business and an area she'd been determined to stay out of.

"I don't know whether it's wise or not," Phil answered. "The whole damn thing's tough either way."

*And tougher this way,* Juliet thought. It was a no-win situation. She wished she could believe it would work out for them. But it was more likely that everyone would get hurt again. She'd seen the pattern in families too many times.

"Juliet, look, they gave me a Santa Claus pen!" Michael came bounding from around the corner with Brady close behind.

"I like it . . . does it write?" she asked, as he thrust it at her.

"Two colors at the same time," he answered proudly. He turned toward his father. "Can we go home now?"

Phil patted Michael's shoulder. "In just a few minutes. First, Brady's going to come with me while I take care of some business. Why don't you wait here with Juliet?"

Michael sat down on the bench by Juliet, who produced a memo pad from her purse. "You want to draw with your new pen?" she asked him.

"Yeah, I guess so."

She watched him fashion the shape of a car and then a big truck on top of it. "Is that how you remember the accident?" she asked him.

Michael started to push his hair out of his face and then grimaced with pain when he touched the big purple lump on his forehead. "Sort of." She could still see the fear in his eyes. "This big truck came barreling down the hill and Mom didn't see it at first and then I got down on the floor in the back seat and there was this awful screeching and then a big crash and then we were spinning and spinning." He buried his head in her lap, his whole body trembling.

Juliet's heart went out to him. It had been so awful for him. First his mother took him and then the accident and now the hospital. "At least everybody is all right and you're going home," she soothed him, gently rubbing his back as he lay against her.

"Me and Dad are going home," he corrected her.

"But Timmy will be all right in a few days," she told him. "And then you'll all be together."

There was a long silence. Juliet felt Michael's muscles tighten. "We won't all be together. Not anymore."

"You mean because of your mother?" Juliet asked. "What if she came home, too?"

Michael kept his face buried. "She won't come," he said in a muffled voice. "And even if she did, it wouldn't matter, because she'd just go away again," he added bitterly. "It would be better if she would just leave us alone." His whole body shook. Juliet could tell he was crying.

She held him for a long time, hurting for him, hating what was happening to him. She would never let this happen to a child of hers, she vowed silently. This was the fallout from ruined marriages. People weren't satisfied with destroying each other. They had to take the children along, too. Michael was right.

Better one parent you could count on than two to tear you apart.

When Phil and Brady appeared, Michael sat up quickly and rubbed his face on his sleeve. "You ready?" Phil asked him, offering his hand. Wordlessly, Michael took it and followed his father.

"Thanks to both of you—for everything," Phil called to Brady and Juliet as they walked away.

Brady slipped his arm around Juliet's waist. "It's been a long day," he said, pulling her close to him. "Let's go home."

Juliet tensed. She was going to have to talk to him. Now. She'd let herself just go along with him, relaxed her guard, let the walls come down. She'd even pretended sometimes that they might be different, and lately she'd been thinking about what it might be like if they were really married. She kept getting in deeper and deeper with Brady, slowly, one day at a time. And she had to stop it.

All the way home, Juliet stared out the window at the ribbons of house lights running up and down the hills. So many people chasing rainbows with lead weights at the end. The pot of gold was only a fantasy. Brady glanced sideways at her several times but didn't try to get her to talk. She was upset about the accident and maybe she needed some time alone with her thoughts. When they got home, he'd take her to bed, and afterward they'd both feel better. They always did.

## CHAPTER THIRTEEN

BRADY TURNED ON the tree lights as soon as they walked into the house, and the living room took on the soft, warm glow of Christmas. Juliet watched uncomfortably as he tossed his jacket on one of the beanbag chairs and opened the fire screen. She was tired, and she longed to curl up with him in front of the fire. But she couldn't forget Michael's face, the bump on his head, his cheeks streaked from crying, his eyes old beyond his years from carrying the weight of his parents' ruined marriage.

She watched Brady methodically stack the wood, two logs across, three on top, tinder underneath. People didn't start out to hurt their children or each other. Juliet knew that. They started out the way she and Brady were starting out, happy and full of dreams. She should never have let their relationship come this far. And waiting would only make things worse.

The match flared. Brady touched it to the wood curls he'd shaved, and the flames crept steadily along the logs. He watched until the fire built in intensity, and then closed the screen and stood up. It was a small fire, but he didn't expect to stay downstairs very long.

Without a word, he turned to Juliet and took her in his arms, leaning down to nuzzle beneath the auburn hair and kiss the sensitive spot along the side of her neck. She smelled good. It was a natural fragrance

that reminded him of spring mornings. He raised his
lips to playfully kiss her earlobe.

"Brady..." The first stirrings of desire already rip-
pled through Juliet, and she realized again how much
a part of him she'd become. It required a conscious
effort to hold her body away from his. "Brady, I need
to talk to you."

He kissed her behind the ear, smoothing back the
flowing hair. "Fine," he murmured. "Come sit by the
fire." His arm tightened around her, guiding her toward the beanbag chairs.

Juliet stiffened and pulled back. "No, Brady, not
here. Let's go into the kitchen."

"Why the kitchen?" He took a good look at her.
He'd never seen her eyes like that, as dark as tree moss
and full of apprehension. *It must be the accident,* he
decided. It had shaken him, too. "We can talk here."
He sat down in the beanbag chair and held his arms
out to her. "The fire's warm and we can look at the
tree. After all, Juliet, whatever else has happened, this
is still Christmas."

Juliet wavered. It was so hard to say no. He'd become a reservoir of strength for her. But that had to
change, too. "I'd like to go into the kitchen, Brady,"
she said again, without explanation.

Puzzled, he followed her.

She sat down at the table, poised on the edge of the
chair. Brady didn't join her. He walked to the refrigerator and found a carton of eggnog. Then he took
two glasses from the cabinet and poured a drink for
each of them.

Juliet took a deep breath. The sooner she got this
confrontation over with, the better. There wasn't any
gentle approach, at least none she could think of. She

might as well be direct. "Brady, this isn't going to work," she said simply.

He put the eggnog carton back in the refrigerator. "What isn't going to work?" He placed a glass in front of each of them and sat across the table from her. She was beautiful sitting there with her hair loose, still dressed in the bright green sweatshirt and jeans she'd pulled on in such a hurry this morning. He picked up his glass and then paused, holding it toward her. "Before you tell me, let's drink a toast to us—and to better ways to spend Christmas," he added, smiling at her.

Her response was an uncomfortable silence. Juliet's face remained impassive and her eggnog sat untouched on the table. Brady put down his glass. "What's going on, Juliet?"

She lowered her eyes. Now was the time to lay it out, clearly and simply. A clean break was the only answer. "Brady, what's happened between us isn't what I'd expected. I never anticipated getting so involved." She hesitated, waiting for him to affirm what she'd said, or perhaps to discuss how he felt about her. He'd never really told her that, not in so many words. But Brady didn't say anything. She could feel him watching her, and she kept her eyes riveted on the table.

"When we signed the contract," she continued slowly, "it was with the understanding that the marriage was an arrangement for the convenience of the baby." Juliet took a deep breath and lifted her eyes to meet his. "What I'm trying to say, Brady, is that I can't live with you anymore, and it's time we move on with the divorce."

Brady stared at her, trying to figure out what could have caused such a radical change in this woman virtually overnight. Yesterday everything had been fine. Before the accident suddenly complicated everything, he'd planned to talk to her about extending their living arrangement indefinitely. He'd figured that would be easier for her to accept than dealing with the future of the marriage which, of course, would also have been extended indefinitely. Now, suddenly, she was talking about ending it all. His stomach lurched.

"Aren't you going to say anything?" she demanded. She'd expected him to at least answer her.

Brady chose his words carefully. "I don't know what to say. A lot has happened between us, Juliet, or at least I thought it had. It may not be the way we'd planned things, but it's the way they are."

His words hurt her still more, and she didn't know why. "That's my whole point, Brady. This isn't right."

"Why the hell isn't it right?" he demanded. "Aren't you happy?"

Juliet stared at her glass, turning it around and around with her fingertips. "It isn't a question of happy or unhappy. It's a question of the future and what we want." She spoke deliberately. "I told you the first time I met you that I didn't want to get married. I agreed to it—" She stopped. Right now it was a puzzle to her why she'd ever gone along with it. She'd sensed even then that it was a mistake, but somehow she'd managed to persuade herself that it was an innocuous one. "I agreed to it because it wasn't a real marriage. We put in the escape clause—"

"That probably wouldn't hold up in court, you know," Brady interjected.

Juliet managed a wry smile. "I know that. I wasn't sure you did." She looked up at him again, a profound sadness in her eyes. "But does it matter? Would you fight it if I wanted out?"

Then it was Brady who looked away. "Of course not, Juliet. Marriages aren't made in the courts. They're made in people's hearts." He tapped his fingers against the table. The whole damn thing made no sense. "But why, Juliet?" he demanded. "Why?"

Juliet shook her head. His was the hardest question of all. "I've already told you why. You know how I feel about marriage." Her eyes pleaded for understanding. "I'd like to think we're different, but that's what everybody wants to think. I'm sure Phil and Eileen thought they were different. You told me yourself what an ideal couple they seemed to be at first—"

"Juliet!" Brady interrupted. "We're not Eileen and Phil. You're trying to tell me because they have problems, we will, too?"

"It's so many people, Brady, and you're never sure till it happens."

Brady ignored her answer. "Besides," he added, "Phil told me Eileen is going to come home for a while until she's feeling better and they're going to see how it works."

Juliet sighed. "I already know that. But they've got the same problems they always had. And look what they're doing to the boys." Her voice took on a hard edge. "Michael has it all mapped out. He said he didn't care if she came home because she'd just leave again." She paused, remembering how Michael's body trembled as he lay against her. "And then he cried, Brady. He hid his head in my lap and he cried. How many nights do you suppose he's fallen asleep crying like that?"

For several moments, Brady didn't answer. "It has been hard on the boys," he admitted finally, "especially on Michael." He was beginning to understand what had happened, and he felt even more powerless than before. What Juliet was telling him had nothing to do with how she felt about him. She must care, or she wouldn't even have tried to explain.

"Can't you see, Brady?" Juliet appealed to him. "This is all wrong for us."

Brady reached across the table and took her hand. "We got married for some pretty flimsy reasons, Juliet. Sometimes things seem a lot different when you look back at them." He took a deep breath. "But what about us, Juliet? Aren't we a reason to be married?"

"I...I'm sorry, Brady." It was harder to say what she needed to with him holding her hand.

The silence gathered around them, a heavy, uneasy silence. "I can't believe you're ready to throw it all away, Juliet. What you're telling me doesn't make any sense at all."

"I'm sorry." Her voice was almost a whisper. She was afraid to try to say anything more.

Brady watched her. There had to be some way he could reach her. "Will you do one thing for me, Juliet?" he asked. "Will you give it a little time and think about it? You're reacting to what happened today—"

Juliet gave her head a vigorous shake. This was one of the things she had determined at the outset she wouldn't do. It had to be a clean break. "I can't stay here with you any longer, Brady. I don't know what we're going to do about the house. We can try to sell it like this. At least we shouldn't lose any money."

He lifted her hand and cradled it in both of his. "I don't give a damn about the house. And I'm not even asking you to stay here with me. Go to the beach house, if you like. All I want you to do is give it a little time."

"Brady," she argued stubbornly, "I'm not going to change my mind."

"No, you're probably not, certainly not if you go back to your apartment and back to your law practice and shut your eyes to everything else." His voice was firm and steady. "That's not fair, Juliet. It's not fair to you or me. You may not like what's happened between us, but not liking it doesn't make it simply vanish. Whoosh!" His hand streaked through the air.

"I know it doesn't, but—"

"Go to the house at the beach, Juliet. Spend some time alone and think about it."

Juliet couldn't quite decide whether his request was reasonable or simply a ploy that she would regret later. He'd managed to persuade her to do some very uncharacteristic things over the past few months. "I don't know, Brady," she hesitated.

"I promise not to disturb you while you're there, if that's what's bothering you, Juliet. You can stay as long as you like."

It was a tempting offer. Juliet knew realistically that making the break with Brady was going to take a lot of rethinking. This meant there would be no baby, at least in the near future. And all those hazy dreams, that had somehow included Brady, were no more. "I suppose it wouldn't hurt to spend a few days at the beach," Juliet relented.

"Thanks Juliet," he responded softly. A shadow of a smile touched his lips.

"Wait a minute," she stopped him. "All I said was I'd go to the beach house."

"And that's all I asked."

"It's a transition, Brady," she warned. "I'm not going to change my mind."

Brady knew the odds of Juliet reconsidering her decision were no better than fifty-fifty, if that. But any odds were better than none right now. He might as well lay it all on the line. This could be the last chance. "There's something I need to tell you, Juliet, something I've never said, but I guess I thought you knew." He took her hand again and looked directly into her eyes.

She watched apprehensively, afraid of what was coming.

His voice was soft when he spoke. "I love you, Juliet, more than I knew it was possible to love a woman. I told you once why I hadn't married—that the woman had to be my reason for being, my family would be my life."

"Please stop," she cried out. "You're only making this harder."

"No," he replied, his gaze never wavering. "I won't stop, because I want you to hear this. You have to do what you feel in your heart is right, Juliet. But I'm not going to let you deny the truth."

"I'm not denying anything." Her voice rose. "I just don't want to hear it."

"Of course you don't. You are ready to destroy something beautiful because you don't have a crystal ball. There aren't any crystal balls, Juliet. We can't live in the future and we can't live in the past. We have to live right now. That's all there is."

Juliet buried her face in her hands. "Don't do this to me, Brady," she pleaded. "Please don't. Please just let me alone."

He stared at her, wanting to take her in his arms but afraid to touch her. There was nothing he could do now. It was up to her to drive out whatever demons haunted her. Nobody could do it for her, least of all him. If he lost her... he couldn't even bear to think about it. The only thing he could do was wait. "I'll leave you alone, Juliet," he told her quietly. "I already promised I would."

She heard his chair scrape against the bare floor, then the clank of the fireplace doors shutting and the click as he turned off the switch on the Christmas tree lights. The front door opened and closed softly. The deadbolt snapped across and a pervasive silence filled the house. Juliet knew without looking that she was alone, very much alone.

THE WEEK AFTER Christmas was sun-dappled and warm, a perfect week to spend at the beach. Juliet hated it. She'd already made her decision. She wasn't sure why she was there.

For the first two days she got up early, took long walks, ate regular meals, and whiled away the long evenings watching old movies on television. She did very little thinking about anything other than having her apartment redecorated and taking a late spring vacation in the mountains to look at the wildflowers.

There wasn't any hurry about anything, really. She didn't particularly want to be at the beach, but she didn't want to go back to her apartment, either. When she'd called Linda to say she wouldn't be in the office for a few days, her friend had urged her to take as much time as she needed. Knowing how much in favor of marriage Linda was, Juliet had expected a lecture, or at least an opinion. But she didn't get either. "I can't give you any advice on this one," Linda had told her. "I'll listen if you need to talk, but you're the only one who has the answers. Just keep thinking till you figure it out." But Juliet couldn't even decide what she was supposed to think about, and after two days she was as confused as when she'd first arrived.

When her alarm went off on the third day, Juliet rolled over and went back to sleep. She awoke with the sun high in the sky and sleepily reached for Brady. He wasn't there. Suddenly she was wide awake and everything came into sharp focus. He wouldn't be there, not ever again. And God! How she missed him!

Pulling on her jeans and an old sweatshirt, she went into the kitchen to make a pot of coffee. Everything reminded her of Brady. His old running shoes, riddled with holes, were sitting by the back door. Two jackets and an old fishing hat had been slung over the wooden rack on the wall. A pottery mug with a picture of two ducks flying sat near the coffee pot. It was Brady's favorite.

She wandered into the living room with her coffee and sat cross-legged on the floor in front of the window wall to watch the surf. She missed the beanbag chairs, but they were back in the house in San Francisco. She remembered the first time she'd seen them, that night Brady had brought her to the house before they got married. Beanbag chairs had struck her as an odd choice, even for a beach house, when she'd looked at them then. That seemed such a long time ago.

That night had been the first time Brady had made love to her. Except he didn't. He'd wanted her to be ready, too, and so he'd waited, and then he'd shown her things about her body she might never have known. Restless, Juliet stood up and walked back to the kitchen. He'd asked her to think about it, but what was there to think about? You either wanted to be married or you didn't. It was easy to delude yourself and pretend that the path would be smooth and you'd walk off into the sunset together holding hands. With Brady that would be so easy. But she'd seen marriages fail so many times.

Grabbing her jacket, Juliet went outdoors, kicking at the sand as she headed down toward the water. The sanderlings were skipping across the beach in tiny steps, a little society all their own that looked suspiciously like a microcosm of San Francisco pedestrians in rush hour. She watched a gull swoop and dive, then she carefully scanned the horizon. She knew there had been whale sightings along the coast. Of course, it was logical that there would have been. It was the time for them, unlike the day she and Brady had gone looking for whales. But that had been as good an excuse as any to go off together. She thought about that sun-warmed rock high on the grassy knoll, and Brady's hands on her back and then all over her body. Picking up a seashell from the beach, Juliet hurled it with all her strength into the waves and then took off running along the water's edge.

She ran past people walking in the sunshine and skirted around children with buckets and shovels digging deep holes in the sand. Farther along she passed a small shark that had washed up, its carcass picked almost clean by the gulls. She studied it all with extraordinary interest, filling up her mind with sights and sounds and smells of the beach so there was no room for anything else.

Her eyes traveled up to the beach houses nestled into hills covered with ice plant. Phil's house was up there. She wondered if Eileen had gone there after being discharged. She looked upward, and on Phil's deck saw two small figures, men probably, by the way they were standing, leaning over the rail. She stopped to study them more closely, and then the one on the left moved. She knew immediately it was Brady. The slope of the shoulders, the way he turned his head, those common, familiar movements she knew so well. It couldn't be anyone else.

She wanted to wave to him and start running up the hill. And then he would come home with her and they'd fix dinner together. Maybe he'd grill steaks and she'd make a salad like they did sometimes. And then they'd spend the evening reading or taking a walk or maybe he'd show her a toy he was working on. Sometimes she gave him pretty good advice. Juliet turned around and began walking back down the beach past the dead shark and the children with their buckets and shovels. The piercing cry of a gull echoed close behind her, but she didn't turn around.

Through the binoculars, Brady could follow Juliet's every move. He'd seen her hesitate. She'd probably recognized him. Even without the binoculars, he'd have known her. But she hadn't come toward him and he supposed he didn't expect her to. He watched her turn back, making her way slowly along the water's edge. She was lithe and graceful, but there was no spring in her step. She walked heavily, like someone carrying a great burden. Brady kept the glasses trained on her back until she was little more than a wisp of color in the distance.

"Any whales out there?" Phil inquired.

Brady grunted, still studying Juliet.

Phil looked at him curiously. "Hey, there aren't any whales that direction. You pick up a good-looking broad or something?"

"Something like that," Brady muttered, lowering the glasses and handing them to Phil. The days had stretched endlessly since Juliet had left. He'd spent Christmas night in a hotel, sleeping very little, mostly pacing the floor and thinking. When he went back home the next morning, he was still clinging to a shred of hope that she might have changed her mind. But he found the house empty. Most of her things were still there, except her toothbrush was missing from her cup in the bathroom and her pale pink robe was no longer hanging in the closet. He'd assumed she must have taken a few clothes and gone to the beach house, but it made him feel better to actually see her and know for sure she was all right.

"Doesn't seem to be much out there," Phil observed, running the binoculars slowly along the horizon and then moving in to scan the beach. "Looks like Eileen and the boys down that way." He studied them for quite a while. "The kids seem to be building one of their sand forts for her." He lowered the binoculars. "She used to love to build with them."

"Isn't she supposed to stay in bed?" Brady inquired.

"That's what the doctor said, but she seems to feel better. I suppose sitting on the beach won't hurt her."

"Is she drinking?" Brady asked.

Phil shook his head. "Not so far. I dumped all the liquor I had in the house, and she hasn't been able to go out." He laid the binoculars on the table. She talked to somebody from Alcoholics Anonymous yesterday. They said they'd help her, but it's going to be a tough battle."

"Yes, but it's a beginning," Brady said. He leaned on the rail, looking out at the pounding surf. He remembered Juliet's conviction that things would never work out for Phil and Eileen and he hoped she was wrong.

"Have you heard from Juliet?" Phil asked him.

Brady hesitated. It was hard for him to talk about their separation. "I didn't really expect to," he answered. "She needs some time."

"And she's at the beach house? Why don't you walk down and see her?"

Brady shook his head. "I promised not to."

"And it's tough as hell, right?"

"Yeah." Brady left the rail and paced across the deck, drinking in the salty wind that gusted off the ocean. "I may have lost it all, Phil. Juliet, the company, everything." He paced back again, his hands stuffed in his pockets. It was hard to admit that it was all gone, everything he cared about. But too much time had passed now and Juliet hadn't called or come home. He'd figured if she was going to change her mind, she'd do it in the first twenty-four hours. After that, the chances were pretty slim.

"I did have one thought," Phil ventured, "not about Juliet but about the company."

Brady paced back across the deck. He didn't want to talk about the company. Right now he didn't give a damn about it.

But Phil persisted. "Don't you personally hold all those patents for the toys and the new furniture line?"

"I guess so," Brady answered absently. "I've been going to transfer them, but—"

"Think about it, Brady," Phil insisted. "If you hold the patents, then what is Talcott Enterprises really?" When Brady didn't respond, he answered his own question. "It's nothing but a shell. As long as you hold the patents, you call the shots, Brady, and there's not a hell of a lot anybody can do about it."

"I guess you're right," Brady answered slowly. "I'd never really thought about it."

Phil was disappointed. He'd solved a major problem and he'd expected at least a thank you. "You don't sound very enthusiastic," he observed.

"I'm sorry, Phil." Brady turned toward him. "I really do appreciate you working it out. It's just ... I guess my mind is on other things."

Phil shook his head. "I guess it is. Six months ago you'd have given anything for that kind of a handle on Talcott Enterprises. Now you're telling me, 'Gee, that's nice.' What the hell are you doing, Brady?"

Brady leaned against the rail again, idly watching the birds march across the sand. "I don't know." He ran his fingers through his hair, trying to find an answer. "Everything's changed. Nothing much seems to matter any more. Nothing except..." He stopped, knowing he might as well lay it on the line. "You warned me, clear back there at the beginning, and I laughed at you. So I guess it's your turn to say, 'I told you so.'"

Phil put his hand on Brady's shoulder. "What are you talking about?"

"I'm in love with her, Phil. Really in love with her. I don't give a damn about anything else. All I want is to have Juliet back."

Almost sharing Brady's pain, Phil closed his eyes. He remembered those feelings all too well, the agony of losing the woman you loved, the sense of power-lessness because there was nothing you could do to get her back. And yet you hoped that somehow, some-day... If she'd died, at least it was over. If you'd walked out, you still had some options. But when she was the one who ended it, there was nothing left. "Have you told her how you feel?" Phil asked gently.

"I told her. Not soon enough, but I did tell her."

"And?"

"And she said she didn't want to be married." Brady picked up the binoculars and scanned the beach, looking for any patch of bright green that might be the sweatshirt Juliet was wearing.

"Did she give you any particular reason?" Not wanting to be married didn't seem to Phil much of a reason for getting a divorce. There had to be more to it than that. He couldn't believe she didn't care about Brady. He'd seen them together too many times. You could tell about a man and a woman, just by the way they were when they were together. And with Brady and Juliet, it was written all over them.

"She's got a lot of reasons." Brady was still study-ing the beach. "Or at least she thinks she does. She's a divorce lawyer, remember. Most marriages don't look very pretty once they get to her." Brady paused, thinking about some of the other things Juliet had said. "I'm not sure that's all of it. Her father walked out when she was ten. She jokes sometimes about how a psychologist would tell her she hates men."

"Does she?"

"Hell no," Brady retorted, "or at least you couldn't prove it by me."

Phil smiled. "That's what I figured."

"What she wants is some guarantee that this will last forever, and there aren't any guarantees."

"No." Phil's jaw tightened. "There aren't any guarantees."

They watched Eileen and the boys walking slowly up the hill toward the house. One boy was on either side of his mother, each holding one of her hands. All of them, Eileen included, were streaked with sand, and they were all smiling. They waved when they saw Phil and Brady, but neither of the boys broke away to run ahead.

"It's nice to see you, Brady," Eileen called out as they approached. "I'm really out of breath," she admitted, sitting down for a moment on the stairs before she climbed up. "Maybe the doctor had a point about a few days in bed."

"Why don't you go take a nap?" Phil suggested. "You've got time before dinner."

"I think maybe I will," she agreed, holding on to the rail to pull herself up.

"I'll help you," Michael offered, taking her hand.

"Me, too," seconded Timmy. Both boys walked with her into the house.

Brady's eyes followed them. "The boys obviously like having her back."

"But they're still afraid she'll leave again," Phil answered.

Brady looked directly at his friend. "Do you want her to stay?"

Phil hesitated. "I'm not sure. We've spent a lot of time talking, more than we have in years. Every so often I catch a glimpse of her the way she was when I first met her... when I fell in love with her."

"That should be good," Brady observed.

Phil stared off into space. "I don't know, Brady. I have a feeling we need to go at this pretty carefully. She's still sleeping in the guest room...." Phil's voice trailed off. "It's almost like starting over again," he said finally. "Even if she does stop drinking, we've got a long way to go."

Maybe Juliet was right, Brady thought bitterly. Maybe marriage was a bad bargain all the way around. But, if that was true, why was he so miserable? There had to be a way to make it work, if two people only loved each other—and trusted each other enough.

THE NEXT DAY Brady stayed home from work. He told himself things were slow during the holidays and there wasn't much reason he really needed to be at the office. But he knew that what he told himself had nothing to do with it. He simply didn't want to go anywhere.

He puttered around the house, mentally cataloguing the work still left to be done. In the small room off the master bedroom, which they had immediately designated the nursery, he ran across a box of pink-and-blue wallpaper rolls waiting to be hung. It had been a ridiculous choice for a house they were about to sell. For a couple with older children, or no children at all, that room would have been a dressing room or a study or maybe a sewing room. He knew that and he'd assumed Juliet did, too. He'd taken the choice of wallpaper as an unspoken agreement that maybe... Maybe what? If he'd said something then, instead of making assumptions, things might have been different.

Brady walked through the other bedrooms and downstairs to the main floor. They'd made a surprising amount of progress in the time they'd had, maybe because they'd enjoyed working together. It had been fun to paint with Juliet. He'd figured that out right away. But the thought of doing it alone was dismal. Objectively he hated painting. He wandered into the kitchen and rummaged through a drawer until he found a list of contractors. As he ran his finger down the names, the phone rang.

Brady stared at it. It could be Juliet. She was the only one his secretary might have told where he was. He picked up the receiver on the second ring.

"Brady, what are you doing at home?" Cass's cheery voice inquired. "You aren't sick, I hope."

"No, nothing like that," he assured her.

"I'm certainly glad to hear that. I assume Juliet must be there, too, since she isn't in her office. Just wanted to let her know we all got back from Yosemite—wonderful skiing this year, and only one broken leg. Fortunately, not mine."

"Actually, Cass, she's not here," Brady told her. "She's at the beach house." The silence was so long that he wasn't sure Cass had heard him.

"What's she doing there?" Cass asked suspiciously.

"She...ah, well..." Cass was so damn blunt it was hard to soft-peddle anything with her. "The weather was nice and she—"

"How long has she been there?" Cass interrupted.

"Oh, a few days," Brady answered vaguely.

"Now, Brady!"

Brady winced. Only rarely had he heard Cass use that tone of voice.

"You can't tell me Juliet's at the beach and you're in the city, staying home from work, and everything is normal. What's happened? Did you have an argument?"

"Well, no," Brady replied. Actually, they hadn't argued. He wished it were that simple.

"Well," Cass continued, "you two haven't been married long enough to have any serious problems. Give Juliet a few days, and she'll probably cool off."

"Yeah, I suppose so," Brady said, deliberately keeping his reply casual. He said goodbye and hung up the phone, turning again to the list of contractors. Cass was smart. He probably hadn't fooled her a bit.

## CHAPTER FOURTEEN

EARLY THE FOLLOWING morning, Juliet sat at the kitchen table in the beach house staring into her cup of coffee. She had awakened before dawn and couldn't go back to sleep. It seemed better to get up and get busy than to toss and turn. But busy doing what? She had no idea. There wasn't anything to do, or even anything she wanted to do. And so she sat at the table drinking coffee and listening to the raucous gulls quarreling over their morning catch.

A sound, different from the other beach sounds, intruded on Juliet's solitude. She listened carefully. It was a car, driving slowly down the beach road. There were never any cars out there this early. Maybe it was Brady. For one long second Juliet's heart stopped. He had promised he would leave her alone, and she was sure he would keep that promise.

She listened again. The car was pulling into the driveway alongside the house. It had to be Brady. There was no one else who would come, especially so early. Juliet stood up and went to the door, waiting for the familiar sound of his footsteps on the deck stairs.

The coffee mug shook in her hand and she set it on the counter. That's when she realized there were no footsteps on the stairs. If it was Brady, he apparently wasn't coming into the house. She hurried into the living room, carefully positioning herself off to one side of the glass wall. No one could see her but she had a clear view of the beach. After several moments all she could see were the birds, and the white-capped surf, and one lone jogger far down the shore.

She was just beginning to feel uneasy, knowing the car was still there alongside the house, when a slim energetic figure appeared in her field of vision. She saw the flaming hair, the billowing gauze blouse. *Who else but Cass?* Juliet watched her mother settle in a secluded spot in front of a sand dune and take a large drawing tablet out of her Kenya bag. Obviously she was preparing to sketch. But Cass wouldn't have driven down the coast before dawn unless she had a very specific purpose in mind. And it was unlikely that purpose was sketching.

Her hands on her hips, Juliet turned away from the window. The only way her mother could know she was here was if Brady had told her. She hoped that was all he'd told her. Cass had zeroed in on the fact there was a problem, or she wouldn't have come. That meant she might have put pressure on Brady. Cass was good at getting information out of people.

Irritated, Juliet pulled on her jacket and headed toward the back door. She wasn't ready to talk to Cass. She already felt dishonest because she'd misrepresented Brady, the marriage, everything. It would make telling Cass about the divorce that much harder. But the sooner she got it over with, the better, Juliet decided, quietly closing the door behind her. She'd simply explain that things weren't working out with Brady and they'd decided…no, she'd decided…it had been decided that getting a divorce now was better than dragging things out.

Juliet saw her mother look up and wave her hand in greeting. With a lightness she didn't feel, Juliet waved back.

"I didn't expect you to be awake this early," Cass called out as Juliet approached. "I thought I'd take advantage of the morning sunlight and work for a while."

Juliet stuffed her hands in her pockets. So, Cass was going to take the casual approach. But she wasn't in the mood for playing games. "You didn't drive all the way down the coast to sketch in the morning sunlight," Juliet said, challenging her.

Cass set her tablet and charcoal beside her on the sand. "Of course not," she answered quietly. "Why don't you sit down and join me?"

Juliet didn't want to sit down. She wanted her mother to go home and leave her alone until she got herself together. But Cass wasn't offering that option, and Juliet couldn't very well just stand there. Slowly she lowered herself to the sand and wrapped her arms around her bent knees. She stared straight ahead, not saying anything, waiting for Cass to give her the opening she needed.

"All you need to do is stick your lip out and you'll look as sullen as you did when you were six years old," Cass laughed softly.

Juliet didn't answer. She didn't like it when her mother saw through her. Besides, she was cold and wrapping herself up was a good way to keep warm. She watched the ocean, studying each wave as it crested to a foamy white peak before it broke and rolled up on the smooth, wet sand.

It was Cass who finally broke the silence. "Would you like to talk?"

Juliet shrugged, still studying the ocean. "Not really. There isn't much to talk about."

"I see," Cass replied. "Well, maybe I will sketch for a little while, then."

Cass picked up her tablet, and Juliet heard the rasping of a charcoal stick as it moved across the lightly grained paper. The sound evoked sharp memories of her childhood, the hours she'd spent in the studio when Cass worked. She could close her eyes and smell the pungent turpentine. She could see the myriad of paint tubes on the table next to the easel, and she could hear the soft classical music in the background blending into the rhythm of the rolling surf. "Whatever happened to that lumpy old chair in the corner of your studio—the one I used to curl up and read in?"

Cass stopped drawing. "I gave it to the Salvation Army right after you passed the bar exam."

"Oh," Juliet answered. It had been years since she'd thought about that chair. She didn't even know she liked it.

"Juliet?" Cass touched her lightly on the back. "I want you to look at my sketch."

Curiously, Juliet took the sketch pad from Cass. Her mother rarely showed her unfinished work. "You sketched me!" she exclaimed.

"That's right."

Juliet studied the stark, hunched figure on the paper, the hollow eyes staring out toward the ocean. "I don't like it." She handed the tablet back to Cass.

"I didn't expect you to," her mother replied. "Art isn't always beautiful, and neither is life."

Juliet hurled a broken shell across the sand toward an approaching wave. "You don't need to lecture me about the seamy side of life. I see it all the time in the office, remember?"

"Maybe too much, Juliet," her mother observed.

"And you're telling me I've set myself up to fail?" Juliet's face was grim. "Look, Cass, if you'd talked to all the people I have who started out full of hope—"

"Just like you," Cass interjected.

"No." Juliet traced a pattern in the sand with her forefinger. "Not just like me. I'm smarter than that. I went into marriage with my eyes wide open. I knew what I wanted and went for it."

"Exactly what was that?" Cass inquired.

"A baby. I wanted to have a baby."

Cass raised her eyebrows. "I didn't think marriage was a prerequisite for having babies nowadays."

Juliet turned and looked sharply at her mother. "How much has Brady told you?"

"Only that you came to the beach house to be alone and think for a few days."

Juliet remained skeptical. "That's all?"

"Yes, Juliet, that's all," Cass answered. "I gather there's more to tell."

Juliet turned away from her mother's penetrating eyes, looking down at the swirled patterns in the sand. "I've really made a mess," she said in a small voice.

Cass reached out and took Juliet's hand. "You aren't alone, dear. We all do it—some of us on a larger scale than others."

"I thought I had it all planned. If only Brady hadn't insisted on marriage...."

"Maybe you should begin at the beginning, Juliet. There's obviously a lot I don't know."

In a slow, toneless voice, Juliet related what had happened. She was barely through the part about advertising for a father for her baby when Cass picked up her tablet and began to sketch again. Juliet knew it was her mother's way of channeling the shock, anger, disappointment—whatever emotions were stirring— while her face remained impassive. The more Juliet talked, the faster the charcoal moved across the paper in broad, bold strokes.

"And so it didn't work out for either one of us," Juliet finally summed up.

For several minutes, Cass continued to sketch without comment. "I'm not sure you've quite come to terms with the problem," she said mildly, laying the charcoal on the sand and turning toward Juliet. "Are you unhappy because you're not pregnant?"

"No," Juliet answered quickly. "I was for a while. But now I'm not even sure anymore that I want to have a baby. I don't seem to be sure about much of anything."

Cass smiled. "You're more sure than you realize, Juliet. You just aren't being honest with yourself."

"I don't know what you mean," Juliet retorted. She wasn't in any mood to have Cass analyze her.

Ignoring Juliet's obvious irritation, Cass asked, "How did Brady feel about you leaving?"

Juliet hesitated. She'd gone this far; she might as well tell everything. "He didn't want me to go. He persuaded me to come to the beach for a while, supposedly to think it all over. I told him I wasn't going to change my mind."

"Exactly what is it you want, Juliet?" Cass asked her.

Juliet's eyes flashed deep green in the morning sunlight. "I can tell you what I don't want," she proclaimed. "I don't want to be married. Getting married means getting hurt. I've seen it over and over again."

Cass studied her thoughtfully. "And so you figured if getting married means getting hurt, conversely not being married means you won't be hurt, right?"

"Right," Juliet agreed, surprised at how quickly her mother seemed to understand.

"Juliet, did you ever study logic?"

Juliet eyed Cass suspiciously. "Of course."

"Well, you should have studied harder. You're asking yourself the wrong questions, Juliet. That's why you're getting the wrong answers."

"I am not," Juliet snapped back.

Cass took Juliet's hand again, and Juliet struggled against the urge to pull it away. "Does Brady love you?" her mother asked.

The question was like a weight bearing down on Juliet. She'd felt so guilty when he'd told her he loved her, guilty and angry because it all seemed so unfair.

"Well, does he?" Cass prodded.

"Yes." Juliet braced herself for the next question.

"And do you love him?"

She wanted to deny it. That would solve everything. It also would be a lie. "Yes, I love him," she admitted slowly. "But a lot of people love each other when they start out, and that doesn't keep them from destroying their marriages and their children and each other before they're through. How can I be sure we'd be any different?"

"You can't ever be sure," Cass replied quietly. "But that isn't the problem, Juliet. What you don't understand is that it's not the marriage that hurts. It's the love, the profound emotional commitment to each other." Cass's face clouded. "That's what tears people apart. You can choose to live with Brady or not. You can choose to divorce him or not. But if you really love him, you're going to hurt sometimes no matter what you do."

Juliet stared at the surf, her head pounding like the breakers. "I've thought about it until I can't think anymore, Cass. I still don't know what to do."

Cass patted her on the shoulder. "You're looking for answers in the wrong place. This isn't the kind of decision you make with your head. You can't make a list of pros and cons the way you do when you're preparing a case."

Juliet frowned. "So what's the alternative?"

"On this one," Cass told her, "you have to follow your heart. It's the only way you'll come up with any real answers."

"But that's not how I make decisions," Juliet protested.

Cass smiled. "Maybe you've never faced a decision like this." She picked up her sketch pad and stood up. "Come on and walk me to the car."

"You're leaving?" Juliet rose slowly to her feet. "Wouldn't you like to come in and have some tea? Or I could fix us breakfast?" As unhappy as she'd been to see Cass arrive, now she didn't want her to leave.

"Not this time." Cass gave her daughter a hug. "Brady was right. You do need some time alone. He knows you well."

Juliet walked with Cass up the dune and around the beach house to the car. She watched Cass's car until it became a tiny red dot in the distance, and then she turned back to the house feeling very abandoned. She wandered around the kitchen for a while and then walked into the living room and sat cross-legged, staring out at the pounding surf. She tried to think, tried to make some sense of everything that had happened, but she couldn't. She only knew that she hurt deep inside, and that as the days passed, the hurt didn't go away.

MICHAEL WAS BORED. He lay on his back on the family room couch and kicked his feet in the air. He'd ridden his new dirt bike all morning, and he was tired of it. There was nobody to play with. Even dumb old Timmy was taking a nap with Mom. His dad had been shut up in the study all afternoon. There was nothing to do.

His eyes wandered to the window. The sun was shining on the beach. Maybe he could go outside and skip stones. But that wasn't much fun alone. He stared at a thin crack in the ceiling. He really wanted to do something neat with someone who was fun. Brady was fun, but he wasn't at the beach house. It seemed like he was never there anymore.

But Juliet was there. He'd seen her walking on the beach. Michael sat up. That was the first good idea he'd come up with. He'd go see if Juliet wanted to do something. She was a whole lot of fun. Pulling on his windbreaker, Michael slipped out the back door and ran down the beach.

As soon as Juliet heard the sound of feet pounding up the stairs, she knew it was Michael. He was the only person who hit those stairs like the lead runner in a marathon. She smiled as she hurried to answer his impatient knocking on the door.

"Hi, Juliet." He was gasping for breath. "I knew you were here."

"Come on in," she invited. His arrival was the brightest thing that had happened to her in days.

Michael shook his head vehemently. "I don't want to come in. I want you to come out."

"All right," Juliet laughed. She pulled on her old green sweatshirt and followed him down the stairs to the beach.

"Do you want to skip stones?" he asked eagerly. "The water is pretty calm today." He began to scuff the sand with the toe of his sneaker, searching out the smooth, flat stones that were best for skipping. "Here's a good one," he announced, handing Juliet a pale pink stone.

Juliet watched him, amazed. Michael looked as though he'd never had a problem in his life. It was hard to believe that this was the same child who had been in a recent automobile accident, the same one who had dissolved in tears because his mother had rejected him. How could he bounce back so fast?

"Watch this!" Michael yelled. He drew back his arm and pitched a stone across the sapphire ocean, laughing aloud when it skipped in three perfect arcs over the top of the waves. "Wasn't that great?"

Juliet knew he wasn't asking; he was stating a fact. Michael was brimming over with confidence today. "My turn now," she announced. She drew back her arm in what she hoped was an imitation of Michael and threw her stone. Instead of skipping, it plopped on top of a kelp bed and sank out of sight. "Not my best skill," she laughed.

Michael skipped another stone across the water. "You should get Brady to teach you. He's really good at this kind of stuff. He taught me."

*Brady.* Juliet hadn't thought about him the whole time she'd been with Michael. That was some sort of a record.

"How come Brady didn't come to the beach with you?" Michael asked.

"He had to work," Juliet explained casually.

"It doesn't seem right, you staying here all this time without Brady," Michael observed.

Juliet didn't answer. She felt the same way, and she still didn't know what to do about it. Absently, she tossed another stone toward the ocean.

"That was a little better," Michael said, praising her. "It must be harder for girls to skip stones. My mom isn't very good at it either."

"How is your mom feeling?" Juliet asked, relieved to change the subject.

Michael's face lit up. "Okay, I guess. She still gets tired a lot." He picked up a shell and examined it before tossing it away. "She made waffles for breakfast this morning,'' he volunteered. ''Real waffles in that waffle-cooking thing. My dad always gets the frozen kind you put in the toaster.'' Poking at the sand, Michael added, ''I hope she'll make real waffles for us all the time now—like she used to.''

Juliet looked at Michael sadly. How easily children were taken in, she thought. How quickly they believed. In Eileen's condition, anything might happen. And here was Michael, letting himself hope that because things had been better for a little while, they would always be. ''You really like having your mom home, don't you?'' she asked.

''Yep.'' Michael crouched down in the sand, digging for more stones. ''I think she's gonna stay this time, too.''

Juliet wanted to protect him. He was opening himself to so much hurt. ''How can you be so sure she'll stay?'' Juliet asked gently.

Michael stopped digging and looked up. ''I'm not,'' he answered quietly. ''I just hope.''

''And if it doesn't work out, then what?'' Juliet prodded.

Michael shrugged. ''Then at least we had today.''

*At least we had today.* At least we had today. At least we had today. The words pounded in Juliet's head like the breakers pounded the sand. It sounded so simple. But, then, Michael was only a child. He didn't have the perspective to look ahead, the maturity to be concerned about his future. He couldn't possibly understand the risk he was taking by loving someone who might leave him.

A stiff breeze blew up from the ocean, and gulls started to squawk. Michael had stopped skipping stones and stood contentedly next to Juliet looking out toward the horizon. "I think I need to go home," he announced. "It's getting late, and my mom might be worried about me."

"Good idea," Juliet agreed.

Michael took off at a dead run along the water's edge. "See you around," he yelled back over his shoulder.

"See you around," Juliet whispered to herself. Maybe it was time for her to go home, too.

Juliet walked slowly up to the beach house. She kept thinking about what Michael had said: "At least we had today."

It was a simplistic approach, a child's way of dealing with uncertainty. But maybe it was more than that. She'd spent all her life planning tomorrows—growing up, working toward law school, preparing for the bar exams, building her law practice so it would be more and more successful. All tomorrows. Even her marriage had been for tomorrow, a way to make a baby who would grow up and have its own tomorrows.

Today, the right now of things, always got shoved aside. All she'd ever done for the moment was make love to Brady. It was the only time in her life when the future hadn't existed for her. She hadn't thought once about whether they would ever make love again or whether it would be better or different. What was, was. It was complete and total and all-consuming.

Juliet went into the house, closing the door behind her. She'd always been so sure of what she wanted— and so determined to have it at any price. But that was before. She sank down on the kitchen chair, her head

in her hands. That was before she fell in love with
Brady.

Now her whole world had changed. Her life was
empty without him. She'd tried to deny it, but it wasn't
any good. She didn't want to go back to her apartment. She didn't want to go to work. The only thing
she'd been able to muster any enthusiasm for in a week
was walking on the beach, and that was because when
she got close to Phil's house she always hoped she
might see Brady.

Standing up abruptly, Juliet hurried into the bedroom and stuffed the few clothes she'd brought into
her canvas bag. She wasn't sure what she was going to
do when she got there, but she knew she was going
home.


JULIET'S PALMS WERE DAMP against the steering wheel
as she turned up the steep street toward the house.
When she got closer she looked for Brady's car, but
she didn't see it. It was early. He might not even be
home. It bothered her that he hadn't called or made
any attempt to contact her since she'd left. He'd
promised not to disturb her, but she'd thought he
might at least check to see how she was getting along.
Maybe he'd done some thinking, too. She felt the cold
knot in her stomach. It hadn't been there in a long
time.

She found a parking spot and started up the front
walk. With its new lighter gray paint, and gleaming
white trim, the house looked very different from when
they had bought it. Having the footing replaced under the corner of the front porch had helped, too. Now

everything seemed solid and square as if the place was ready for another hundred years.

As she approached the front steps, Juliet caught sight of something alongside the porch and went to investigate. In the fading light she couldn't see it very well, but she was sure it hadn't been there when she left. When she rounded the corner of the porch, she knew immediately what it was and she cried out.

Their Christmas tree, stripped of its lights and its ornaments, was on its side, discarded and forlorn. From the way it was lying there with the burlap hanging off the root ball, it was apparent that Brady had dragged it that far and left it to die. An overwhelming sadness surged through her. The tree was alive. Brady had proudly told her that when he gave it to her. She'd thought they were going to plant it in the yard where it could grow.

She stood staring at the tree for a long time before she understood. No wonder he'd left it there. This was their tree, the symbol of their first Christmas together, and now Brady didn't want to plant it. She couldn't really blame him. Christmas was over, and maybe everything else, too. With brimming eyes, she reached inside the branches and took out a paper bird Brady had missed. Carefully she straightened out one of the crumpled wings.

Slipping the bird in her purse, Juliet inspected the tree. She didn't want it to die. Until right then, she hadn't known how much it mattered. She walked all the way around it. The ball of dirt was dry and crumbling, but except for a few brown needles, the tree itself still looked healthy. Maybe she wasn't too late.

She found a discarded paint can near the back door and filled it with water. It took a dozen trips before she was satisfied that the roots were thoroughly soaked. She tried to prop the tree upright so its branches wouldn't get bent or broken, but it was too heavy for her. It would take Brady, or better yet both of them, to maneuver it. Dusting the dirt off her hands, she walked back around the house. At least their tree would live for a little while longer.

When she walked into the house, she felt its emptiness. "Brady?" she called out from the foyer. Her voice echoed through the rooms. She knew without asking that Brady wasn't home.

With the silence clinging to her, Juliet went up to the bedroom and dropped her canvas bag on the unmade bed. When she hung her robe back on its hook in the closet, her eyes were drawn down to the jumble of shoes on the floor. His shoes had started out on the left and hers on the right, but somewhere along the line they'd gotten all tangled up together. She and Brady had talked about building a rack to keep them separated, but they hadn't done it. It hadn't seemed too important.

Juliet wandered into the adjacent room they'd decided should be the nursery. She knelt down beside the roll of wallpaper laid out on the floor and traced the pink and blue design. They'd laughed when they'd chosen it. You needed both colors, Brady had said, because you never knew whether it would be a boy or a girl. She'd thought at the time maybe one or the other might already be growing inside of her. But that had been another dream. Maybe they weren't intended to have children. There was no way of knowing. As Juliet walked out of the nursery, it occurred to her that the room would make a wonderful study for someone without babies. They'd made a really dumb choice of wallpaper if they were going to sell the house.

She went down to the kitchen and considered fixing dinner, but she didn't know whether Brady even came home for dinner now. At loose ends, she made herself a peanut butter sandwich and since there wasn't any milk, she drank a Coke. She wished Brady would arrive, and at the same time she was almost afraid to see him. She didn't know why.

The kitchen was almost finished, she noted with satisfaction, except for painting a couple of door frames and the chair rail. Then all it would need was curtains and maybe some hanging copper pans. Juliet stopped herself. This wasn't the time to be planning homey touches for the kitchen. She was facing other decisions first. But at least she could paint the chair rail.

She opened the paint can and stirred it patiently, until the swirls of blue blended into one solid color. She could understand why Cass took such pleasure in painting. Of course, Cass created pictures. Juliet just liked the feel of the brush in her hand and the way the paint flowed onto the wood. She had finished the wooden strip of chair rail along one wall and was starting on the next when she heard Brady's key in the lock. She kept on painting, a chill spreading inside her. She didn't know what to say to him. She didn't know what to say to herself.

Brady's heart was pounding as he fumbled with the deadbolt. The lights were on inside. That meant Juliet had come home. Maybe it was only to pack, to leave for good. But she was there. He jiggled the key impatiently. It was the first time for months he'd had trouble with the lock.

When he finally got it open, Brady literally ran inside. "Juliet!" he shouted. "Where are you?"

"In the kitchen," she answered. Her fingers were trembling and the paint oozed over the edges of the wood onto the wall. She put down the brush and dabbed at the splotches with a damp rag.

When he reached the kitchen door, Brady stopped dead still. "You're painting!" he exclaimed.

She didn't know how to answer. Obviously she was painting, and she was doing it because she wanted to. Still on her knees in front of the chair rail, she wiped a blue streak off the wall and picked up the brush again. "I thought we needed to get it done. And I guess I like to paint." It was an easy thing to say while she forcibly calmed her trembling body. She focused totally on her brush strokes, never looking up, never meeting his eyes.

Brady wasn't quite sure what was going on. Whatever he'd expected to find when he walked in, it wasn't this. He'd thought she might be packing. Or maybe she'd be at the table waiting for him. Or she might be pacing the floor agitated and upset. But from the way she was acting, she might never have left. On the other hand, she might have come back only to work—to hold up her end of the bargain. That would be like Juliet. Either way, she didn't seem in any hurry to talk about it. "When did you get back?" he asked her.

"This afternoon. I was going to fix dinner," she explained, "but I didn't know whether you would come home." Home. As her lips formed the word, it echoed in her mind. This really was home. They'd made this house a home, by sharing it and working on it and caring about it. But home implied so much, such an enormous commitment.

"I always come home," he said softly. "I always hope maybe I'll find you here." Unwilling to wait any longer, Brady crossed the kitchen in three long strides and gripped Juliet's shoulders. "Juliet, talk to me," he commanded. "What's going on? Why did you come back?"

Her paintbrush zig-zagged across the wood in a wavy line before Juliet pulled it away and set it down on top of the paint can. "I thought about it for a long time, Brady." Her voice was barely louder than a whisper. "I wanted to come home."

He dropped on his knees beside her and took her in his arms. He hadn't lost her. All those nights he'd waited, so sure that she wasn't coming back, were over now. "I've missed you, Juliet," he whispered. "Oh God, how I've missed you!"

She rested her head against him, feeling full and complete for the first time since she'd left. If only life could be this simple, if she could just live one day at a time. "I'm all snarled up, Brady." Her voice dropped lower until it was barely audible. "And I think I'm afraid."

He stroked her hair, cradling her against him. "Afraid of what, Juliet? Not afraid of me?"

"I think I'm mostly afraid of me." She leaned hard against his shoulder. "I'm changing, Brady. What I always wanted, or at least thought I wanted, isn't the same anymore."

His arms still around her, Brady leaned back against the wall and looked at her. She'd obviously struggled over the last few days. At least she'd faced her fears. That was the first step. He stroked her hair. "But what are you afraid of, Juliet?"

"I'm afraid of marriage." She hesitated. "And I'm afraid because of how I feel about you. I'm afraid because I love you." She'd never admitted all that before, and it was very hard to talk about now. "I've always made my own decisions, set my own goals. I go after what I want. But this is different, Brady." She met his eyes. "I didn't decide I wanted you. It just happened. And now I don't know what to do about it. I don't know for sure we can make it work."

His arm tightened around her. "But if we don't try, we'll never know. We'll never know anything beyond what we have now unless we try." He paused, wanting her too much to make promises to her that he couldn't keep. "There aren't any guarantees, Juliet. We have to trust each other."

She moved away from him slightly, wrapping her arms around her knees and hugging them tightly to her. Brady let her go, sensing that he'd touched a raw nerve in her. "I don't know if I've ever completely trusted anybody, Brady," she said thoughtfully, "except maybe myself." She buried her face in her hands. "Oh, Brady, why does it have to be so complicated? Why can't I just get married and have babies and take my chances like everybody else?"

"Because you're not like everybody else." He gently took her hand. "And, you know Juliet, maybe it isn't marriage that's the problem. Maybe you're not ready to have a baby."

Startled, Juliet sat up straight. "But having a baby was the whole reason for getting married in the first place," she protested.

"I know," Brady agreed, "and not a very good reason."

"But I've always wanted to have a baby by the time I was thirty—"

"And if you don't, then what?"

Juliet thought that over. Having a child had been one of her goals, like making the dean's list and passing the bar exam. A slow smile lighted her eyes. "I guess, if I didn't, maybe I could have a baby when I was thirty-five."

"Right." He laughed and gave her a hug. "We aren't in any hurry, Juliet. We've got years and years to have babies if that's what we want to do."

Juliet hesitated. "I don't know, Brady. That's how I'd planned it for so long—"

He shrugged. "Plans change." He looked at her for a long time. "Do you love me, Juliet?" he asked her. He had to hear her say it again.

"Of course I do, Brady," she answered quickly. "I already told you. That's partly why I'm afraid."

He put his hand under her chin and turned her head gently toward him until their eyes met. "No, Juliet, I mean really love me, the kind of love that lasts forever."

Juliet hesitated. She knew what he meant. He was asking for the kind of commitment she'd been afraid to make all her life. It was the question she'd wrestled with all those lonely days at the beach. But it wasn't until she looked into his eyes that she found the answer. "Yes, Brady," she finally told him. "I do love you. That's why I had to come home."

He pulled her close to him, and held her, rocking her gently back and forth. It was what he'd wanted to hear. "Then we'll make it work, Juliet." His eyes were dark with emotion. "But it will take both of us." Brady gently touched her cheek. "We haven't had much time together, Juliet. Most people start out going to dinner and taking walks in the park. They do it for months, or even years. We started out by getting married."

Juliet laughed, seeing the irony. "I'm glad I didn't get pregnant, Brady. That would have been all wrong."

"It needs to be just the two of us for a while," he agreed, "and then maybe we'll know each other well enough by the time the baby comes along—"

"That we could be three without losing each other?" Juliet finished for him. She felt like a weight had been lifted off her. "But we can keep the wallpaper for the nursery just in case," she added happily.

Brady laughed. "In the meantime, we'll buy some bookcases, and I'll use the room as my study," he announced.

"Wait a minute!" Juliet's eyes flashed and she sat up. "Whose study?"

Brady's eyes were still twinkling. "We'll argue that one later," he said taking her in his arms again. "And if that's the biggest problem we're facing, you can be damn sure we'll make it."

Juliet snuggled against him, letting his lips feather tiny kisses down the side of her face. "Brady," she said tentatively. "There's one more thing."

"What's that?"

"Our Christmas tree. I don't want it to die."

Brady stood up, pulling Juliet up with him. "Then I suppose we should go out and give the root ball a good soaking.

Juliet smiled. "I already took care of that."

"You watered the tree?"

"I did, and now I want to go plant it in the backyard.

Brady looked out the kitchen window. "It's starting to get dark. Couldn't we wait until tomorrow?"

"No, I want to do it right now. I want to plant it, and water it, and feed it—"

"And watch it grow over the years?" finished Brady.

"Yes, that's exactly right. I knew you'd understand."

"Of course I do." Brady pulled on his jacket. As he reached in his pocket for the key to the garden shed he felt something else. "Hey, look what I found." He grinned as he took out Juliet's gold wedding band. "This doesn't belong in my pocket."

"No, it doesn't," she whispered.

Brady took her hand in his and slipped the wedding band on her finger. "That's more like it," he said, kissing her gently.

Juliet held him tightly. "I'm glad you kept it, Brady," she murmured. "I didn't feel right wearing it before, but now it seems to belong there."

"It does belong there, Juliet." His voice was husky. "It belongs there, just like we belong together."

Juliet smiled up at him. "I love you, Brady."

He stood quietly studying her for a moment. "The last time I gave you that ring, we had a ceremony, and went on a honeymoon...do you want to do those things again, Juliet?"

"Once in a lifetime is enough," Juliet answered emphatically.

"Good," Brady agreed. "Then this time we'll do it our own way."

"Our own way?" She wasn't sure what he meant.

With a broad grin, he pulled her toward the door. "What's the most romantic way you can think of to celebrate a marriage?"

Suddenly understanding, Juliet leaned up to kiss him, and her laughter blended with his. "Get the shovel, Brady. Let's go plant a tree."

# *Harlequin Intrigue*
## Adopts a New Cover Story!

### We are proud to present to you the new Harlequin Intrigue cover design.

Look for two exciting new stories each month, which mix a contemporary, sophisticated romance with the surprising twists and turns of a puzzler . . . romance with "something more."

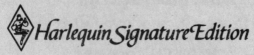

# Penny Jordan

## *Stronger Than Yearning*

### He was the man of her dreams!

The same dark hair, the same mocking eyes; it was as if the Regency rake of the portrait, the seducer of Jenna's dream, had come to life. Jenna, believing the last of the Deverils dead, was determined to buy the great old Yorkshire Hall—to claim it for her daughter, Lucy, and put to rest some of the painful memories of Lucy's birth. She had no way of knowing that a direct descendant of the black sheep Deveril even existed—or that James Allingham and his own powerful yearnings would disrupt her plan entirely.

Penny Jordan's first Harlequin Signature Edition *Love's Choices* was an outstanding success. Penny Jordan has written more than 40 best-selling titles—more than 4 million copies sold.

Now, be sure to buy her latest bestseller, *Stronger Than Yearning*. Available wherever paperbacks are sold—in October.

# *Harlequin Superromance*

## COMING NEXT MONTH

**#282 THE TENDER TRAP • Jane Silverwood**
Zookeeper Faye Johnson loves working with all the
creatures at Wilderness Worlds. But animal
behaviorist David O'Neill is puzzled by the strange
goings-on there. Could Faye be involved in
something illegal?

**#283 FOR ALL THE RIGHT REASONS •**
**Suzanne Ellison**
When Nick Morales accompanies botanist Kelley
McKinney to a remote Mexican village, he knows the
journey won't be easy. But scorching desert,
rattlesnakes and smugglers are nothing compared to
the danger his heart is in....

**#284 NORTHERN KNIGHTS • Bobby Hutchinson**
RCMP Corporal Michael Quinn thinks Dawson City,
Yukon, is no place to have a lady as his right-hand
man. Constable Christine Johnstone disagrees, and
she's determined to make her boss see things
differently. In the land of the midnight sun,
disagreements are often settled in unusual ways—
especially when the best man for the job is a woman!

**#285 DILEMMA • Megan Alexander**
Shannon Gallagher is about to become Mrs.
Matthew Rossi. Her previous marriage, a very brief
union with a young sailor, is so far in her past that it
seems more like a dream. But for Shannon that
dream is about to become a nightmare....

# Take 4 best-selling love stories FREE
## Plus get a FREE surprise gift!